HAWTHORNE

Molly Sheppard

Bloomington, IN  Milton Keynes, UK

AuthorHouse™
1663 Liberty Drive, Suite 200
Bloomington, IN 47403
www.authorhouse.com
Phone: 1-800-839-8640

AuthorHouse™ UK Ltd.
500 Avebury Boulevard
Central Milton Keynes, MK9 2BE
www.authorhouse.co.uk
Phone: 08001974150

This book is a work of fiction. People, places, events, and situations are the product of the author's imagination. Any resemblance to actual persons, living or dead, or historical events, is purely coincidental.

© 2006 Molly Sheppard. All rights reserved.

No part of this book may be reproduced, stored in a retrieval system, or transmitted by any means without the written permission of the author.

First published by AuthorHouse 3/3/2006

ISBN: 1-4259-1012-2 (sc)

Library of Congress Control Number: 2006900074

Printed in the United States of America
Bloomington, Indiana

This book is printed on acid-free paper.

This book is dedicated to my hometown.

PROLOGUE

IT WAS A BEAUTIFUL, balmy May day, a Sunday morning, in the little town of Hawthorne. Goldie Bassett, the proprietor of The Bassett Bed and Breakfast, was giving her prize geraniums their morning drink of water and at the same time hosing the sidewalk leading to her establishment when she was greeted by Sarah Livingston. Sarah had reserved a room at the bed and breakfast in order to soak up the small-town flavor. Much had been written about the town, but Sarah wanted to do something more in depth in the column she was writing for the National Dispatch.

"The person I told you about is having a cup of tea in the dining room while she waits for you, Miss Livingston," Goldie informed her.

Sarah proceeded directly to the dining room and introduced herself to the young lady. "I hear you are the one for me to talk with if I want to know the full story of Hawthorne. I thank you for giving me this time."

"My husband is working today, and I am free, so time is not a problem. Goldie told me you were looking for someone to help you with an in-depth story of Hawthorne. Well, there is nothing, really, that I don't know about the people and happenings here. I am very close to the people and events of the past year. How long are you going to be in town? I could probably talk for days. Of course, I wouldn't want you to print any details of a personal nature about the people I will be telling you about."

"I can stay as long as it takes for me to feel I have everything I need in order to do my column justice. You probably know I am the editor of the Community and Human Interest Department. Most of the paper's reporting about this town has come from the Associated Press, and, I have to tell you, every day, we get a significant number of letters wanting to know more about Hawthorne and its people. We all thought interest in your town would slack off but quite the contrary. You can tell me everything you know and rest assured that I won't print anything before I get your approval first," promised Sarah.

"The only way I can do this is to tell it in my own words, and you can take it from there. I might get a little wordy, because there is so much to tell, and I don't want to leave anyone out of the story."

They ordered more tea…a teapot this time…settled back and the storytelling began.

HAWTHORNE

THE SKY WAS dark and dreary and on the verge of weeping. At the same time, the heavens were exploding with thunder and lightning and railing against the universe. She sat in her executive office high above the city watching nature act out this scene of sadness and anger and knew she was experiencing the same feelings. What was causing these moods she had been experiencing more and more in the past few months? She had always been the cheerful and optimistic one, who felt that no hill was ever too high to climb, and she had been able to reach the top of those high hills by her determination and love of work.

After graduating from the university, Kathryn Hawthorne had answered a "help wanted" advertisement for the position of secretary to Marcus Thayer. Marcus Thayer was a kindly, energetic man, who was forming a new advertising business. He liked the fact that Kathryn's courses of study were varied and included American history, art, music, and composition. During the interview, he discovered she was from a small town in the Midwest and had no inclination to return but wanted to live and work in the city. As she told him about some of her history, he took in her beauty: long auburn hair, brown eyes, peaches-and-cream complexion, and a beautiful, wide smile. He couldn't help but think his daughter, who had died when she was ten years old, would have been about Kathryn's age. She was hired immediately and offered a salary higher than he had planned.

At the university, Kathryn had excelled in all her studies and been the leader of her peers. Now she was eager to take the next step in her life and find her niche in the world of business. Kathryn had been endowed with optimism, a spirit of "can do," and all of this was fueled by boundless energy. It didn't take long for Marcus Thayer to realize the jewel she was, and Kathryn became his protégé. Mrs. Thayer, Emily, took Kathryn under her wing and introduced her to all their friends and thought of her as a member of their family. The Thayers came to love her as their own, and that love was returned in full measure.

Now this stormy day, she sat in her beautiful, plush office high atop the prestigious Thayer Building, feeling empty and depressed. It had been happening more and more lately and was so foreign to her nature that it felt like an overwhelming sickness. She had everything she had ever dreamed of having; most of her goals had been met, but she had lost that something-new-around-the-next-corner feeling that she had always owned, the challenge of each new day. Why was this happening? She knew no pill could fix it. It was up to her to find the cause and cure.

Kathryn looked at her watch and realized it was time for Marcus and her to leave for the Thayer estate, where she was spending the weekend. As she was clearing her desk, Marcus bounded through the door and gave her a huge bear hug.

"Where is your luggage? This has been a hectic week, and a relaxing weekend will do both of us a lot of good. I know Emily is looking forward to having you with us for the weekend; you've become like a daughter to both of us. Emily was devastated when Sissy died, but she's had you to mother for the past few years. I hope you know how much we love you."

"Marcus, I don't think I tell you often enough how much you and Emily mean to me. I love you too—more than you will ever know. I can't imagine my life without you."

When they reached the street, Otto, the chauffeur, was waiting at the door with umbrellas to escort them to the limousine. Thankfully, they could leave the driving to Otto while they discussed the past week's ideas for many future promotional deals. They had never lost their enthusiasm for the work at Marcus Enterprises and could spend hours talking about their various accounts and plans. However, this evening, Marcus sensed a reticence in Kathryn.

"You seem tired and a little withdrawn tonight. Is something bothering you, Kathryn?"

After a pause, Kathryn nodded her head. "I know it's nothing physical, Marcus, but I have been having these feelings off and on for a month or two, feelings of emptiness, uselessness, and sadness, and to compound the uneasiness, I feel guilty having these feelings, because there's no reason for them. I have you and Emily, the work I love, friends, and well...everything I have ever dreamed of having. What is wrong with me?"

Marcus's suggestion that she might want to see a doctor was met with an emphatic "No." Marcus put his arm around her and said, "Don't worry about it so much, my dear. We'll have a good talk with Emily, and I'm sure we can get to the bottom of your depression. You're too strong and bright a girl to give in to this doom and gloom. We're going to fix it."

As they drove along, the skies cleared, and by the time they arrived at the Thayer home, the air was clear and cool, and all the countryside was renewed after the showers. In her mind, Kathryn hoped this was a good omen.

Emily Thayer had inherited the manor house and the extensive acreage surrounding it twenty-five years ago, but Marcus and she had not renovated it or lived there until Marcus had been able to afford it. He was a proud man and had always refused to use any of Emily's fortune. When Marcus became successful and rich in his own right, he decided it was time to move into the manor and the work had started. Marcus and Emily had poured over blueprints for the renovation of the home and the plans for the use of the many acres included in the estate. It could not have been done any more tastefully. Kathryn particularly loved the iron gates with the name "THAYER" incorporated in the grillwork that opened to the oak-lined corridor leading to the main house. As soon as they entered the gates, a peace seemed to settle on them. It was a beautiful haven.

They found Emily reading on the back patio. Her face lit up when they approached, and she opened her arms to both of them. Kathryn always marveled at the love and devotion Marcus and Emily exhibited. Their love for each other was so very apparent, and Kathryn was honored to be a part of it.

"I know you're anxious to get comfortable. Kathryn, I bet you have had a hectic week, so why don't you go to your room and freshen up a bit?" said Emily. "You might even want a little rest before cocktails. Take a little time for yourself."

Kathryn gave her a hug and agreed that she needed a little time to unwind. She had her own suite of rooms filled with all the comforts she loved. She even kept some of her wardrobe there so that she wouldn't need to travel with much luggage. The Thayer estate was her second home.

After a leisurely bath, Kathryn stretched out on her chaise intending to read a journal that lay nearby, but she fell asleep. She woke with a start a short time later feeling refreshed and relaxed. Since it was to be only the Thayers and she for the evening, she dressed comfortably in a soft, long skirt topped with a silk blouse and tied a scarf around her long hair, forming a ponytail.

Emily and Marcus were exchanging reports of their days and making plans for the weekend when Kathryn joined them. She thought, *What a beautiful couple they are and so suited for each other.* Marcus, six feet tall with graying hair but a youthful face, was wearing his Harris tweed jacket and grey slacks. Emily was in her violet, two-piece dress, the violet of the dress enhancing the same color of her eyes. Her unlined face was framed by naturally wavy hair tinged with grey, which she made no effort to hide. However, it was her warm smile that drew everyone to her. Aside from their handsome appearance, the defining things about this couple were integrity, kindness, and gentility.

"We're having martinis. What can I get for you, my dear?" asked Marcus. Kathryn opted for white wine, her usual choice.

As he handed the wine to her, Marcus remarked, "Here you are, dear. I hope you had a good rest. You look a little perkier to me."

"Thanks, Marcus, I do feel much better."

Emily was always very intuitive, and she had been feeling that something was not just right with Kathryn. It was at this point that Marcus told her about the earlier conversation he and Kathryn had regarding Kathryn's uneasy feeling. Emily listened as a mother might listen when told something disturbing about her child. "What can we do to help you, Kathryn? This is not like you at all. Something is bothering you deep down, and we must fix it. Do you think some therapy would help?" Emily was full of questions. There was no doubt about her concern.

"Please, you two, I don't want you to worry. I'm sure it will pass. I really don't have a clue as to what brought it all on. As I told Marcus, I have everything I have ever wanted…and more. Most especially, I have both of you… You are a treasure. I'm sorry I even told Marcus about all of this. Let's just forget about it. It will pass."

Realizing Kathryn didn't want to discuss the subject any longer, Emily turned the conversation to the plans for the following evening. They were going to have a few close friends in for dinner and some good conversation. Kathryn always enjoyed all the friends of the Thayers. They had made their mark in the business world and professions. Their interests included travel, sports, the arts, and current affairs, which made for interesting discussions. Most of the ladies were involved in promoting the arts and contributing time to working for the less fortunate. All of them, as far as Kathryn had observed, felt the need to contribute to society by volunteering in philanthropic organizations. They gave many hours to these endeavors, and Kathryn admired them for that. It was never a dull evening when this group was together.

The next morning, Kathryn woke early and decided that the thing she wanted to do more than anything was to have a ride on her favorite horse. Horses had been a passion of hers since her early childhood when her grandfather had taught her to ride and care for horses. Her grandfather, whom she called Poppy, had been one of the greatest influences in her life. Yes, she wanted nothing more this particular morning than to ride Figero. The Thayer estate was made up of many acres that were ideal for riding. After the rain of the previous day, all of nature seemed to sparkle and the air was brisk and clear. It was just the tonic Kathryn needed.

After her ride and a refreshing shower, she joined Emily and Marcus for breakfast. All of them were rested and looking forward to a leisurely day. The staff would take care of all the arrangements for the planned dinner. Marcus suggested they play some tennis later in the morning, and Kathryn took up his challenge laughingly. Activity was just what she needed at this time.

The dinner guests were Phyllis and Arthur Irving, Mary and Wallace Ames, and their son, Joshua. Arthur Irving was a mover and shaker in the world of finance, and Wallace Ames was a renowned lawyer. Joshua had joined his father's firm and was making a name for himself. They arrived at six o'clock for cocktails, a handsome group. Before entering the room, Kathryn stood back from the group for a short time, admiring each of them and wondering how a girl with her small-town roots had ever arrived at this place.

Joshua hurried to her side, and his joy at seeing her was apparent. Kathryn and Joshua had become the best of friends and were often thrown together at these affairs. Kathryn did not have a steady man in her life, and Joshua was rebounding from a failed marriage. They enjoyed each other's company and had many deep talks about their hopes and goals. Joshua accompanied Kathryn to many affairs: Broadway shows, operas, and benefits. They were a striking couple and they always made the society columns whenever they appeared in public. It was a joke to them that people expected some romantic conclusion, but they knew it would do no good to try to dissuade that thinking, so they laughed at the misconception the press was giving the public.

Kathryn had accepted invitations from many men, but she had found no one who interested her romantically. Most of them had moved too quickly to the roses and romance phase of the relationship. When this happened, Kathryn always found a way to let them down gently. Joshua was another story. He was her best friend, and there was nothing of a romantic nature between them. Kathryn hoped Joshua would find a lovely girl, who would be devoted to him and would make him her first priority. He deserved nothing less.

It was a lovely evening, and cocktails were served on the patio under a canopy of stars with a soft breeze serving as a gentle fan. Kathryn and Joshua found a spot away from their elders and caught up with each other's activities since their last meeting. All the others had much to discuss, too, and the time passed swiftly.

Emily enjoyed entertaining. It was an outlet for her artistic and homemaking talents. On this particular night, she had used springtime as her theme. The two low centerpieces were comprised of crocuses, lilies, and jonquils. Each napkin was formed and tied with a large yellow satin bow into which had been inserted a beautiful jonquil. The china was yellow and white, and the room was lit entirely by candlelight. It was enchanting. Of course, Emily had planned the menu with their superior chef, and everything was perfection. They all raised their glasses in a toast to Emily.

After a leisurely dinner, they engaged in a fiercely fought game of bridge. All were avid bridge players, and there was a lot of friendly competition. This night, the honors went to Phyllis.

Shortly after their guests had departed, Emily said, "We've all had a busy day, and I suggest we retire. Let's have a leisurely morning with a late brunch." Kathryn and Marcus agreed with Emily's plan for the morning, and after their nightly hugs and saying, "See you in the morning" and "I love you," they were off to a good night's sleep.

As Kathryn prepared for bed, she thought back over the evening and the fine people she had shared it with... especially Joshua. She realized that Joshua was really her best friend in the city, and she wondered, for the first time, why she had so few close companions. *I simply never made room for many people in my busy life*, she thought. Marcus and Emily had been all the people she had needed because her work had filled her life. Perhaps she would never have gotten to know Joshua if the Thayers had not invited him to their affairs so often. The strange part in all this, she felt, was the fact that it had never occurred to her before. When she was younger and living in her little hometown, she had been surrounded by friends and had spent many hours with her special confidante, Emmie. Somehow, since living in the city, she had lost that part of herself. How and why had it happened? Kathryn was not given to pondering her private life, and so she shook her head and sighed. "Oh well...who knows?" She went to bed, turned off the light, and allowed the spring breezes to lull her to sleep.

As the dawn began peeking over the horizon, Kathryn was reluctantly letting go of the dream she was having. The dream was like a crazy quilt with odd pieces that held pictures of people she had known in her childhood, and the large centerpiece was a vision of Poppy, her grandfather. Some of the pieces were blank. Could they represent her unknown future? She wanted to keep the dream alive, so she could experience the friendships of her younger years, but the dream faded, her eyes opened, and she was in the present. She was enjoying the luxury of lying in bed all safe and cozy, because most mornings, she was up and out early.

As she lay thinking about a myriad of things, she heard a mockingbird entertaining her with his version of all the other birds' songs.

As she listened, Kathryn spun a little fairytale about the mockingbird. In her story, he was the most talented of birds because of his ability to sing all birds' songs. However, she wondered how the other birds felt about his copying their compositions. More importantly, she wondered how the Mockingbird felt about himself. Did he have a song that was just his, that he had composed and that was original? Was he fated to never really be accepted by the other birds or to have a song of his own? This fantasy became a real question to her. Was she like the mockingbird, always searching for her own song?

They all gathered in the beautiful glassed morning room for their late brunch, well rested and full of talk about the previous evening. Emily was, once again, complimented on her talent for entertaining. As they were finishing their brunch, Marcus suggested they all take the horses out for a nice canter through the woodlands on the beautiful April morning.

"I think that's a marvelous idea, Marcus," said Kathryn, "but I have something else to tell you before we go riding. There's something I just realized this morning. It came to me in a flash, but I know, as sure as I'm standing here, that it's something I have to do. I need to go back to my little hometown of Hawthorne and reconnect with Poppy for awhile. He's my dear, dear Poppy, and I have not spent enough time with him these past few years. Oh yes, I know he's come here to see me on many occasions, but I've missed being with him on the farm. I know this is sudden, but this morning, I'm overwhelmed with a deep need to do this."

"Kathryn, I would never stand in your way when something is important to you. Of course, you must go. How long do you intend to be away?" was Marcus's quick response.

"This is so sudden, I haven't really thought how long I need to be there, but in order to make it meaningful for Poppy and for me, I don't want it to be a rushed visit. I want time to find out how he's doing and time for a lot of reminiscing. For want of a better phrase, I need to get in touch with my roots, I guess. Do you understand what I'm saying? Does this make sense to you?" she asked as she searched their faces.

"Something has been troubling you lately and perhaps this is part of it. The hard part for me is that you seem to suddenly have this problem of identity and purpose. You always have seemed so sure of yourself," was Emily's observation. "I think, anything you want or need to do, you must certainly do."

Kathryn was so touched by their demonstration of love that tears welled up in her eyes as she went to them for an embrace.

After Kathryn had her emotions under control, she turned to Marcus and said, "If I had to choose a time to be away from the office, it couldn't be better than at this time. Because we work so far in advance, we have most of the promotions in place for the fall season. Summer is always a slack time, when I mostly look for inspiration and ideas for future television and print promotions, and really, I can do a lot of that while I'm with Poppy. I'll have my computer systems installed at his home and can be in touch with you all the time. While I'm away, Alma can forward mail and take care of the day-to-day office work. She's a wonderful assistant, who has been with me a long time and knows just how I operate. I think it will work."

As she spoke, organizational plans seemed to pour from her. She was overtaken with excitement.

"I'm getting a little worried here, Kathryn, because it's beginning to sound as though you're planning to be gone a long time. I don't want to lose you."

Kathryn paused for a few minutes before answering. "Marcus, how would you feel about six months? I could be back by the end of October. Why don't you two plan a trip to Hawthorne and a visit with Poppy and me? He has wonderful riding horses, and you would love the countryside, I'm sure. I'd so enjoy showing you around."

"I'm going to miss you terribly, so a visit with you might help fill some of the void," said Emily. "We will surely plan to visit with you whenever it's convenient for you and Nathan. He's such an interesting and lovely man."

After their ride, the rest of the day was filled with talk of Kathryn's trip back to Hawthorne. As they talked, Kathryn became more and more positive she was doing the right thing at this time. She hadn't realized how much she needed to go back. It was ironic that she needed this trip so much, because after high school graduation, the only thing she had wanted to do was kiss it all goodbye, live in a city, and make her mark. Now that she had reached that goal, all she wanted to do at the present time was to return. She was realizing life takes many twists and turns.

Kathryn called Poppy and told him about her plan. He was ecstatic and said he would be waiting "with bells on." She took a week to get all her work-related matters organized, make lists with Alma, and order her needed computer equipment to be installed at Poppy's. She decided that even if it took her two or three days to get to her destination, she wanted to drive. This would give her time to let go of her business life for a short time and to just relax and think in the quiet of the drive. Kathryn was beginning to see that although she had loved every moment of her work, she had been on a treadmill for years, and now, she would relish some solitude.

She drove the secondary roads that were so beautiful this time of the year with trees budding, wild flowers appearing, fields being plowed for planting, and oh, the long-forgotten odor of newly turned soil. Several times, she parked the car and walked to the side of a country road and leaned on a farm fence while she allowed her senses to absorb it all. How could she have forgotten the beauty of springtime in the country. As she drove through the small Midwestern towns, memories of her hometown came flooding back. Long-forgotten memories surfaced that she was ready to relive. She wanted to remember her early years that she had buried for such a long time.

Kathryn smiled faintly as she thought about dear Poppy. He had always been her guiding light, her staunch supporter, mentor, and her place of refuge. To Kathryn, his name was Poppy, but his real name was Nathan Hawthorne. The Hawthornes had settled her home area in the 1700s. Kathryn remembered the story she had been told as a youngster of the Hawthorne family's history.

The early Hawthorne settlers had traveled to the Midwest in a covered wagon along with six other families from New

Jersey. Isaac Hawthorne was a sturdy man with strong convictions and was very wise. He was soon recognized as the leader of the group. Our country was new and the young government was encouraging people to settle and clear the land by deeding property to those strong and dedicated enough to clear and till the land they chose. Isaac took advantage of this offer and claimed hundreds of acres in a beautiful valley surrounded by rolling hills, many forested, through which ran creeks and a clear river. While many of the people gave up because of the hardships they encountered, Isaac's family labored to clear the land, build a log cabin, plant seeds, and make a pasture for their cow and bull. As more and more people found this paradise, Isaac gave some land to be set aside for a village. The village was named Hawthorne.

Several years after they had settled in the valley, the dynamic of Isaac's family began to change. One by one, the daughters married and went to their new homes. There were three sons, and two of them decided against working the land and started a little trading post farther west. That left the eldest son, John, who loved the valley and the farm. John was heir to all of Isaac's holdings. It set the pattern of the eldest son receiving the responsibility for the Hawthorne legacy. Down through the generations, the heirs revered the land and tended it lovingly, always remembering their strong patriarch, Isaac.

NATHAN AND ANNA

YOUNG NATHAN WAS happy to know he was the next in line to carry on Isaac's dream. When he was a small lad, his father bought him a pony so he could ride along as they inspected the fields and livestock each day. He was given small responsibilities at first, but as he grew and matured, the responsibilities became more complex. Nathan never shied away from any of the jobs he was given. The farm was his passion.

Nathan was a handsome young man in a rugged way. He was tall with the physique of a man who has worked hard at many jobs on the farm all his life: muscled and fit.

His eyes were brown and set in a face tanned and square jawed, and his hair was thick and wheat colored. It was this handsome young man who set off in his teens to the university to study farm management. The course was redundant in his case, because after his life on the farm under the tutelage of his father, he could have taught the course. Since the farm management course did not live up to his expectations, he decided to study law. It was during that time he met Henry Jorgenson, and they became lifelong friends.

Henry invited Nathan to accompany him to his parents' home one Sunday afternoon. The Jorgensons were a warm and welcoming family, but it was their daughter, Anna, who captured Nathan. It was love at first sight. Anna was an exceptionally beautiful young lady, who was interested in art and music. She was statuesque, brown-eyed, light-complexioned with long brown hair filled with red highlights, and had a smile that dazzled. She had studied music from her early years and was recognized as an accomplished young pianist. When not at the piano, she enjoyed setting up an easel before an attractive scene and spending many hours trying to capture the time and place on canvas. Everything she did was perfection as far as Nathan was concerned, and he could think of nothing else but her after their first meeting. Thankfully, she felt the same way about Nathan, and within a year, they were married in a lavish wedding at her parents' home.

Nathan positively worshiped his beautiful Anna and wished he could give her the world. The next best thing was his plan for their honeymoon…a trip to France. They traveled by rail to New York where they boarded a large, ornate ocean liner for the balance of their voyage. A trip of this magnitude was a first for both of them. The two young lovers drank in all the sights and sounds of Paris and the surrounding areas. After attending musicals and operas and visiting the museums in the city, they traveled to Provence. Nathan had always heard about the beautiful agricultural lands and homes in that particular area of France, and he spent many hours talking with the farmers there, while Anna spent most of her time sketching people, buildings, and happenings for a portfolio she would complete when she returned to her new home.

They basked in the beauty before them and in their love, but as idyllic as their time in France was, the time came when they both yearned to set sail for their Hawthorne home. The Hawthornes had always referred to their land and home as "Isaac's Dream." All the caretakers down through the years had done their job well, and the land had been kept intact. The first Hawthorne home had been a cabin that still stood and was maintained to remind the family of their roots. The log cabin had been replaced as home in the 1800s by a very large Victorian-style house which had been refined and added to several times. It stood proudly on a high hill as testimony to the different generations who had called it home. Nathan now had custody of his heritage.

On the east side of the house was Nathan's study. He spent many hours there attending to the operation of the farm, to read and contemplate. He loved this room and had surrounded himself with all the things that gave him pleasure. The walls were lined with books chronicling the great wars, the settling of this great country, and texts on land management. In the center of the study was a huge oak mission-style desk that had been used by several generations of Hawthorne men. The only decorations in the room were very fine paintings of horses and horsemen. Daily journals that had been started by Isaac and continued by following generations were now recognized as real family treasures. In order to preserve them, Nathan had added a small room next to his study which was kept air conditioned and humidity controlled. Nathan used the study not only for daily work, but it was a refueling station for his soul, his sanctuary.

On their way home from France, Nathan told Anna he wanted to add a room on the west side of the house that would be Anna's room. He wanted her thoughts on just how she would like to have it done. He told her, "I envision floor-to-ceiling windows which would open to a terrace... a large terrace. In the room, you must have a fine piano, a desk for your writing and accounts. You shall furnish it to your liking. I think it very important that you have your own sanctuary."

Anna had never expected such a treat, and she was overjoyed. She could think of little else and immediately had ideas for her room. Tears welled up in her eyes as she raised her hand to caress his cheek. He was so wonderful, and she was overwhelmed with her love for him. Nathan saw all this as he looked deep into her dark eyes.

After the boat docked, they eagerly boarded a train for home. Young Ben, one of the farm workers, met them at the station. He remarked that he had never seen Mr. Hawthorne look so well. Anna took Young Ben's hand and thanked him for meeting them, and he was devoted to her ever after. Anna's beauty and gracious manner won every heart. From that first day, she wanted to get to know each of the caretakers and their families. Most of the families had lived in neat, comfortable houses on the farm and had worked for the Hawthornes for generations. Each family was responsible for some part of the farm operation, and they took pride in their work. There were those who planted the acres of vegetables. Others tended the trees, the forests, and the orchards of apple, peach, and berry trees. Some worked with the livestock, horses, and the diary stock. It was a huge operation, but many of the people had worked for the Hawthornes all their lives, and they considered the land their home, too. They were loving stewards and completely devoted to the Hawthorne family. Most people would have described this home and land as an estate, a manor, or even a ranch, but the Hawthornes called it simply, "the farm."

As they approached the hill leading to the house, Anna asked Young Ben to stop. This, her first homecoming, was not to be rushed. She wanted a moment to take it all in and tuck this moment into her memory bank. This moment was to be savored. Young Ben stopped and not a word was spoken, because they knew this was Anna's private time. She took in the beauty of this large white house with the green shutters and the wrap-around porch. Two large maple trees shaded the front of the house and other varieties of trees surrounded the sides and back of the house. As she gazed at her new home, Anna heard bird song and cattle lowing, and hovering over it all were large puffy clouds in a pale blue sky. *I must paint this someday*, thought Anna. After a few moments, Anna told Young Ben he could move on, and they traveled up the gravel road to their home.

There were several people waiting to greet them at the house. Nathan introduced Anna to Mrs. Kite, Jewel, and her daughter, Gemma. They were the cooks and housekeepers of the house, along with Mrs. Kite's husband, Olly. The Kites had been with the family for many, many years and lived in an apartment at the back of the house. Anna would be working closely with the Kites, and she was delighted that she liked them from this first meeting. Jewel had a round, happy face with hair pulled back into a tight knot at the base of her neck. Anna was sure Jewel would prove to be a good cook as her physique displayed a love of food and eating; she was short, soft, and round. Gemma had not reached the proportions in body size of Jewel, but other than that, she was pretty much a carbon copy of her mother. Olly came puffing around a corner of the house. He was tall, thin, and bony with a nest of thick grey hair and a big toothy smile. Anna thought of him as Jolly Olly.

While Young Ben and Olly carried their luggage to the master bedroom, Anna and Nathan toured the house. Anna felt at home immediately; the enormous living room was furnished with mostly Victorian furniture and oh, the beautiful huge fireplace. The living room and the grand dining room could be separated by heavy, sliding pocket doors affording privacy for each of the rooms. The kitchen was a very large room, a typical country kitchen with a monstrous table in the center of the room so that many people could be served. Anna turned to Nathan and said, "Everything is so right except one thing. I wish we could have a small, more intimate place for our meals when we are alone."

"I would never have thought of it, because after a day of work, I usually just sat at the big table in the kitchen and ate with the Kites. Now things will be much different, I'm happy to say...so we will add a small dining area to our plans."

When they came to Nathan's study, Anna surveyed it all carefully, turned to Nathan, and said, "It's positively perfect and could be no one else's room but yours. Oh! You wonderful man, what did I ever do to deserve your love?"

Nathan gathered her in his arms tenderly, kissed her, and continued to hold her as he said, "We're so lucky that in this huge world, we found each other and can share our life together. Our love is strong and will be forever. If only I had the words to tell you how much I love you."

They held hands as they climbed the great staircase to their bedroom. It was a very large room with a bay window to the east. One of the generations had built a bench in the alcove which made it a cozy spot from which to view the grounds and to watch the dawn. Adjacent to the bedroom was a dressing room that had been installed by Nathan's mother and beyond that, the bathroom. All the furniture was massive and of the Victorian era. Anna thought the furnishings were perfect for such a large room. Once again, they came together, overwhelmed by their love and the perfection of their day. And to think, it was only the beginning.

◇◇◇

After his month away from the farm, Nathan was swamped with details that needed his attention. All the farmhands had done their jobs well, but Nathan was needed for decision making, and he was the anchor of the entire operation. While he was occupied with his responsibilities, Nathan told Anna she was free to plan any changes in the household routines.

Immediately upon their arrival, Anna had called the farm "home." She spent a lot of time with Jewel, Gemma, and Olly talking about the house routines, and she was always quick to compliment each of them for all they did and the fine results of their efforts, thus endearing herself to them even more.

High on her list of priorities was planning for the house addition that Nathan had suggested when they were on their honeymoon.

The addition was hers to plan as it was to be her special room, and she set about doing just that. Being the artist she was, Anna was able to draw her vision of the room she would like to have down to the last detail. As Nathan had suggested, she would have floor-to-ceiling windows and French doors, which would open to a large terrace. The room would be furnished in French country, a more delicate style than the rest of the house. There would be a small fireplace for the cool fall and cold winter days. Of course, the central item in the room was to be a piano, not only for her daily pleasure, but she envisioned inviting fine pianists to play for their friends. When she was satisfied the drawing was complete, she showed it to Nathan. After perusing each and every detail carefully, he threw his arms around her and said, "Is there anything you don't do to perfection? I think it will be beautiful and a reflection of you, my dearest love. We must get the builders in right away."

After Nathan had approved the plans for her room and the terrace, she set to work planning the small, intimate dining area they had discussed. It was to be opposite the kitchen and open onto the terrace, also. Her plan called for floor-to-ceiling glass windows, as were planned for her room, so they would have a beautiful view of the changing seasons. She wanted it to be sunny, bright, and intimate.

Nathan called in the finest local builder, and Anna set about searching for just the right furnishings. She wrote to her family so that she could share her happiness and to invite them for a nice long visit. In her letter, she described her room, and by return mail, Henry said her parents insisted they send the piano from their home to her....It would always be her piano. Anna was touched deeply by the love of her family. God had smiled on her when he placed her in their lives and now again, by leading Nathan to her. Her happiness knew no bounds.

Anna watched the building of her room and spoke with Mr. Bodey, the building contractor, each day; it was a joy to watch her drawings come to life. After her daily discussion with Mr. Bodey, she would visit with one of the families who lived and worked on the farm. Gradually, she met them all. She was accepted into each of their homes warmly, because they could tell she was genuinely interested in each of them. She always complimented them on their cozy homes and would say, "I know this is a happy home." She knew they were fine people and devoted to Nathan. The love and esteem all the families had for Nathan were now extended to Anna.

A very special day came when Nathan took her to see the first home of the Hawthornes when they had settled the land: Isaac's log cabin. It was larger than most frontier cabins we see in history books, and it had a porch across the entire front of the cabin. Some of the original hand-hewn furnishings were still there. Anna asked Nathan if it would be all right if she hired some people to clean the cabin inside and air it out. It had stood untouched for a long time. Anna could almost feel the ghosts of the early Hawthornes who had dwelt there, as though they were speaking to her. She wanted to buy some rocking chairs for the porch, because she knew that with this cabin, she had another very special retreat. In fact, as she took it all in, Anna realized this would be just the place for her to have all her art supplies, and she told Nathan about her plan.

"You have perfect taste, Anna, and I know this old cabin could not be in better hands."

This became a project dear to her heart, and she strived to make no changes that would harm the integrity of the building.

The days of summer saw the young couple busy with their special projects and living in such a glow of happiness that it touched everyone who met them. The new addition to the house was completed along with the lovely terrace, and Anna had seen to the cleaning of the cabin, hung new calico curtains, and put rocking chairs on the porch. Another big project undertaken by Anna was the planting of oak trees along the road leading to the farm, and with Olly's help, she planted hundreds of annual and perennial flowers all around their home. It was a sight to behold, and Anna wanted her family to see the result of her efforts and to have them share in her happiness. They were invited to the farm after harvesting in the fall. She and Nathan had some exciting news to share with her parents and brother: Anna was pregnant.

Anna took great delight in showing her family their beautiful home, and as her brother, Henry, watched her, he thought, *Married life and pregnancy become her...She is more beautiful than ever, if that's possible.* She took them to the cabin and told them its history and her plans to use it as her painting hideaway.

Nathan took them on a tour of the farm, introducing them to the employees and explaining all the operations. They especially admired his stable of fine horses. It was good, too, for Henry and Nathan to spend time together as they had remained the best of friends ever since their university days. Henry was getting established as a lawyer and was enamored of a young lady who was a teacher. He confided to Nathan he was going to ask for her hand, and he said, "I only hope we will be as happy as Anna and you."

Nathan smiled, patted his friend on the back, and replied, "You have set a high goal, my friend, but if she's anything like my Anna, it could not be otherwise."

While the Jorgansons were there, all the employees and their families were invited to a Harvest Celebration, the brain child of Anna. This was to become a yearly celebration. Tables were set up under the trees, barbeque pits were readied, and the women spent days preparing special foods. The adults visited while the children enjoyed games, and in the evening, after their huge repast, several of the men brought out their banjos and guitars for a sing-a-long. To make it all perfect, Mother Nature supplied them with a gentle breeze, a starry sky, and a full moon. Anna thought, "This is like the setting for a fairytale."

It was not long after the Jorgansons' visit that fall bowed out, and winter set in. Anna looked forward to the holidays and made elaborate plans for decorations and entertaining to celebrate her first Christmas in her new home. Old Doc Weis admonished her about all her activities and told her she must slow down. He took Nathan aside and reiterated that Anna should not overdo it. Nathan put a stop to any entertainment on a large scale. He told Anna she must not do the decorating of the house herself but should direct Jewel and Gemma to follow her instructions, and they could do the work. So Anna became the boss-lady telling Nathan what kind and size tree she wanted for decorating and the greenery she needed for wreaths and swatches. Nathan found beautiful old decorations for the tree that had been stored away in the attic for many years. When everything was finished to Anna's satisfaction, their home was beautiful. They invited several couples from Hawthorne that Nathan had known for years to a candlelight dinner. After dinner, Anna played carols, and they all sang. Everyone agreed the farm had never looked so beautiful as it did that night, dressed in its finery of green garlands and swatches with poinsettias in every nook and cranny and oh...the most beautiful tree filled with all the antique decorations. Anna had insisted on candlelight everywhere. It was a memorable celebration.

Anna had been working for a long time on her gift for Nathan. Unbeknownst to Nathan, she had sketched their home and then taken the sketch to the cabin, where she spent hours painting it. The painting was titled "Isaac's Dream" and was to be hung in Nathan's study. Nathan was overwhelmed. "I have never been given anything that has meant so much to me. Anna, Anna, you know just how to touch my heart."

For Anna, Nathan had selected a beautiful, large pure diamond which could be worn on one of two chains he had purchased for it. One was a choker length and the other a long chain so that one of them would fit whatever costume she might select. She had never seen so large a diamond, and with her eyes brimming over, she told Nathan, "This most beautiful token of your love must be passed down generation to generation; I want it to always stay with the lovers in our family."

After the holidays, winter set in with a vengeance; the ponds froze over, and there was so much snow that the area resembled a fairyland. If Anna had not been pregnant, she would have gone for a ride in their big sleigh with two large horses pulling them, and, of course, she thought, there would be many sleighbells. Or they could have joined many of the farm families for skating on the pond, but that, too, was out of the question. In place of too much activity, she spent most of her time playing the piano, writing letters, sketching, and reading. She asked Nathan if she might read the journals. She found them fascinating, and she was able to see how each generation had made its mark on the family: Each had made a special contribution, and now, it was their turn...

The time for the baby's delivery arrived on a cold blustery day in March. A little girl was born, who lived for only one day. They were devastated, and Anna cried out, "Why?! Why?! What did I do that was wrong? I must have done something to cause this."

They named the baby Ann and buried her in the Hawthorne plot on the farmland, where all the Hawthornes had been laid to rest.

After the death of her baby, Anna seemed to close down. Jewel tried to tempt her with her favorite foods, but she shoved them away; she no longer smiled her beautiful smile, no longer did she spend time at the piano or sketch or even spend much time reading. She lost herself in sleep, and when not sleeping, she would sit and stare at the snowy fields. Nathan spent his time trying to awaken Anna once again to the world around her. He would tell her about happenings in Hawthorne and on the farm, encourage her to eat, and he tried to find books that she might like so that he could read to her but to no avail.

Finally, Nathan wrote to her brother, Henry, explained the situation, and asked for some guidance. Henry decided to visit with them, and while he was there, he sat down with Anna and very pointedly asked what had happened to her great love for Nathan. "You lost your baby and that was surely a tragedy, but it didn't happen only to you, Anna. Nathan is suffering, too. He not only lost the baby, he thinks he's lost your love. I always thought you two could face and conquer any adversity, but I see no sign of it from you. Nathan is a wonderful man, who loves you, and you're torturing him every day that you push him away. Come on, Anna, you have to move ahead to the wonderful future you and Nathan can have. I'm sure you don't want to turn your back on that. Your husband really, really needs you now. Wake up, girl!"

Anna had always adored her big brother, and as he spoke to her so earnestly, a cloud seemed to pass from her eyes, tears fell, slowly at first, and then she sobbed as she clung to him. She cried until there were no more tears, and finally, she said, "I see you are right. How could I have been so blind to Nathan's sadness; I've been thinking only about myself and locking him out when he needed me. Oh, thank you for setting me straight...We need each other.

He's in his study, and I'm going there right now to beg for his forgiveness."

After Henry's visit, Anna gradually returned to her old self, and Nathan and she became even stronger and more devoted...He had his Anna back. By the time the fruit trees were in bloom and the new planting was being done, Anna was back to her piano and her daily trips to the cabin to paint.

Since the loss of her baby, Anna was more aware of the children who lived on the farm...Each one seemed so precious...One day, she had an inspiration. Why not teach them about art and how to paint? Then she realized that she might even teach piano to those who were interested. She had not been so excited in a long time, and she could hardly wait to begin.

Nathan could sense there was something exciting on her mind from the glowing expression he saw as they sat down to their dinner that evening. It was not long before she was detailing her plan for him. "That is positively wonderful!" he said. "An inspiration. I'm sure many of the children will jump at the chance." As they spoke, she became more excited and eager to begin. She planned to buy all the supplies for the children as a treat for them. The art group would meet on the porch of the cabin for their lessons, and the piano lessons would be given privately in Anna's room at her grand piano. Her cheeks were flushed with excitement, and her eyes sparkled. Nathan was overjoyed to see her so happy. His Anna was truly back. The very next day after she had told Nathan of her plan, she set off to visit all the homes on the farm and speak with the mothers, who promised to let her know if she might have a pupil from that house. A few days later, she had heard from all the mothers, and she had four girls and two boys signed up for the art lessons and two girls for music instruction. She ordered her supplies and made out lesson plans. *I may not have my own little girl, but I can have these children with me some of the time,* she thought.

In May, right before her lessons were to start, Anna found out she was pregnant again. Dr. Weis told her not to be afraid that what had happened before would be repeated. He said she was very healthy and should be able to do anything she wanted within reason. "Oh dear God," she prayed. "Thank you for this baby I'm carrying. Please, may our baby be strong and healthy." Her little group of adoring pupils filled her time...They were delightful and responded to her teaching. Her months of pregnancy flew by.

In the spring, they greeted their strong, healthy son, and they named him Matthew Hawthorne. He was to be an only child.

MATTHEW HAWTHORNE.

NEVER WAS A child more loved or doted on. He might have become a haughty, selfish brat, but with the loving guidance of his parents and living by their standards, he was a fine lad and liked by all who knew him. He learned from both his parents. From his father, he learned to revere the land and delight in all that nature provided. His father taught him to be a very good horseman, and they spent many hours roaming the fields on horseback. From his mother, he learned about music, art, and the love of reading. Most of his friends lived on the farm, and they played like children have always played;

they built forts, played cowboys and Indians, hiked the fields, climbed the trees, fished in the pond, and played games every evening till the sun went down. It was a good, well-rounded life.

When he reached his teens, everyone said, "You can surely tell he's Nathan Hawthorne's son, because they have the same mannerisms and look alike." Matthew was over six feet tall, had thick, dark, wavy hair, a wide smile, dark... almost black...eyes, and broad shoulders; the same strong physique and manly good looks as his father.

Ever since his boyhood, Nathan had been grooming Matthew to be the next caretaker of "Isaac's Dream." Near the end of his senior year in high school, Matthew sat down with his father and told him that as much as he loved the farm and the home there, the only future plans he had were to be a teacher. It was obvious to Nathan that Matthew had given his choice much thought as he expanded on his plan to be a teacher at the high school level; he wanted to somehow inspire young people to have a reverence for learning, and he said, "I firmly believe we have to start instilling in young minds a love of learning before their university years." He explained it was his opinion there was something lacking in the high schools and that young people needed to be taught how to study and prodded to keep their minds open to all the wonders around them. They also needed guidance in choosing their life's work.

He wanted to have a hand in helping young people find their rightful niche in life.

Nathan listened attentively and in awe of the maturity his young son displayed. He was disappointed that Matthew wanted to chart a new course for himself, but he felt the passion with which his son spoke, and he nodded his agreement to Matthew's future plans. As they rose, Nathan embraced Matthew and with great emotion, said, "I'm very proud of you, son."

◇◇◇

Anna and Nathan supported him in his chosen field, and Matthew enrolled in one of the nation's most respected universities as the first step in reaching his goal. He was completely at home in the university environment; he enjoyed it all. Even though he was scooped up by the leading fraternity and he participated in many extracurricular activities, he could be found most of the time at lectures or in the vast library reading everything he could find on the art of leading and teaching. He was popular with boys from all walks of life. He had the special gift of making each person feel special.

Holidays and school breaks Matthew spent at the farm with his parents and the farmhands. He took long rides with his father, listened while his mother entertained at the piano, and admired her latest works of art. Matthew had heard stories from some of his classmates about their less-than-happy homes which included such problems as infidelity, abuse, and many of his friends had been sent away to school at an early age while their parents spent their time traveling and indulging themselves. These young men were aimless and shallow with no knowledge of a real home...They were free-floating, never looking beyond the present. After hearing their stories, Matthew always felt sad thinking of their hollow childhoods. All this made him realize more than ever how blessed he had been with the parents and home he had been given.

When he was home, he always went to the old cabin and sat on the porch for a spell, surveying the beauty before him. It was one of his favorite places. He made good use of the rocking chairs his mother had placed on the porch many years ago. Being there in that place and with his parents never failed to be a time of renewal for him.

Matthew graduated at the top of his class and headed back to Hawthorne. He was recruited by several prestigious private schools and even some universities, but he remained true to his original dream, and that was to teach in Hawthorne. When his application was received by the Hawthorne School Committee, it was acted on immediately. He would teach social studies and American history.

Matthew reestablished himself in his room at the farm. During the summer, he rode with Nathan as he made his daily inspections of the various farm operations. Nathan touched base with all his foremen each day, and at the end of the day, he followed the Hawthorne tradition of writing in the journal. Anna would watch as they rode off together on their daily tour and think how much they looked alike. It was hard for her to believe her little son was this handsome man, and she thanked God that he had come back to Hawthorne to teach. In the evenings after dinner, they usually gathered on their large porch to watch the sunset. They, who live close to the earth, enjoyed the simple evening country rituals...watching the birds heading for their nests and listening to the merry voices of children echoing as they played at twilight.

Labor Day passed, and it was time for school to begin. Matthew was ready, and still it felt very odd to him to walk through the doors of his old high school as a teacher. He vowed he would keep his pledge to teach to the highest standard, to hold the students to the same standard, and to make learning a priority for them for the rest of their lives. Most of the teachers, who had been there for a number of years, could not help but quietly deride his idealistic approach to teaching, because their enthusiasm had been tarnished by the lackluster performance of most of their students. Teaching had become just another job to them.

To each other, they made comments such as, "We'll see how he feels in a year," "He'll find out this is a far cry from the halls of academia he is used to," "These, so-called students will run roughshod over him in no time…"

Every year, on the first day of school, there was an assembly and all the teachers sat on stage while the superintendent welcomed the students back for another year with the promise that it was going to be the best year ever. He then introduced all the faculty; after which, there was mild, unenthusiastic applause from the student body. After the assembly, the students went to their assigned homerooms where they were given their schedules for the year.

Everyone in the town knew the Hawthornes and had only the highest respect for them, but they had not seen this young Matthew Hawthorne much during his university years. Needless to say, he was very impressive with his gentlemanly manner, his quiet personality, and good looks. The young, unmarried women teachers wanted to know him better, and the girl students had romantic dreams of him just as they might have about celebrities. All this adulation by the female school population did not deter the men and boys from liking him immensely. Matthew was unaware he was having this effect on people, which endeared him to all of them even more.

Each day, as he drove to the school, he looked forward to the day with enthusiasm and was more certain than ever that he was in the place he wanted to be and doing what he wanted to do. He did inspire his students, most of them, and helped them understand that this time in school and what they were learning, along with their daily experiences, were building blocks for their future. It was up to each of them to take control of their future; no one else could do that for them. He had each of them write goals for themselves. This they would do at the beginning of each year, and by the time they graduated, these yearly goals would be returned to them. "I will be writing my goals, too," he told them, "and we will see how these goals change from year to year." After the goal setting, he pledged that he would do all in his power to make their studies meaningful and asked for any suggestions from them that would be of help in the courses he taught. The students had never been spoken to this way before, and they responded positively. He had their attention...They were intrigued.

American history was presented so well that the students felt they had been a part of it, which led them to a new respect for all the sacrifices that had been made by their forefathers. They came to realize freedom is not free or for the faint of heart, but that we all have and will continue to have the responsibility for protecting this freedom. Matthew said, "It is our generation's turn now to guard the freedoms that were secured for us by the Puritans, settlers, and all generations before us." He touched a chord in all of them.

One of their first assignments was for each of them to study their own family history and write a report about their ancestors and their place in history. "Remember," he said, "today will be history one day, and we're all contributing to it in our own way. You decide if your contribution is a good one."

It would be wrong to say that every person in his classes was inspired by his leadership, but the majority of the teens were enthusiastically following Matthew's lead in the study of history. They were fired up over the assignment to research their genealogy, and their parents became interested and involved in their research. Students went to the senior center and talked with the elders of the town about the early days. It became a topic of conversation all over Hawthorne, and as they talked and became conscious of their backgrounds, a sort of pride in themselves and their town began to manifest itself. The editor of the *Hawthorne Weekly News* was delighted to have a column in the paper weekly, chronicling the history of Hawthorne's families using what the students were uncovering in their research. Not only did all of this have an effect on his students, but some of the hardened teachers began to realize that maybe there was a way to inspire young people, and they started looking at the tired approach they had been using.

Matthew was oblivious to the fact he was the school's star and that he had set a high standard for the teaching profession in Hawthorne. Everyone admired him for his unassuming manner, and many were heard to say, "He was truly born to teach." As for Matthew, he didn't aspire to do anything other than what he was doing, and his days were happy and fulfilling.

Each young woman in the town had been hoping she might be noticed by Matthew and had been shyly pursuing him. Most of these girls had been schoolmates of his, and he had known them all his life. Now that he was back and going to different socials, he invited one or the other to be his date, but Matthew experienced no romantic feelings for any of them...That was about to change.

Ivy Baines arrived in town. Her parents had died several years before she appeared in Hawthorne, and she lived with her two brothers, Roy and Russ. They had been good students of their parents on how to avoid work whenever possible. They drifted from town to town, perpetrating scams and mooching on the unsuspecting citizens for as long as their luck held, and then they moved on. They didn't particularly want their sister with them, but, on the other hand, it was good to have someone to cook and do laundry for them. Their home was an old trailer that was towed by a rusty vintage car. They always seemed able to convince some farmer to allow them to park the trailer on the edge of his land for a small fee.

Ivy's reading material consisted of movie magazines, fashion magazines, and the society columns in the newspapers. Some day, she vowed, she would be living like the people she read about, and they would be writing about her in the society columns. Ivy was well-named because she was a climber.

When they arrived in Hawthorne, they had no money, and the car was badly in need of repairs, which were going to require some new parts. Therefore, Roy and Russ applied at a small manufacturing company and were hired. Ivy wanted to earn some money, too, in order to buy some new make-up, nail polish, nylons, and maybe even to earn enough for a new dress. Most of her clothes had been bought at Goodwill stores or consignment shops. She was fortunate they needed a sales girl at the local Newberry's Five and Dime store, one of her favorite places to shop. Miss Bertha was manager of the store, and she decided this pretty, vivacious girl would be a refreshing change from the last drab sales girl, who had left to do the accounts for the Kroger store. Ivy was hired.

The first thing every morning, Ivy and Miss Bertha would carry certain rather large items out to the sidewalk in front of the store. For some reason, it was thought this might tempt people walking by. As they were performing this ritual one morning, Ivy spied a handsome young man entering the bank. "Oh, Miss Bertha, who is that good-looking guy? He looks just like a movie star."

Miss Bertha told her the young man's name was Matthew Hawthorne, and he was a member of the family for whom the town was named. Miss Bertha was so happy to have someone who knew nothing about their leading family, so she could tell the Hawthorne story. Everyone in town knew the story. Some day, she told Ivy, she should drive by the Hawthorne land in order to see the beautiful home they had. She informed Ivy that Matthew was the town's rising young star, and everyone was waiting to see which one of the local girls he would choose for his wife. As Ivy listened to all Miss Bertha told her and had her questions answered, she set her sights on Matthew. If she had her way, he would be her man; this was her ticket to a better life.

Everyone shopped on Main Street, and Ivy knew she would be seeing Matthew again. She watched for him and observed he had a pattern of going to the bank every Saturday, usually just before noon. She had to have a plan to make him notice her, because, she was sure, there would never be an occasion for an introduction. One Saturday, just before the noon hour, she asked Miss Bertha if she could hurry over to the bank. The timing was just right;

Matthew was approaching the bank. She hurried across the street and managed to collide with Matthew. "Oh, I'm so sorry," he said, while she clung tightly to him as though she might fall.

"I think I twisted my ankle...I can't seem to put any weight on it. Will you please help me to that bench in front of the bank?"

As he helped her to the bench, Matthew's concern was apparent. "I hope it isn't seriously injured." They sat down, and he turned to look at her. Who was this gorgeous girl, small and delicate, with a flawless cameo complexion, bright blue eyes, and magnificent red hair that lay in ringlets? He was smitten, and Ivy knew it.

Ivy lowered her eyes and began massaging her ankle. "I do believe the pain is going away, so if you could just help me back across the street to Newberry's, I'll rest during my lunch break, and I'm sure I'll be alright. You have been so kind."

Matthew replied, "Oh, so you work at Newberry's? I'm sure Miss Bertha would understand if you went home for the rest of the day. Why don't I talk to her, and then I can drive you home?"

Ivy insisted she would get along fine. She went on to tell him that Saturday was their busiest day of the week, and she just wouldn't think of leaving Miss Bertha to manage alone. He helped her as she limped back to the store. The Main Street shoppers observed this event with great interest. Who was this flashy new girl? That Saturday afternoon, Newberry's had more customers than ever before after the grapevine had done its duty. This outsider, who had captured Matthew Hawthorne's attention, had to be inspected by the many locals who could make it to Main Street that day.

Matthew had never met a girl like Ivy Baines, and there was no way he could dismiss her from his thoughts. By the time school was dismissed on Monday and he had counseled three students, his need to see her was so compelling that he literally trotted out to his car with hardly a nod or wave to other teachers and students who were leaving at the same time. He drove slowly as was ordered in the town, but his heart and mind were racing. What if she had injured her ankle more than they had thought, and she wasn't at the store? What if she was in love and engaged? What if she...? and on and on. He parked his car and tried to appear casual as he walked into Newberry's. Miss Bertha greeted him at the door, but she was quick to realize it was Ivy he had come to see. Ivy was at the candy counter filling and weighing bags of goodies. When she saw him, she flashed a huge smile, and her eyes lit up. "Well, we meet again. I'm so glad, because I want to thank you once more for being so nice and helpful to me. It's just as I thought...my ankle is much better."

As he looked deep into her bright blue eyes, Matthew's fate was sealed. "I was worried that you might have a bad sprain or worse, so this is quite a relief. It must be quitting time soon...Why don't you let me take you to Walters' Restaurant for dinner to make up for my clumsiness, and so I can get to know you better?"

"I don't think it was any more your fault than mine," she said, "and you don't owe me anything."

He would not take "no" for an answer, and it was agreed she would meet him at the restaurant, which was situated on Main Street.

After Matthew left, Miss Bertha sauntered over to the candy counter with a sly smile and said, "You look like the cat that swallowed the canary. I must say it didn't take you long to get your hooks into him...and done very cleverly, too. I'm going to enjoy watching this."

Ivy was very pleased with herself. She spent the time between the late customers straightening up the counters—especially the lipsticks, nail slicks, and jewelry which were her favorites. She also looked through the latest movie magazines to see what the stars were wearing and how they were having their hair done. The store was never very busy on Mondays, because most of the women were busy with household chores, so the time seemed to drag, and Ivy thought the clock would never register six o'clock.

At 5:30, she and Miss Bertha started carrying in all the items they had put outside in the morning, and then Miss Bertha began tallying up the day's sales while Ivy did some organizing of the counters so they would be ready for the next day. Promptly at six o'clock, they put the closed sign on the door, locked up, and Ivy hustled to the restroom to check her make-up and fluff her hair. She didn't want to hurry too much because, in her mind, it would be good to keep him waiting...She didn't want to appear anxious.

Matthew was waiting for her in a booth in the restaurant, and when she appeared, everyone else in the room faded for him. She was not like any of the girls Matthew had known; she was like a bright light exuding boundless energy and excitement, and yes, she was so lovable. His adulation was not lost on Ivy and did not go unnoticed by the other patrons in the restaurant. This meeting would fuel many hours of speculation in town. Ivy loved being center stage but Matthew had no idea of the stir they were causing, because he had eyes only for Ivy.

The Walters' Restaurant had been an institution on Main Street for many years. There were wooden booths around two sides of the large room and tables in the center of the room. One side of the room was filled with a large counter and stools where many individuals preferred to sit and visit. The huge window across the front looked out on Main Street and was left bare except for a small ruffled curtain that ran across the bottom of the window. Of course, as with most of the stores on the street, there was a huge awning for shade in the late afternoon. The restaurant was owned by Jim and Barbara Walters. Jim did most of the cooking while Barbara took the orders with the help of Mrs. Cooley, who worked part-time. Barbara's mother, Olive, made all the pies, and people came from all over the county to enjoy a slice of Olive's pie. Olive arrived at the restaurant every morning by five a.m. to start her baking. She was an early riser, and she liked to be in the kitchen without anyone interrupting or bothering her. Jeff Moore, the police chief, started his day early, too, and so he always checked on Olive while they had their first cups of coffee for the day. Jeff was the only person permitted to share her mornings.

As soon as Ivy was seated, Barbara placed the daily menu before them, took their orders for coffee, and returned to her cash register in order to give them time to make their selections. Matthew told Ivy she must have a piece of the best pie that could be found anywhere, so she decided to have a salad and a slice of chocolate pie. Matthew opted for a more substantial meal and apple pie. After their orders were taken, Matthew told Ivy he wanted to know all about her.

Ivy had known this moment would come, when he would want to know more about her. She was aware, that in a small town, everyone would know she lived with her brothers in a broken-down trailer, so she would have to tell him the story of her life in the way she wanted him to hear it; she shaved and embellished the truth to suit her purpose. With a sad face, she told him her father had been sickly and weak, and her mother had spent her days taking care of him, so they could never afford a real home. They had to live in a trailer going from place to place for her father to find work, which always turned out to be part-time because of his illness. She and her brothers had not had much education due to the fact that they were never in one school long enough to grasp the lessons. When her parents died a year ago, that had left her and her brothers searching for a place where they could settle down. Oh, how she wanted a real home. Now, her brothers had decided that California would be their land of opportunity and that was where they were going when the car broke down in Hawthorne. Her brothers were working at a local manufacturing plant in order to make enough money to repair the car, and then they would continue their trip to California. She was working to help them.

Her story didn't make Matthew any less entranced with her. On the contrary, he listened with deep compassion to her story and admired her all the more for her strength and stamina against all the odds. Her story had the affect she had intended, and she was certain she had found her protector.

Matthew took her hand and said, "I have never known anyone as brave as you. I would like to take you to the farm where I grew up so you can meet my parents. I'm sure they will like you very much. Besides, you should see how beautiful this part of our country is—maybe even as pretty as California."

"Oh, I'd just love to do that. I'm sure your parents are super people to have a son like you, and, you'll be surprised to know, I've never visited a farm." As she gave him one of her smiles, she thought how Miss Bertha had told her to ride by the Hawthorne farm some day, and now she was actually going to visit.

As they lingered over their second cup of coffee, it was decided that Matthew would pick her up on Sunday around noon. He told her to dress casually, because they would probably want to hike around the farm.

Ivy's brothers had been fortunate to get temporary jobs at the local manufacturing plant due to the fact that the company had just gotten a rush order. They worked the night shift—eleven at night until seven in the morning, after which they came home, ate a huge breakfast, and tumbled into bed. Days went by when they barely saw Ivy, but she did manage to let them know she had a friend who was taking her to his house Sunday, and she would appreciate it if they would stay out of sight when he came to get her. They asked no questions, because the family had always lived by their wits, and they figured this was a plan of Ivy's to foist herself on some unsuspecting male. The truth of the matter was that they really didn't care what Ivy did as long as she found someone to latch onto, so they would be free of her. They would soon have enough money to repair the car, and then they were heading for California. They were happy to cooperate with Ivy.

Ivy spent the week trying to decide what to wear. He had said to dress casually, and since they lived on a farm and Matthew said his father had beautiful riding horses, she decided to wear her denim cowgirl outfit with silver studs and fringe and western boots. She had found the garments and boots at a Goodwill store, and this outfit was a favorite of hers.

When Matthew arrived at the trailer, she was at the door, ready to go, so he would not expect to enter or meet her brothers. She told him they had gone away for the day. Matthew had never seen anyone dressed like she was, but he was so enamored of her and naive when it came to girls that he thought she looked very special.

When they arrived at the foot of the hill leading to the house, Matthew stopped and proudly, with a sweep of his arm, he said, "This is it...my home."

Ivy was thinking, *What have I gotten myself into?* because this was foreign to any of the places she had ever been; in fact, whenever, she and her brothers had traveled through rural areas, she had always been very bored. She liked the action of the cities. As he turned to her, Matthew's smile faded. He mistook her quietness for sadness. He was sure it had sounded as if he were bragging, and he must have hurt her. Matthew was touched to think how her father had barely eked out a living, and it caused him to feel even more protective of her. Ivy managed to murmur that everything was beautiful. Matthew wanted to leave that awkward moment quickly, so he pointed the car toward the house.

Anna and Nathan were in a high state of anticipation, because she was the first girl he had ever brought home for them to meet. They knew her name was Ivy Baines, and he had told them all about her sorry childhood, so they were ready to accept and treat her gently. However, they were not quite ready for the real Ivy Baines. When she approached them, her red curls blowing in the breeze and oh, the costume she was wearing, Nathan thought, *Where did she come from? All she lacks is the cowboy hat, but then, she wouldn't want to cover that magnificent head of hair.* Anna smiled, held out her hand to Ivy, and thought, *She is a beautiful young girl, who has had a hard life. If Matthew cares for her, so will we.* Anna could tell how proud her son was of this girl, and she knew, as mothers always do, that Matthew wasn't going to see any other girl from that time on.

Ivy had never been entertained by such gracious people before or in a home of such refinement. Anna and Nathan led the way through the house to the terrace so they did not see the look of awe on Ivy's face as she ogled the interior of the house, the stylish antique furniture with its rich patina, Anna's piano, the huge dining room, and the many paintings. Matthew walked beside her, pointing out his mother's paintings and suggesting that they might persuade her to entertain them later at the piano. Ivy could not believe the number of books lining the walls, and she thought, *Who could read all this stuff?* It was obvious to Anna and Nathan how happy Matthew was to have Ivy in his home with his parents. When they reached the terrace and sat down, Gemma appeared with delicate sandwiches, little cookies, and iced tea and lemonade. The linens were crisp and white and the glasses chilled. The house servants had changed a bit after Olly's death and Jewel, due to her age, had passed the point of managing the housekeeping. Therefore, Gemma and her husband, Jake, had assumed the duties. Jewel was still able to work in the kitchen on a lesser scale. On this day, everyone complimented Gemma on her presentation as she blushed and nodded a "thank you." After marriage and the birth of two little boys, Gemma had surpassed her mother in plumpness.

They sat on the terrace and enjoyed getting to know each other. Matthew was plainly showing off Ivy, this treasure he had found, while his mother and father talked about the farm, its history, and the people who lived there. Even though Ivy had heard the Hawthorne history from Miss Bertha, it was different hearing it told in detail by the Hawthorne family. Matthew had told his parents about Ivy's sad history so Anna had reminded Nathan that they must be sensitive and not query her about her past life. Instead, they asked questions such as how she liked Hawthorne, how she got along with Miss Bertha, and other questions not too probing.

After their light repast, Matthew suggested Ivy and he take a hike on the property. He wanted to show her the horses and stables, the old cabin, the Hawthornes' burial ground, the pond where he had learned to swim, and maybe she would meet some of the farmhands. They excused themselves and his parents watched as they walked away hand in hand and thought, *This is a most unusual girl—and she has captured our son.*

It was a beautiful fall day, the air crisp and cool, with a sky full of puffy white clouds, and all the trees dressed in their bright finery as they heralded the year's most colorful season. Their first stop was at the stables where she met

Marcy Ellis. Marcy's father, Abe, had been in charge of the stables and horses for years, and she had always lived on the farm. In fact, she had been one of the children Matthew played with as he was growing up, and now she was a teacher in the same school as Matthew. Marcy had always loved the horses and spent more time helping her father at the stables, than she spent in the home with her mother. Abe had taught her well, and she was a fine equestrian.

From the stables, they walked to many other sites, and finally, they came to the cabin. Matthew had saved it for last, because it was the most special place to him. They sat on the old rocking chairs and drank in the view. "I keep this scene with me all the time," said Matthew reverently, "and somehow, it always grounds me...brings me back to my roots."

By the time they had finished their walk, the sun was starting to set, and the sky was afire. Matthew convinced Anna that she had to play a tune or two for them, so they proceeded to Anna's room. *Imagine having a room like this just for yourself,* thought Ivy as her eyes cataloged everything: the beautiful grand piano, Anna's delicate desk, the cases filled with books, and Anna's paintings. There was a small fire in the fireplace to take the evening chill from the room, and they took their places while Anna played some of her favorites. Ivy was not familiar with classical music and really didn't like it at all, but she repeated her usual line,

"It's lovely." After the short concert and dinner beautifully served in the formal dining room, it was time for Matthew to take Ivy home. Ivy told them she had really enjoyed it all and thanked them.

Anna said, "You must come again soon."

Anna and Nathan sat on their porch and watched the couple drive down the lane. Nathan had been unusually quiet during the day, due to the problem he had warming up to Ivy. Anna said, "Poor girl, she's had such a dreary life moving from pillar to post. We have to overlook her rough edges and try to help her. It's obvious how much she means to Matthew, and I think she's probably here to stay."

"I think you're right, my dear," Nathan replied softly.

Miss Bertha never had a beau. She had always been a plain-looking, plain-dressing lady, who lived with her mother in a little house near Main Street. Her father died when she was young, after years of custodial and other menial jobs that had allowed for little savings. Therefore, it became Miss Bertha's duty to provide for and tend to her mother. She had been a shy child and always held herself aloof from others, never cultivating friends. Her life centered around her home and church on Sundays. When she was hired to work at Newberry's, it was such a big step for her that she became devoted to her job. Her dedication and reliability did not go unnoticed by the representatives of the company on their monthly visits to the store; she was promoted to store manager. The store was her life and her identity, and she felt great pride in being the manager. Her mother had died a few years before Ivy came to town, and from then on, Miss Bertha lived a solitary but contented life in the little home.

Ivy had no friends in Hawthorne, so she naturally made Miss Bertha her confidante. The day after Ivy's visit with Anna and Nathan, she arrived at the store fairly exploding with the excitement caused by the previous day's visit. Miss Bertha had gone to the store earlier that morning in order to have all preparations for opening out of the way, so she would have time, with no interruptions, to hear Ivy's report of her visit to the farm. Ivy had become her friend...her first friend.

They had a few minutes before it would be time to turn the sign hanging on the door to OPEN, so they sat on stools at the back of the store while Ivy told Miss Bertha every detail of her visit. She described her meeting with Nathan and Anna, the lunch on the terrace, and the areas of the farm Matthew had shown her, especially Isaac's cabin. Miss Bertha wanted to hear all about the interior of the home, because she had only seen it from afar, and she was never likely to ever see the inside of the home. She listened intently to Ivy's description of Anna's room, the piano, book-lined walls, Nathan's study, the terrace, and how they had been served by Gemma. "I felt like royalty," said Ivy.

"I can't believe it, girl. You have only been in this town for a few weeks, and you've been entertained by our royal family. I have lived here all my life, and I have never stepped on their property. I have to admit, I've spent many hours dreaming about what it would be like to live in that grand house. You surely have captivated that young man, you lucky girl. Thank you for sharing with me."

Ivy leaned toward her and said breathlessly, "Oh, Bertha, you're my best friend. I just had to share all of this with you. They said they wanted me to come back sometime. Do you think they really meant it?"

Miss Bertha had a ringside seat to Matthew's courtship of Ivy. He came by the store every working day, took her for drives, to the movies, and out to dinner. Matthew was in love for the first time, and it was apparent to everyone. He was with Ivy so much that people wondered how he was able to prepare lesson plans for each day. They were the talk of the town, and everyone watched this romantic tale unfold...The grapevine had never been so busy.

Matthew's closest friend in Hawthorne was Dr. Dan Hurley. Dan had set up his practice in Hawthorne about the time Matthew began his teaching. Dan's wife, Martha, was his nurse, who was not only a golden-haired beauty, but a gentle, compassionate person loved by everyone she tended. Matthew had met them at several socials and events, and they had just naturally gravitated to each other. Dan and Matthew were both young, energetic men... idealists, who had chosen professions in which they could help others. They enjoyed sports and were friendly rivals at tennis. Dan and Martha were welcome guests at the farm where Anna and Nathan were always delighted with their company.

Dan and Martha were the first people Matthew told about this wonderful, exciting girl named Ivy that he had met. It was evident to them that this was not just any girl in Matthew's life; she had captivated him.

The Hurleys invited Ivy and Matthew for Sunday dinner and with crossed fingers, hoped there would be no health emergencies that day. They had bought one of the older houses in Hawthorne, which was located on Adam's Hill, a section of the town with fine old homes. Martha liked the character of their old house which had been home to several earlier generations. They had purchased some of the furniture from the previous owner, and now, Martha was taking her time finding just the right antiques for the furnishings. Because she was with Dan in the office every day, and sometimes for long hours, they had hired Mildred Woodin, a widow, to be their cook and housekeeper. Mildred lived with them in a suite located on the sunny side of the house.

In order to protect Ivy from prying questions about herself and her family, Matthew had, once again, sketched a short recap of her disadvantaged upbringing and suggested Dan and Martha not probe into her past. Therefore, on the day of the dinner, Ivy was greeted warmly by these friends of Matthew and very few questions were directed her way. They talked about how the three of them had become such good friends, about the goals they had for their lives, and what a wonderful place Hawthorne was to make your home. They were glad she was a part of it all, they told her. Of course, Martha was sure Ivy, like most women, would like to see their home, and so she took her on a tour, proudly pointing out all the plans she had for each nook and cranny and said, "I will probably be at this for the rest of my life. I guess, I'm what you would call a 'nester' because I really do get a lot of joy from my home."

Being rooted in one town and tied to an old house was all new to Ivy, and she wasn't sure just how she felt about it, but as Martha showed her around, she smiled a lot, oohed and aahed, and nodded agreement to everything.

That night, after they had bid their guests goodnight, Dan put his arm around Martha, kissed her lightly on the cheek, and said, "I thought I was the only man to be so besotted over a girl. Poor old Matt, he really has it bad. I wonder how long till the wedding."

Fate took a hand in speeding up the inevitable. Ivy's brothers announced one Saturday that they were ready to pull up stakes and continue their trip to California. Ivy turned to Miss Bertha with her problem. She didn't want to leave Matthew and her chance at the good life, but she would have no place to stay after her brothers left, and she didn't have enough money to rent a room. Ivy was surprised to see a smile of delight cross her friend's face. "Why do you look so happy about all this?" she pouted. Ivy was told that she must pack all her things as soon as possible and move in to Miss Bertha's home. After her mother's death, living by herself had become very lonesome, and Miss Bertha welcomed the company of this vivacious girl who had so much going on in her life. Ivy hugged her friend and said, "Good things just keep happening to me since I came to Hawthorne. You're the best!"

This event set the wheels in motion for everyone concerned. Ivy gathered her few possessions from the trailer and moved into Miss Bertha's spare room. Roy and Russ left town, glad to be rid of their sister. Matthew felt free now to visit Ivy in her new place of residence, and Miss Bertha felt privileged to have a Hawthorne in her modest home. It was not long after her move that Matthew proposed marriage with a promise to take care of her and give her everything she would ever want. He wanted to love and pamper her so that he might erase her memories of all the hardships she had endured in her past.

Anna and Nathan were happy for their son, because they could see that Ivy made him happier than they had ever seen him, and even though Nathan harbored some reluctance, they gave their blessing. Since Ivy had no one but Miss Bertha, it was decided they would have a small, very intimate wedding in the garden at the farm with only Matthew's parents, Miss Bertha, Dan, and Martha in attendance. However, a large reception was planned for after the wedding. It would be held at the farm, and the guests would include all the farm employees and their families, Matthew's fellow teachers, and other old friends from Hawthorne. Miss Bertha could never, in her wildest dreams, have imagined she would ever be included in such a celebration. She wanted to buy Ivy's wedding dress as her gift to the bride. Matthew drove them to a nearby city where there was a bridal shop. Ivy playfully told Matthew to "get lost" while they shopped. In a short while, they had found a gorgeous, princess-style satin dress that was perfect for the petite Ivy. A tiara was selected in place of the conventional veil so that Ivy's flaming curls would not be covered. At Ivy's urging, a soft blue lace dress was selected for her dear friend. The sales lady called the blue dress "the mother of the bride" dress. *Well*, thought Miss Bertha, *I am like her only family.*

Planning for their future revolved around where they would live. Both of them wanted to build their home. Nathan and Anna suggested they live at the farm while their home was being built and even suggested they might want to build their future home on a section of the farm. If it had been Matthew's choice, he would have liked the idea of living on the farmland, but Ivy was not thrilled with the prospect of living there. She conceded that she could live at the farm while their home was being constructed, but she had found a new upscale section in Hawthorne that appealed to her. They went to look at the new development and chose an oversized plot of ground for their home. Ivy's excitement over her very own home delighted Matthew. He knew he would miss the farm, and he was surprised at the style of home and furnishings that appealed to Ivy, but he wanted her to have what was going to make her happiest. They chose the house plans and engaged a fine builder to erect a low, rambling modern ranch house.

IVY AND MATTHEW

DUE TO PERFECT planning by Anna, the wedding was done to perfection. Ivy looked positively beautiful, and Matthew was, what you would have to describe as, giddy with joy. Ivy made her entrance on the arm of Nathan after descending the huge staircase. Dan was Matthew's best man, and Martha was the matron of honor. They took their vows standing before the huge fireplace in the beautiful old living room that was filled with flowers and lit by candles. After the ceremony, they exited to the terrace, where all their friends waited to greet and congratulate the new Mr. and Mrs. Matthew

Hawthorne. The entire terrace area, where everyone gathered for the reception, was lit with tiny lights, which were strung over trees and bushes. Anna had engaged a harpist to provide soft background music. It was a heavenly sight.

Due to Matthew's work schedule, the honeymoon had to be brief, and they were soon back at the farm after only a week in the mountains. Matthew surprised Ivy with a car of her own...a small red convertible. She had never felt so free. She spent as little time at the farm as possible and could be seen every day checking on her new home and visiting with Miss Bertha, who remained her closest friend. Many days, she would be gone for the entire day, because she preferred going to the city for her purchases. To her, the women's clothes sold in Hawthorne were not the latest styles and were too provincial for her tastes. She was always looking for something more striking and out of the ordinary for herself. Ivy also preferred the furniture sold in the city stores, because she wanted sleek modern instead of what she thought of as the heavy, dowdy styles most people in Hawthorne had in their homes. She knew that Matthew's trust fund, which had been put in place for him till he reached maturity was now his, and since he had told her he wanted her to have everything that would make her happy, she felt free to buy everything that caught her fancy. Oh, what a good life! To think, she even had her own checking account.

After several months, their new home was finished, draperies were hung, and the furniture was all in place. It was time to settle into their new life.

Anna and Nathan had mixed feelings about their leaving the farm. They had hoped to get to know Ivy better and to help her in any way they could to meet some of their friends or advise her in any way about her new home. However, they soon found that she had her own agenda, and it did not include them, so they stepped back and decided she would let them know if she needed their help. In no way did they want interfere. On the other hand, they were happy for their son, who delighted in everything Ivy did. Anna said, "I guess, all people love and live in different ways, and we can't expect our children to be clones of us. All we can do is rejoice for them and hope all their dreams come true as ours have. Oh, Nathan, you've always made me so happy, and I do so treasure your love. I just want them to be as happy as we are."

The newlyweds settled into their new life. Their home delighted Ivy, and she could hardly wait to show it off to Bertha (she had dropped the Miss) and her new neighbors. It was all her creation...the modern chrome and teak furniture throughout the low, rambling house with the interior primary color being shades of purple with accents of apple green. In her wildest dreams, Ivy had never imagined she would have such a home. None of the other houses in this new section of town were nearly as large as her new home, and she was sure none of them could compare with the interior decorations she had selected. Matthew continued trying to make up for all the years Ivy had lived as a vagabond, so he stood aside enjoying her delight.

Ivy had very little in common with the young people in Hawthorne that Matthew had known all his life. Bertha still remained her special confidante, and she spent many hours with Ivy in her new home. Ivy made it a point to meet her new neighbors and to cultivate their friendship by inviting the women to lunch and the couples to little parties. Ivy knew nothing about entertaining, so she relied on Bertha to be her guide. Bertha replaced the mother Ivy had hardly known. She blinded herself to the flaws in Ivy, thus missing any chance to correct any of her behavior or to guide her in other ways. She loved her unconditionally.

One day, Matthew said, "Ivy, I've missed seeing Dan and Martha. Let's invite them to dinner. I'm sure they'd like to see our home, and, you know, Dan is my best friend." He saw the frown appear on Ivy's face and realized she was nervous about entertaining. "We'll keep it really informal. I'll do all the cooking on the grill, and that will make it easy for you." He knew Ivy had no hostessing skills, and once again, he thought it was due to her deprived youth.

One thing Ivy did enjoy was showing off their fabulous new home, and in her mind, she just knew how much Martha must be envying her. On the contrary, it was Martha's turn to smile and keep saying, "Lovely" to everything, while all the time, she was thinking, *Poor Matthew, this must be a nightmare for him.* Martha and Ivy had little in common, and therefore, conversation between them was brief. However, Dan and Matthew were so glad to be together, they kept conversation moving. They set a date to play tennis and suggested Ivy might want to take tennis lessons, so that someday, they could play doubles, but she declined, saying she didn't think she would be very good at it and really was not interested.

Ivy and some of her new friends did take bridge lessons, and they had regular dates to play in their homes. These women were new to the area. Their husbands were climbers in their professions, most of them working for large corporations in Wayville. Ivy was impressed to know they were all climbing the corporate ladder, and she was embarrassed when she told them Matthew was a teacher in the local high school. However, the name Hawthorne carried a lot of weight, and Ivy was determined to be a member of this group of country clubbers. She became the instigator of the bridge parties, shopping forays, anything for fun. However, she still spent a lot of time with Bertha, who loved being privy to all the gossip.

The young people, who were buying into this new upscale community called Mayfair Estates, were working toward becoming the leaders in big business and manufacturing. They all worked in Wayville, a city about twenty miles from Hawthorne and had very little interest in the little town of Hawthorne. The men traveled a lot and worked long hours, which gave their wives plenty of time for their own pursuits, which consisted mostly of whatever fun they could plan. They all belonged to the Wayville Country Club and played cards and lunched there often. Ivy aspired to be like them in all they did; she loved their lifestyle. In her search for social standing with the new crop of young people in her community, Ivy overlooked the hometowners who had been Matthew's friends all his life.

Matthew was more dedicated to his teaching than ever and spent much time preparing lesson plans and giving time to the many extracurricular activities at the school. He felt very strongly about being available to any student who needed his council, regardless of the problem. The students always knew he was there for them and was never judgmental but always understanding; they could always count on him. Parents, too, came to him quite often for advice regarding a problem they might be having with their teenager. Matthew spent long hours at school, and he felt fortunate that Ivy never rebuked him about the time she had to be without him. She was always busy, but she made sure she left his dinner in the refrigerator if she were going to be out. There were many nights he ate alone. He missed having her there to greet him at the end of the day. There were many times he longed to have someone with whom to share his thoughts and ideas, but he understood Ivy had been without friends for so many years of her life, and now, she was making up for lost time. On days when he knew Ivy would be gone for the day, he tried to visit with his parents for a short time. He had seen very little of them since his move to Mayfair. Anna always enveloped him in a warm, motherly hug, and Nathan gave him a fatherly pat on the back before they settled down for a short visit. The farm had been his home for many years, and, Matthew realized, it still felt like home.

When the school year was over the first year after their marriage, Matthew surprised Ivy with tickets for a cruise. After all, they had not been able to have a long honeymoon, and this would make up for it. Ivy was overjoyed with the idea of a cruise, and she thought, *Now I can buy all the right cruise clothes.* Preparing for the cruise was going to be most of the fun as far as she was concerned. *I will have a lot to tell my friends when we return, and they will be so envious* was her second thought. Matthew had suggested to Dan that he and Martha should join them, but they had to decline because they couldn't leave their patients at that time. Actually, Martha could not imagine spending long periods of time with Ivy. They had so little in common. What would they do? What would they find to talk about?

By the second year of marriage, Matthew and Ivy had pretty much established a daily routine: She was gone most of the day with friends during the week, and he spent longer hours at school. On the weekends, they were either going to a party or entertaining in their home. Ivy was living life at a frantic pace, and Matthew could see no prospect of her slowing down. The rut they had established grew deeper until their paths scarcely crossed. Sex was practically nonexistent...an occasional act. Matthew had thought it strange she had never responded to his sexual advances, but when they were first married, he attributed it to shyness. Now, he was sure she regarded lovemaking as a duty, not the ultimate love act.

During their fourth year of marriage and after much soul searching, Matthew had geared himself up for a serious talk with Ivy. He had known for sometime that neither of them was fulfilled in their marriage, never sharing their inner thoughts and dreams...never sharing intimacy and love. It was time, Matthew knew, for each of them to move on from what he perceived as their humdrum existence. He was tired of her friends, their never-ending parties, and their superficial lives. He wanted out. Before he had a chance to talk with Ivy about their failed marriage, Ivy announced she was going to have a baby. Matthew was stunned, and yet, as he got used to the idea, he was happy. He would have this little one he could teach, protect, and love. He set his sights on a new view of the future. Matthew's first thought was to rush to Anna and Nathan with the news. He knew they would be overjoyed at the prospect of another generation of Hawthornes.

As for Ivy, she wasn't looking forward to the nine months ahead when she would gain weight and, in her words, look grotesque, but most of her new friends had babies or were expecting. Now, she could be a part of all the baby-planning sessions. She had never thought that she had measured up to Anna and Nathan's standards, but now, when she presented them with a new little Hawthorne, they might hold her in higher regard.

Dr. Hurley pronounced her healthy and said she showed no sign that she would have a problem pregnancy or delivery. However, Ivy convinced Matthew that he would have to be very careful of her because she wanted to do nothing that would harm their baby. Matthew cautioned their housekeeper, Lila, to see that Ivy ate the right foods and got plenty of rest. Lila mumbled to herself, "Ivy will do just what Ivy wants to do."

Ivy spent nine months being pampered in every way, shopping for the most expensive and attractive maternity clothes, and being treated to a grand baby shower. Except for the extra weight which made her a bit clumsy, she enjoyed it all.

They rejoiced in April when their beautiful baby girl was born. Matthew was sure something this wonderful could never have happened before; his daughter was a miracle...his daughter had to be the most beautiful baby ever. He leaned over Ivy, and with tears in his eyes, he thanked her for this miracle. He asked Ivy what they should name her, and since Ivy's favorite movie star was named Kathryn, that was the name she chose. She liked the name Susan, too, so their little girl was christened Kathryn Susan Hawthorne.

Two days after Kathryn's birth, Dan and Martha greeted their new daughter. They named her Emma but always called her Emmie. Kathryn and Emmie were destined to be best friends all their lives.

KATHRYN SUSAN HAWTHORNE

KATHRYN HAWTHORNE WAS a beautiful, happy baby....chubby with a round, rosy face, a head of auburn curls, and she had inherited her father's deep brown eyes. Anna and Nathan adored her from the first moment they laid eyes on her, and she became Katie Sue to Nathan. Anna yearned to have this beautiful baby girl in her arms, and whenever Matthew took her to the farm, Kathryn was placed in those loving arms.

As a young child Kathryn probably received more kisses than any other child ever had, because Ivy gave her goodbye kisses when she left and hello kisses when she returned; her mother came and went a lot. Whenever Ivy returned from an outing and after the hello kiss, she always tweaked Kathryn's chin and asked, "What have you done today?" Kathryn would babble on about her toys, games, and different things she and Lila had done. Her daddy was different, because he picked her up, twirled her around to make her laugh, and he would ask, "What shall we play now?" Her world took on a different hue when he was around; everything seemed brighter and safer. Matthew read to her every day, and they took long walks while he pointed out all the wonders of nature and took time to answer her many, many questions. The farm was a favorite of theirs, and they explored every inch of it. Except for her dad, Granna and Poppy were her favorite people, whom she knew loved her no matter what. One of her favorite places on the farm was the stable with the beautiful horses. Poppy bought her a pony when she was small and her love of riding was born. Instead of fairytales, Poppy told her stories about all the past Hawthorne generations, who had lived at the farm, about Isaac and the settling of the land. On Kathryn's fifth birthday, Ivy had a luncheon to attend at the country club.

"I'm sorry, dearie, that mommy can't be with you today, but Daddy is going to take you to the farm, and you can have fun with Granna and Poppy," Ivy said to Kathryn.

Then to Matthew, "She'll never miss me, and I really want to go to the luncheon."

Poppy and Anna surprised Kathryn with a golden retriever puppy, whose name was Barney. "A puppy of my very own! Oh, Granna and Poppy, I love you!" Kathryn nuzzled her beautiful new friend. She had every kind of toy, but this was different, a real puppy instead of a stuffed one.

She was so overjoyed with Barney that Matthew hated to dampen her spirits. "Barney is a wonderful gift, Kathryn, and I know you love him, but I'm afraid he will have to stay at the farm. You know your mother has always said we can't have any animals in the house like a cat or dog. Besides, Barney will like it here, because he won't have to be tied up, and he'll be able to run free all the time."

As she snuggled with Barney, huge tears formed in Kathryn's eyes and slid down her cheeks. Nathan and Anna could hardly bear to see their granddaughter so unhappy.

Matthew tried once again to sooth Kathryn. "You know Poppy and Granna will take good care of Barney. And just think of this...we'll come out to the farm more often now so you can play with him. You'll like that, won't you?"

She knew her dad was bound to be right so she dried her eyes with the back of her hand and contented herself with playing with her puppy. She liked the idea that Barney would give them an excuse to spend more time with Granna and Poppy.

Kathryn's most special friend was Emmie Hurley, Dr. Dan's daughter. The friendship between Dan and Matthew had deepened over the years, which was especially good for Matthew because he needed someone to confide in whenever he was troubled. There was little Dan could do about Matthew's sad marriage, but his listening with a kindly ear was soothing for Matthew. Whenever they had any free time, they spent it together, and these times usually included their daughters.

Many times, when Matthew and Kathryn were going to the farm, they would invite Emmie to join them. When Poppy realized they were likely to have two little girls with them often, he bought another pony, and both girls had riding lessons. These were happy, carefree days, and as they grew older, they were set free from their elders to explore all the areas on the farm. They loved to go to the old log cabin and pretend they were the first people to live there. Other times, they played games with the children who lived on the farm. Barney followed everywhere they went, always barking at any intruder he thought might be apt to harm the girls. One of the farm children they liked most was Alexander Adams, whose grandfather had been in charge of the stables for years. Alexander liked having an appreciative audience that would listen raptly to his expounding on the care of horses, naming the different breeds and each breed's characteristics. He had learned it all from his Grandpa Ellis. Someday, he said, he would be doing what his grandpa did, training horses. The girls were in awe of him and his vast knowledge of horses. Alexander enjoyed impressing them. Often, when they were around the age of ten, they liked to take books to the farm and head to their special place to have a picnic and to stretch out under a huge maple tree and read while their devoted protector, Barney, took a nap next to Kathryn. This favorite spot overlooked a pond that seemed to be a favorite gathering place for all the ducks on the farm. The sounds of the farm were all around them, the mooing of the cows, the ducks quacking, and the many birds presenting their musical chorus. Kathryn and Emmie instinctively knew these days were to be treasured forever.

When she wasn't romping with friends or riding with Poppy, Kathryn was with her Granna, as she called Anna. In her mind, Poppy always knew the answers to everything, could fix anything, and told the best stories. Granna was just as important to her in other ways. Granna was gentle and loving. Always, when she was tired, she climbed on Granna's lap and listened to one of her lullabies. As soon as she could reach the keys, Granna started teaching her simple melodies on the piano, and from an early age, they would sit for hours drawing pictures. One of their favorite places for drawing and coloring was in the huge kitchen, where they sat at the long table with their art paper and paints spread out, while Kathryn created some fantasy. Sometimes, one or two of Gemma's children would join them. Granna helped them all, but she recognized Kathryn's outstanding talent. When she got older, Granna took her to the cabin where they would set up easels and both of them would paint. Other than her father, Granna and Poppy were the greatest influence on Kathryn's life. Seldom has a child experienced such a strong bond with her grandparents.

When they were elementary school age, Kathryn and Emmie were free to explore every area of their town. They knew all the stores and the owners, their teachers greeted them on the street, and the police and firemen were cognizant of their every move. The children were always watched over and protected by everyone in the town, because they were members of the town family. That was small-town life in those days. It was understood by all the children that their families expected them to behave in a way that would not dishonor their family, and they came to realize that they not only represented their family, but their town. If they ever did get into any trouble, their parents would surely be informed by the grapevine. Hawthorne was not a town where no one did any wrong, where fights did not happen, or tragedies did not occur, but it was agreed by everyone that it was just about as good a place to live as anywhere else and better than most.

Hawthorne was Kathryn's world, and she was happy and secure in it. Her mother took her to Newberry's often so that Bertha could see what a pretty daughter she had, and while in the store, Kathryn was always treated to a little toy, trinket, or candy. Bertha doted on her just like a grandmother, and for birthdays and Christmas, she would lavish gifts on her.

Matthew was always delighted to have Kathryn by his side, and they spent a lot of time on Main Street. Sometimes, Matthew had business to attend to, and sometimes, they just went to Main Street to the ice cream parlor and visited with Wilma and Frank Emerson. The Emersons had leased this space several years before and installed a marble soda fountain with a mirror on the wall behind it. There were no booths, but the room was furnished with little round tables held up with heavy wire legs and chairs to match. The Emersons served coffee, tea, sandwiches with chips and pickles, and the best ice cream concoctions to be found anywhere. They always made double-dip ice cream cones, not puny one dippers, and their sodas, sundaes, and banana splits were something to behold. Emerson's was an institution in Hawthorne.

Main Street was the gathering place for everyone. The street was laid out in a square with a green space in the center, and there was a store for every need: Burke's Clothing Store, the Evans Family Grocery Store, Fred Harris's Drugstore, Sara and Louise Knowles Dry Goods, Root's Hardware, Clark's Meat Market, Ike Pappas Shoe Repair and Dry Cleaning, Charles and Edna Murphy's Shoe Store, and Jean Rizzo's hair salon. Lewis Purvis was the jeweler. Of course, as mentioned before, there were Newberrys', Emersons', and Walters' restaurant. There was also the bank and offices for doctors, dentists, and attorneys. The Ott's owned the Roxy Movie Theater. All the businesses were owned by townspeople except the Kroger store, but it was managed by a local man, Frank Orman. Many of these businesses had been in the same families for many years, having been passed down by earlier entrepreneurs. Main Street afforded "one-stop" shopping. Quite often, Matthew would take Kathryn to Main Street on Saturday evening, because that was the best time of all. Everyone went to do their weekly shopping, and the townspeople were joined by all the farm families around the area. The young people went to the Roxy and after the movie, migrated to Emerson's. Their elders did their shopping and walked leisurely around the square greeting and visiting with all their friends. It was an innocent and fun time.

The years seemed to roll by too quickly to suit the older members of the Hawthorne family; they could hardly believe Kathryn was now a teenager. She was popular with all the young people and involved in most of the school activities, including cheerleading as co-captain of the squad along with Emmie. Kathryn excelled in all her studies but mostly in the arts. Emmie remained her best friend and confidante, but they spent hours with all their friends at parties, movies at the Roxy, and loafing at Emerson's. Some of the best parties were held at the Hawthorne farm where Nathan had installed a large pool, and there was an extensive area for their games. It was a treat for all the teenagers when they could go there and likewise, a treat for Anna and Nathan. They loved to hear the joyful screams and happy laughter filling the air.

Matthew was still teaching at the high school and had earned his position as the most esteemed teacher on the staff. He had been offered the position of principal, and then the school board tried to tempt him with the superintendent's job, but he declined both offers. He did not want to leave the classroom, where, he felt, he had more influence on the young people. He certainly didn't need the added money, and he was fulfilled completely working closely with the students. He was glad to be where he could observe Kathryn often during each day, but he made sure he watched from afar. Ivy would have liked for Matthew to accept the position of superintendent because of the prestige it would bring, but she had lost all influence on Matthew's life. For years, they had been going through the motions of a happy marriage. Matthew felt it was worth continuing this sham marriage in order for Kathryn to have a stable home life.

Ivy was busier than ever with her friends, playing bridge, shopping, going to the spa, and she still went to see Bertha regularly. When Bertha had free time from the store, they often went to the nearby city for a day of browsing in the stores and to have lunch at a favorite restaurant, while they caught up on the gossip about people and happenings in Hawthorne.

Ivy liked to advise Kathryn on her choice of clothes, hairstyle, and friends. She was delighted Kathryn seemed to be the most popular girl in her school and was always glad to receive compliments from her friends on her rearing of such a fine young lady. Kathryn wanted to please her mother and tried to follow her advice on most things, but some of the advice was difficult for Kathryn to process in her mind. The most troublesome advice had to do with sex. As soon as Ivy realized her daughter had reached the age to date, she began warning her about boys and their sex appetites. She wanted Kathryn to realize, she said, that the only thing all boys and men were interested in was sex and that they would go to any lengths to get it; they would try seduction, even tell you they love you, give you gifts, and finally, they would grasp and paw you, and she said, "Believe me, it's not pleasant. So," she told Kathryn, "before you give in to any of that, be sure you have captured a man who can give you a good life…It is easier to live with a man of means for life than a poor one." This was Ivy's council to Kathryn, council she repeated many times. All of this was very difficult for Kathryn to believe when she thought of her tender, loving father. On the other hand, why would her mother say such things if they were not true…a mother just wouldn't say such things if they weren't true! No one ever knew why Kathryn seemed friendly but aloof around boys and men—all, that is, with the exception of her father and Poppy.

Toward the end of her junior year in high school, Kathryn had to deal with the death of her parents. Ivy and Matthew had gone to a social event in the nearby city, and on their way home, driving on icy roads in a blinding snowstorm, they were killed in a head-on collision. Kathryn and Emmie were staying the night together and had just returned from a basketball rally at the high school, after which all the teens had gone to Emerson's, as was their habit. When the girls arrived at Kathryn's home, they were exhilarated and happy. "How about a mug of hot chocolate to help us unwind?" suggested Kathryn.

They were replaying the antics of the evening and producing gales of laughter when the doorbell rang. Their mood changed quickly when they saw Poppy at the door with Alex Adams.

"Oh, Poppy, what's happened?" Kathryn managed to ask. She was sure something bad had happened to Granna. Poppy looked shaken and old to her as he entered the house, and she thanked a grim Alex for doing the driving.

It was almost more than she could bear when Poppy gave her the sad news. She couldn't believe that her spunky mother and wonderful, strong father were gone....gone and would never be there with her again. "Gone" was such a final word. In an instant, her life had changed.

Ivy and Matthew were buried in the Hawthorne plot at the farm after the largest funeral there had ever been in Hawthorne. The world would never be the same again for Nathan and Anna, but they stayed strong for Kathryn. She was so young and lost. They were by her side continually as was Emmie. No one was more stricken than Bertha; Ivy had been like a daughter to her. The Hawthornes thoughtfully included her in all the family rituals and kept her near them so she would not mourn alone. When the services were over and they were alone again, they, along with Bertha and Emmie, sat in Anna's room and talked about the past and the good times they had enjoyed. Yes, they told Kathryn, her parents had died too young, but their lives had been full and happy.

Kathryn had no desire to return to the home her parents had built, and so it was decided, she should move in with Nathan and Anna. The farm had always been a haven to her, and now, more than ever, it seemed like the most soothing place she could stay, and she would be with the two people she most loved and admired. Anna told her to choose which room she wanted, and she chose a large room on the west side of the house. Emmie helped her gather all her belongings, and they spent many hours fixing and arranging everything to Kathryn's liking.

The summer after she moved to the farm, Kathryn spent a lot of time reading, riding, and remembering. She realized that Granna and Poppy needed her as much as she needed them...They had lost their only child...so she made sure to spend quality time with them. They all supported each other, and their pain became less acute. Also, during the summer, Kathryn realized she had only one more year in high school and should be starting to think about which university she wanted to attend. She and Emmie poured over college guides and spent hours discussing their dreams for the future. Emmie was sure she wanted to be a nurse just like her mother, and someday, she wanted to work with her dad, Dr. Dan. Kathryn didn't have as clear an idea of her future, but she knew she wanted to learn more about art, history, and music…all the things that Granna and Poppy had nourished in her. At this point in her life, more than anything, Kathryn was sure she wanted to move from Hawthorne and the sadness of the last years, and so she applied to schools located in cities in the east. Finally, she selected a university close to New York City.

Every morning she entered high school during her senior year, Kathryn thought about her father and felt a knot in her stomach. It was still hard for her to say, "I will never see him again." She was a more subdued girl since the tragedy, but her friends, especially Emmie, held her up and carried her along. Emmie and she were the head cheerleaders, and she had many girlfriends and suitors among the boys. The suitors, she kept at a distance. Finally, the school year drew to a close, and it was time to observe the rites of graduation. She accepted Jack Root's invitation to the senior prom. He was the outstanding athlete in the school and was going to college on a football scholarship. She was the envy of many of her friends to have snagged Jack Root for the prom. Granna and Poppy enjoyed all the preparations for the prom, and Granna was delighted when Kathryn asked for her help in choosing a gown for the special night. After much searching and a few rest periods for Granna, Kathryn chose a long gown of chiffon the color of sea foam. The skirt was voluminous, the neckline draped softly, and there was a stole of the same chiffon. They both agreed, it was the right choice.

"You are the closest thing to a princess I have ever seen," said Granna proudly. "Wait till Nathan sees you. Just one more thing you must add—my pearls."

The night of the prom arrived, and when Nathan saw her coming down the huge stairway, all he could whisper in awe was his special name for her, "Oh, Katey Sue." There were tears in his eyes; their little girl had grown up and would be leaving them soon.

Her classmates had paired up, and they all looked beautiful and handsome sporting their formal attire. Emmie's date was John McMillan, who was leaving after graduation to study law. They had dated off and on during the year, but Emmie knew they probably would only see each other rarely after this night. Alex Adams from the farm, who rarely attended any school functions, had brought one of the young girls who lived on the farm. Kathryn had seen a lot of him when they were youngsters, but he was always busy with his grandfather at the stables when he got older and never seemed to care about high school activities. It was good to see him joining with all the other seniors on this special night.

Kathryn had never been much interested in dating which led many to call her a snob, but on this night, they were all together. She felt honored being with Jack Root, the star athlete. The dance was held in the school gymnasium which had been decorated by the junior class. A small local orchestra had been hired which would never have been classed as good, but the dancers didn't seem to be aware of the ragged play. The dance went on until midnight when the crowd moved to the Roxy Theater, which had been kept open for them. After the movie, they moved to a local lodge where the members were serving a late buffet for them. All of this was offered after the prom in order to keep the prom-goers in Hawthorne and entertained, so they would not be tempted to go out on the highways. They all stayed together and had a memorable time.

It was toward morning when Jack took Kathryn back to the farm. As they approached the farm on the long lane leading to the house, he stopped the car, leaned over, put his arms around her, and kissed her. Kathryn tried to accept his kisses as she knew the other girls did, but as the kisses became more amorous and insistent, she stiffened and pulled away.

"Please, Jack, don't do this," she said.

"What's with you?" he smirked. "Just come down off that pedestal and enjoy yourself." He pulled her back to him, and she began to struggle. Her dress was torn, but she continued to fight him off. *Oh*, she thought, *Mother was right...men are ugly.*

Finally, Jack acknowledged he didn't want her that bad. Jack had never been rejected before, and his pride was hurt. He turned from her, started the car, and said, "I don't need this...You aren't worth it." As soon as he stopped in front of the house, she ran from the car without a word. It was a sad ending to an evening that should have held sweet memories for her. All she wanted was to shed her clothes and climb into the safety of her bed. Her mother's years of talking about how sex was a dirty act and enjoyed by men only and that only after marriage did a woman permit it, because it was then an obligation, had hit its mark. Kathryn was sure she would never let it happen to her again. This was Ivy's legacy to her daughter.

Graduation night was special in Hawthorne, and all the seats in the auditorium were filled with proud parents and grandparents, most of them shedding prideful tears and sad tears, too, when they realized their child would be leaving the nest. Granna and Poppy had invited Bertha to join them at the suggestion of Kathryn. After all, she had been Ivy's best friend...really like family...and had always been good to Kathryn. Bertha didn't seem to have any family and since Ivy's death, had become a recluse except for the days she still spent at Newberry's. She was more than delighted to be included in their celebration.

Except for Granna, Poppy, and Emmie, Kathryn, with the fervor of youth, was anxious to leave Hawthorne for good and start the next chapter in her life. She looked forward to the city and the world outside her hometown.

HOME AGAIN

KATHRYN HAD ONLY a few miles left before she would arrive at the farm. Traveling along with no schedules or time limits, she had been able to remember in detail the events of her early life with her parents and grandparents on the farm and in the little town of Hawthorne. Memories of those years had been buried deep ever since her flight to the city, and now, they were laid bare. She felt an urgency to be back home again. However, she encountered very little traffic and thus was able to drive slowly so as not to miss any of the landmarks she remembered. The names of the people who had lived in the little neat houses along the road came back to her, and she wondered if the same families lived there still. The fruit trees were all in bloom, and most of the fields had been plowed and were being planted. She had forgotten that nearly every house had a porch where families spent the twilight hours resting and visiting. It was spring and the porches had all been cleaned, and most of the swings and rockers were freshly painted. Spring flowers were in bloom everywhere. The women had always taken pride in their flowers. Window boxes and hanging baskets were bursting with bloom at almost every house. It was obvious the people who lived in these modest homes were proud and industrious; there was not one sign of neglect anywhere. *How reassuring,* thought Kathryn, *that some things never change.*

Kathryn had only been back to the farm once since she left as a teenager and that was to attend the funeral for Granna. Granna had died peacefully in her sleep while sitting with Poppy on the terrace one late afternoon. Thankfully, she had not been sick and had not been ravaged by old age but had grown more beautiful each year. She had been Poppy's love...his life...ever since their first meeting, and after losing her, he might have given in to depression, given up on life, but he carried on as he knew she would have expected him to do. Kathryn had spent almost two weeks with him at that time, and all the farm families surrounded him with their love. On that sad visit, Kathryn had never left his side, but now she felt remorseful because she had not done more. Her dear friend, Emmie, visited with him often and always reported to Kathryn that he seemed to be doing fine. She thought, *None of us ever realized how deep the hurt went, because he was never one to share his sadness. I'm really happy to have this time to be with him.*

She finally came to the lane leading to the house, and, as Anna had done years ago, Kathryn stopped the car and got out in order to drink in the sight. The hundreds of flowers that Granna had planted had multiplied and were blooming in profusion, and the trees that Granna ordered planted during her early years on the farm were now huge and lined the lane which afforded a majestic entry to the house. After her long look at the house and surrounding fields, she drove slowly up the lane and parked near the terrace. *I don't know how I've stayed away so long,* she thought.

Kathryn was aware that Poppy had no idea of her arrival time, so he was probably visiting the different areas of the farm as he did each day, but he would be home soon for lunch. While she was parking by the terrace, Gemma appeared at the door. Jewel, their old housekeeper, had died before Granna's death, and her daughter, Gemma, who had taken over the housekeeping duties many years ago, was aging now and teaching her daughter, Jade, to assume more responsibilities. All the families had lived on the farm for generations it seemed and had passed on their duties to their children. Early in the life of the farm, when help was needed, only the most dedicated and industrious were hired. Land was set aside for each of them on which to build a little home, and most of the original families still lived in their little homes. *There is never a break or disruption in the farm schedule*, thought Kathryn, *which is very unusual. They're all like one big family.* Gemma greeted her warmly and introduced her to Jade, who had hurried to the door when she heard the car.

"You don't have any idea just how happy you've made Mr. Hawthorne, Miss Kathryn. When he told us you were going to be with him for a spell, he was all smiles, and, I swear, he grew younger right before my eyes. We're all happy to see you Miss Kathryn, and we're hoping you can stay for a long time."

"Your family has taken good care of Poppy for many years, Gemma, and there's no way I can thank you enough. I know you all love him, and believe me, that love is returned in full measure. I'm so glad to be here with you all again. Right now, I wonder, could I have a glass of iced tea while I just sit here on the terrace and enjoy the peace of this place?"

As she sat there sipping her tea, she thought about the farm, its history, and the past generations, her father, and the families on the farm, and she was overwhelmed with a feeling she could not describe or name. Her thoughts took her to Granna, and she could almost feel her presence on the terrace. The terrace had been her creation and one of her favorite places. And she thought of Poppy, not until she had reached this point in her life could she fully appreciate the man. Oh yes, she had loved him dearly all her life, but she had never really thought about the man and his life. Now, as she lay back on the chaise with her eyes closed, she remembered hearing Granna and Poppy talking about the "powers that be" wanting him to run for a high government office. After all, he owned one of the largest land holdings in the country and operated it meticulously. With his personality, strength, and background, they said, he could take the country by storm. Poppy had thought about it for only a short time and refused, saying he did not want to give up his life and happiness on the farm and added that he was doing exactly what he wanted to do with his life. The movers and shakers realized he was firm in his refusal, but they did continue to come to him often for advice and direction. Yes, Kathryn thought, he did always live his dream...just like Isaac had done, and she was sure, her father followed his dream, too. It was a Hawthorne trait.

Thinking of Poppy without Granna would be an incomplete picture; she was so very much a part of Kathryn's past. *I have been fortunate to witness their great love and devotion*, she thought, *because a love such as theirs is rare.* They were truly soul mates. Only one other couple she knew had ever displayed the same kind of love and that was Emily and Marcus, her dear friends. A smile crossed her face as she enjoyed thoughts of their love, but suddenly, it came to her that her parents had been far from experiencing that kind of love. How sad their lives must have been…She had never given their marriage much thought before.

As she sat musing in a half dream, Nathan appeared, and at the sight of her, his face lit up, and he proceeded to smother her in his arms.

"Oh, my Katey Sue, you are here at last…I thought you'd never get here. It is so right for you to be sitting in Anna's chair on her terrace. I'm sure she's looking down and smiling on us right now. I hope you don't think me weird, but I do know she's with me all the time."

"Poppy, I'd never think of you as weird, you are the sanest person I know, and I agree, she's surely here and will always be a part of this place," she said as she reached her arms up to encircle his neck once again; he had always been her haven. Isn't it strange, she thought, the house in town, where she had lived for years, had never really been home to her...this was home.

After Anna's death, Nathan could not bring himself to sleep in the large bedroom suite they had shared. He moved to the west side of the house. Now that Kathryn was with him, he wanted her to have their room, so he had all her computer and business items placed in there. She was surprised to learn of this, but she realized it made Poppy happy to know it was being used by her. When she was a little girl, Kathryn had spent many happy hours with Granna in their room helping her brush her beautiful chestnut brown hair with the red highlights, wearing Granna's high heels that always clopped on the floor, trying on hats and gloves, and even sometimes being allowed to try a little lipstick. Memories were everywhere.

After a good night's sleep, Kathryn was renewed and anxious to jump into all the things she had made mental notes to do while she was driving the many miles to the farm. She dressed hurriedly in a pair of jeans and a soft white shirt, tied a scarf around her long auburn hair, and hurried downstairs to join Poppy for breakfast. After Anna's death, he had reverted to eating in the kitchen, but this morning, he was waiting for her in the small dining nook. Gemma provided a very adequate farm breakfast for them, the likes of which Kathryn had not eaten for many years. This was a far cry from her city "grab and run" toast and coffee and eating alone. They talked over their plans for the day. Poppy would saddle his horse and spend the morning visiting the different farm sites. Kathryn planned to spend the day getting settled, but the first order of business for her was to call Emmie. Also, she had to get her computer equipment installed and then she would get in touch with Marcus and her New York office. After all, she told Poppy, she had work to do while she was at the farm. "My most important task this summer is to design a new ad campaign for an elite costumer. It has to be in place well before Christmas. I'll probably be spending quite a bit of time working while I'm here. Marcus is so generous in giving me all this time away from the office, I can't let him down. I'm sure you'll understand, Poppy."

"Of course, I understand, and I'll try to stay out of your way when you are working, but this morning, before we do anything else, I just have to show you a surprise I have for you."

Poppy was fairly bursting at the seams to tell her of his latest gift for her...a beautiful black stallion.

For a moment, Kathryn was speechless as she looked at him with unbelieving eyes. "You never cease to amaze me with your extravagant gifts, Poppy. You just keep spoiling me!"

After a tender hug and a few happy tears from Kathryn, Poppy told her that Abe Ellis was no longer able to manage the stables and that Abe's grandson, Alex Adams, was now in charge, and they, Alex and Poppy, had searched for the horse together. Alex had trained and groomed this horse to perfection, but he said, "We have not named him...That is for you to do."

"You know, Poppy, years ago, when we were kids running all over the farm, Alex said he was going to do just what his grandfather did someday. It's the only thing he has ever wanted to do, another man following his dream."

After complimenting Gemma on their delicious breakfast, Kathryn hurried to phone Emmie before office hours would start for her. Emmie had replaced her mother, Martha, as her father's nurse. Martha still assisted them when they had a heavy schedule, but she was happy to be able to spend more time in the home she had made her family's special nest. Now she could devote more time to the gardens and home and still have time to enjoy the results of her labors.

Emmie was an early riser and always arrived at the office by seven o'clock every morning in order to have the examining rooms in perfect order, to review the files of the day's appointments, and to make and have a cup of coffee. She had just sat down with the files and her coffee when the phone rang, and she heard her best friend's voice.

"Hey, you finally got here...thought you'd never make it...We've been waiting for days, it seems. This is like old times. When are we going to get together? We have a lot of catching up to do." She was the same old Emmie...bubbling over with enthusiasm.

A smile of delight crossed Kathryn's face as she heard the perky voice of her dear friend. She replied, "I have so much to do here today getting my computer installed, unpacking, and arranging my room. Poppy has put me in the room he and Granna shared. I can hardly believe it, but he seems so happy having me use the room. I suppose it's been hard for him to see it vacant. I'm sure you can understand I really want to spend this day with Poppy, because even with all the daily activity on the farm and many visitors, I know he's been lonely. How about Saturday for you and I to get together? You don't have office hours then, do you? Why don't we meet at Walters' Restaurant? It's still on Main Street, isn't it?"

"Oh yes, Walters' is still in its same location. Why don't we meet at noon for lunch and plan to spend the rest of the day together. I want to hear all about your work and life in the city."

The local computer expert arrived to install Kathryn's equipment. Previous to his arrival, she had enlisted Gemma's husband, Jake, to help her rearrange some of the furniture in order to accommodate the installation. However, she was careful not to change the room too much, because she, like Poppy, wanted it to stay just the way Granna had arranged it.

She phoned Marcus to let him know all was well and that she had enjoyed her drive back to the farm. She could hear the relief in his voice when he answered her call. "Emily and I miss you more than you can know, and I must say, we've fretted these past days when we didn't hear from you. You certainly took your time getting back to the farm."

"I'm sorry if I worried you, Marcus, but I so enjoyed taking my time and enjoying the beautiful countryside and frankly, enjoying the solitude. I have to thank you again for allowing me this time...It means the world to me."

"Well, the office won't be the same while you're gone, and Emily and I will miss you terribly, but we want you to do what is best for you," he said.

"I want to let you know that I have my computer installed and will be in touch with my office there regularly. In fact, I'm going to call Alma today and give her a list of items to take care of for me. When you have time, will you please touch base with her, because I know you'll be able to tell if she is comfortable handling everything there. I just don't want to swamp her. And don't worry, I will be working toward the designs for the fall campaigns. I mustn't keep you too long, but do say 'hi' to Emily and give her a hug for me please," she said as she signed off.

Once again, she thought, *I have certainly been blessed to have Marcus and Emily for my dear friends.*

The morning seemed to fly, and by noon, she was happy to have accomplished so much. Her clothes were unpacked, the luggage stored, and her new home office was all in place. Now she was ready to settle in and soak up the aura of Isaac's Dream. As she stood at the bay window looking toward the east, Poppy entered the room. *How right this is,* he thought, *having Katey Sue in Anna's room.* She was the only family he had now, and to him, she was perfection. Kathryn felt his presence, turned, and smiled lovingly while thinking, *There could never be another man to measure up to him. He's strong, yet gentle and so very handsome even at his advanced age.*

After lunch, they walked to the stable so Kathryn could see her magnificent stallion. Alex knew it wouldn't be long after her arrival that Nathan would want to show her his surprise, and he was there to greet them. Kathryn had only seen Alex briefly since they were children romping over the fields, and she was amazed to see the man he had become. He was about an inch taller than Poppy, stood tall and straight, and he had a strong physique. His tanned countenance was framed by a square jaw and topped with a thatch of sun-bleached hair. He smiled broadly at the sight of her, displaying warmth and easy charm. *I can't think who he reminds me of,* she thought, *but there is someone.* He looked at her with his piercing blue eyes while he reached out his hand to welcome her.

"Alex, I see you're following the dream you always talked about when we were kids; you always said you were going to do just what your grandfather did: train horses."

"Yes." He nodded. "Every day, I thank my lucky stars I'm doing the work I love and that I can do it right here. You know, I always feel this farm is a little piece of heaven on earth. I'm glad you're going to be here for awhile to enjoy it."

"Training horses isn't all Alex does," Nathan added. "He's a crack pilot. He spent some years in the United States Air Force and, in my book, he's one of the best. Whenever I have to make a trip that is quite a distance from here, Alex is my pilot."

"Do you charter a plane?" she asked.

"No, I bought a four-seater and keep it in a hanger in Wayville, where they have a little aviation group. I thought about having my own landing field here, but I didn't want to tear up any of the fields, so I just rent space over there. Comes in handy when I want to take a quick trip."

Kathryn hadn't known about all this and was a little flabbergasted. "You never cease to amaze me. I'll have to fly with you two while I'm here. I would love to see this area from the air."

"Just name the day," said Alex.

"Why are we standing here when there is a high-spirited stallion waiting to meet his new owner?" Nathan could contain himself no longer, and they moved inside the stable where Alex led her to the stall, and she got her first look at her horse. She walked up slowly and while speaking in a soft tone, she stroked his face. She could see the fire in his eyes, but he seemed to feel her gentleness, and he responded by remaining still and receiving her soft touch. When Alex felt Kathryn and her horse knew each other well enough, he led the horse out of his stall and walked him around while Kathryn stood aside and looked in awe at this magnificent creature. She was sure there had never been a steed to equal this one.

"If you want to ride now, I'll saddle him for you," said Alex.

"Oh yes," she replied, "I'm still breathless at the sight of him. Poppy, you have given me so many presents, but you surely outdid yourself with this one. I know for sure I'll be spending many hours riding. Wish I had a good name for him."

When she returned from her ride, Kathryn's cheeks were rosy, her hair was windblown, and she was truly in high spirits. As she removed the saddle and prepared to cool and rub down the horse, she told Alex she had never ridden such a spirited stallion. "He's something from legends I've heard. You are probably going to laugh at the name I've chosen, but there is only one that will do. I'm calling him Rhett after one of my favorite fictional characters. They are both handsome, beguiling, fearless, and slightly reckless. Just have to name him Rhett."

Alex couldn't stifle a chuckle as he said, "Well, it certainly wouldn't have been a name any man would have given him, but I guess most of your women friends will understand."

"I might have known you'd say something like that, but I won't change my mind. Rhett, it is. I do want to thank you for all the help you gave Poppy in selecting Rhett and training him for me. He handles beautifully, even though he's very spirited."

Saturday morning, Kathryn rose early, as was her custom, poured herself a large glass of orange juice and proceeded to the stables. She had been riding Rhett every morning since Poppy had presented her with the stallion; sometimes, she even took an evening ride. She enjoyed both times of the day; morning, with the east throwing light on the new day and the evening, when the west was aflame with the dying embers of the day. She realized this closeness to nature had been one thing lacking in the city. The high rises, the paved-over earth and the constant din of voices and traffic formed an impenetrable barrier to nature. Alex was always at the stables when she arrived, and day by day, they were getting to know each other better. She told him her ride would be short that morning as she was going to meet Emmie Hurley for lunch.

"Oh yes," he replied. "I remember her when we all went to Hawthorne High together. Didn't she go away to medical school?"

"Yes, she's now working in her father's office as his nurse."

"Tell her I said 'hello.'"

As she drove to town, Kathryn realized she was excited about seeing Main Street again, and best of all, this was Saturday so there would be a lot people there...just like old times. She drove onto Main Street and thought she must be in the wrong place. There were only three cars parked there and very few people. It was quiet and deserted. *What has happened?* she thought. Thankfully, Walters' restaurant was as she remembered it, except it sported a new modern facade. She stood for a time taking a long look at the entire square. Many of the stores were closed, more cheap-looking modern facades covered many of the old brick buildings; everything looked tacky and unkempt. It was hard for her to take in. When had all this happened? She turned slowly and entered the restaurant. Emmie was sitting in one of the booths enjoying her first cup of coffee. When she saw Kathryn, she got up quickly and moved toward her with open arms and a huge smile.

"There's no way for me to tell you how good it is to see you again. You look wonderful, so I guess life is good for you. I want to hear all about your exciting life in the city."

"Oh, Emmie, I've missed you, too. I don't have any friends that I feel as close to as you. By the way, you look like life is agreeing with you, too," Kathryn replied as she surveyed her friend. They were both about medium height, lean and well built, but Emmie had a heart-shaped face and honey-colored hair which she wore short in order to promote her natural curls. Kathryn had the square jaw of the Hawthornes and wore her wavy auburn hair long. They attracted a lot of stares from the breakfast crowd at the restaurant. The patrons all knew Emmie, but they had not seen Kathryn for years. Finally, someone whispered to another, "Isn't that Nathan Hawthorne's granddaughter?" On closer inspection, heads nodded yes.

After their greeting, they scooted into the booth, and a young girl came to take their orders. "Do you still have your wonderful pies?" asked Kathryn. When she learned they were still serving their famous pie, she said, "I don't usually have much dessert, but today, I'm going to indulge. I would like the coconut cream, please."

Emmie chuckled, "Remember all the times we used to have coconut cream pie together when we were teens? And remember Emerson's? We have so many happy memories, don't we?" They moved to the land of "remember when," and after a time, progressed to "tell me about your life now." No one was ever rushed at Walters', and they felt free to occupy their space as long as they desired.

It took a long time for Kathryn to tell Emmie all about her work at Thayer Enterprises and about Emily and Marcus. Emmie wanted to hear it all and prodded Kathryn to tell her more and more by asking questions about her daily schedule and the renowned clients she served. Letters could not tell it all. At their fork in the road, they surely had taken different paths, but that had in no way dimmed their friendship.

They had finished their large wedges of pie with a "yum-yum" and ordered a second cup of coffee. Now, it was Emmie's turn to tell her story. Emmie's story of her present life took a much shorter time to relate, but it was evident she was extremely happy working with her father and helping to treat the local people she had known all her life. Her life was safe, almost stress-free, and very rewarding. Kathryn asked about Dr. Dan and his lovely wife, Martha, and she was told that Martha had pretty much retired, and Dr. Dan had slowed down considerably, so he now had an associate, Dr. Mark Taylor.

"It must be very hard for this Dr. Taylor to get established in Hawthorne, because everyone loves your dad so much, and he's been their doctor for years. I'm sure all his patients want only him when they're sick."

"You are so right; it's slow going for Mark, but he's patient and kind, and gradually, the people are accepting him, and Dad keeps telling them what a fine doctor he is. Mark is really over-qualified to be a small-town doctor and could have been on staff at several renowned hospitals, but according to him, he always wanted to be a general practitioner in a small town like ours. He and Dad get along famously, and I think if Dad had ever had a son, he would have been just like Mark."

"I'm so happy that your dad has some help, Em." A frown appeared as she went on. "Speaking of small towns, what has happened to ours? I haven't recognized a soul in here today, and that's probably because I've been away for a long time, but I hardly recognized the square when I drove here. I almost feel like a displaced person. Let's walk around the square, and you can fill me in, but before we go outside, start with this restaurant. I know Olive can't still be baking the pies, and where are Jim and Barbara Walters, who were always here?" Kathryn asked as she looked around the large room, which had not changed much in all the years she had been gone.

"You're right. Olive died several years ago. I always think she must be baking pies in heaven these days. After she died, Barbara took over from her mother, and the pies are still delicious...I guess she'd been taught well. She even comes in early every day to bake, just like her mother did all those years. Jim and Barbara's son, Bill, and Bill's wife, Jen, have the business now and their daughter, Susie, helps out. They hire a high school boy to do clean up, and since they don't have a lot of business, that's all the staff they need. We're all so used to having Walters' Restaurant here on Main Street; I don't know what we'd do without it. It's just plain, real good home cooking, and that's the way we like it. The menu never seems to change much."

They stepped out into the afternoon sunshine and started walking slowly toward the bank. So much had changed that Kathryn was surprised to see there was still a large bench in front of the bank. "Let's sit here while I try to absorb this devastation." Kathryn sighed.

"I really hadn't thought how this would appear to you. You haven't been here for so many years," replied Emmie. "It all happened gradually. Many of the merchants thought it would benefit them to 'spiff up their stores,' as they called it, by modernizing, and that explains the tacky storefronts. I told you it happened gradually over a number of years. One of the factories relocated some of its departments to another state, and they left only a skeleton crew here, so men lost jobs. But the main culprits were the large discount stores that located in Wayville, close enough to hurt the local businessmen. Everyone left town to shop there, and that was the death knell for our Main Street. Another sad part of the decline was the fact that several of the aging proprietors of our Main Street stores had turned their businesses over to their children or someone else in the family. These young people had grown up learning from their parents and had started out full of enthusiasm, but that was soon blunted by the 'discounts.' Some have closed their doors for good, and others are trying to hang on, hoping for a miracle. We've all watched it happen over the years, but no one knows what to do about it. Makes us all sad."

"I just can't take this all in. It's the saddest thing I've seen for a long time. I guess I was naive to think all of our little town would never change, but this is too much change, the wrong kind of change. Just look where Newberry's was. It's a cheap outlet store. I have so many memories of going there all the time with my mother to see Miss Bertha. Oh, poor Miss Bertha. I've lost track of her...Is she still living here?"

"Yes, she still lives in the same little house. You know, she always looked matronly and older than her age, and now, she doesn't look much different to me. Poor woman, I don't think she does anything but go to church on Sundays and work in her little flower beds. You ought to stop by to see her...It would mean a lot to her, I know."

"I'm surprised the people in this town don't care enough to do something about this erosion. I know I shouldn't criticize, because I left years ago and haven't done anything to help here, but when you've lived in a city for a number of years, you realize that living in a place like this used to be was pretty close to heaven, a place where people knew and helped each other, where they shared each other's pain and each other's happiness...That's what is important in life. If they only knew what they're letting slip through their fingers." Kathryn surprised herself with this outburst. "Listen to me. I didn't mean to speechify."

"Gee, Kathryn, I can see why you are so successful creating advertising and promotions. When you really care about something, your passion is catching. You always did have a way with words, and now, you're even better."

From Main Street, they drove all around the town. It was noted that the same families were living where they had when Kathryn was in school. All the neat, freshly painted houses surrounded by vegetable and flower gardens lifted Kathryn's spirits a bit. They went to the athletic field by the school, where they had spent so many hours cheering on their teams. Kathryn's heart skipped a beat when they passed the high school as memories of her dad came rushing in. She parked the car for a few minutes by the school entrance. Neither of them spoke as each remembered those long ago days.

"One more place we have to go is the park...I hope it's still there," said Kathryn. Emmie nodded in the affirmative, and they drove on. They bought ice cream cones and sat at a picnic table under a huge maple tree in the highest part of the park, so they could see a large part of the town. *What a wonderful little town*, thought Kathryn. *I was so lucky to have lived here for so many of my years.*

Both were interested in the other's love life, but neither had much to report. Emmie explained that she had dated several men, but the spark was never there. So far, she said, she was happy with things as they were but knew she wanted to have a family some day, and she didn't want to wait too long. "Just haven't found the right man yet, and I can't do it alone," she smiled.

Kathryn had never told Emmie about her aversion to being close to a man, and so she just said the spark had never been there for her either. She did tell Emmie about her good friend, Joshua, and their "just friends" relationship. She had been too busy, she told her friend, to have really given much thought to being married, and living alone suited her just fine.

They lingered at the park watching the little children on the swings and the youth baseball teams practicing for their summer games. Memories flooded in on them as they sat quietly thinking of all the days when they had been doing just what the present-day children were doing. It was good to know some things never changed, they thought.

The town swimming pool was being readied for the season and would open in a week. That was one thing that had changed, because there had been no pool when they were young, but maybe they had more fun swimming in the clear waters of the river that ran by the town. The river had a sandy shore which had been crowded every day in the summer. There had been no lifeguards...people just kept watchful eyes on the swimmers, and fortunately, there had been no catastrophes. Yes, they thought, it was the same with everything they did in Hawthorne...People watched over you and kept you from harm. That's what it meant to be a member of their town family.

After a period of quiet, Kathryn started to ask Emmie about some of the people she had known and about some of their classmates. The majority of those she asked about were still living in Hawthorne. Most of them had followed in their parents' footsteps, doing the same type of work or were carrying on the business their parents had left to them.

"I'm just heartsick over the condition of Main Street," sighed Kathryn again. "There just has to be an answer. I always work on the premise that for every problem, there is a solution."

"I don't know," replied Emmie. "I'm afraid it's a losing battle. There's been a lot of grumbling, but no one seems to have a solution."

The sun was starting to lower in the sky, and they continued to sit and ponder. Kathryn thought, *Is this the fate of all beautiful small towns that don't have a huge discount store?*

Suddenly, Emmie said, "Gosh! I just remembered there's going to be an alumni reunion next Saturday. We just have to go. Everyone will be there, and you can catch up with all your old friends. Don't know why it took me so long to think of it. What do you say?"

"I think you're right...I'd love to see everyone. Where are they having it?"

"It's to be in the VFW hall because they need a place large enough to accommodate a large crowd, and that's the only place big enough in Hawthorne." After a moment, Emmie continued, "You and I will probably be the only women there without an escort. Darn...I wish we had a date for the evening, but who? Do you have any ideas?"

This brought a smile to Kathryn's face, because she didn't think it would be so bad to make an appearance without a man at her side, but it seemed important to Emmie. "You know, I've been gone for so long, I don't know anyone anymore. Only person I know who is our age is Alex Adams from the farm. I've gotten to know him rather well and could broach the subject to him...I'll feel pretty silly asking him, if he already has a lady friend...but I'll give it try...Do you have anyone in mind?"

"I know of one person who might be available, and that's Dr. Mark Taylor, Dad's associate. Don't get any ideas," she said as she saw Kathryn raise her eyebrows. "We're good friends, and he is a wonderful person, but no, there aren't any romantic feelings between us. If he doesn't have any medical appointments, he just might be glad to go."

The sun was setting on their day, and they had to leave the park, but now, they had something to look forward to and plans to make. Kathryn was surprised at how excited she was about it all, and she hoped Alex would be able to go with them.

"I'm happy to see that the park has not changed," said Kathryn. "This has been a good day." Then she giggled softly and said, "I hope you get your date for next Saturday. Let's call each other as soon as we know something."

The next day, Sunday, Kathryn and Poppy went to church, and she saw people she hadn't thought of in years. People remarked to each other that Nathan looked younger since Kathryn was with him again, and they all agreed she was the most beautiful girl they had seen in years.

"Too bad Anna isn't here to enjoy her granddaughter," they said.

Kathryn had not felt as relaxed and happy for a long time as she did being with her Poppy on that Sunday morning. It was a most beautiful spring day; the air clear and cool, and the trees dressed in their new gossamer finery. After the church service, Poppy drove her down some scenic back roads where they viewed the newly planted fields and all the spring wildflowers. Their destination was a small restaurant, The Little Cove Restaurant, that was frequented by people with discerning palates. It was quiet and secluded; the perfect place to be on this spring day. Their orders were taken, and as they enjoyed their wine, Kathryn told Poppy about the upcoming reunion. She told him about how she and Emmie were searching for dates for the evening and asked him if he knew whether Alex had a girlfriend or not. Poppy said he'd never heard Alex mention a special girl even though, he was sure Alex must date a lot, because he was a handsome young man.

"Do you think I would be out of line in asking him to accompany me to the reunion?" asked Kathryn. "He's the only eligible man I know here." Poppy assured her he thought it would be fine for her to instigate a date...adding that it couldn't be with a finer man.

The Little Cove Restaurant served a beautiful dinner of Caesar's salad, leg of lamb with mint sauce, new potatoes, corn soufflé, rolls, and coffee. As they ate, Kathryn told Poppy how distraught she was over the condition of Hawthorne. "It's dying!" she said. Nathan didn't go to town very often anymore and really had not been aware of how the town had deteriorated.

Nathan replied, "Why don't the town fathers do something about it? I guess those discount stores have played havoc with a lot of privately owned businesses, but I feel sure the Hawthorne citizens don't want a discount to move in to save the town. There ought to be something they can do. I've always believed that for every problem, there is a solution."

Kathryn smiled to herself. That was the exact phrase she had used the previous day when talking with Emmie. That must have been a lesson Poppy had taught her sometime in her past, and it had stayed with her.

"Have the people in Hawthorne ever had an issue that they all had to work together to solve? Is there any way to bring them all together?" she asked.

"I can't think of any time they've faced anything like this. The town always just went along with few ups and downs, but nothing like what you're describing to me now. You're really upset about this, aren't you, Katey Sue? I wish I had some suggestions."

The following morning, after an early breakfast, Kathryn went to the stable for her early morning ride. As she walked toward the stable, she tried to plan how she was going to broach the subject of the alumni reunion to Alex. She had never asked a man to accompany her anywhere, and she felt awkward. Alex greeted her with a warm smile saying, "You surely are an early bird...thought I was the only one around here. I think your horse is really ready for a good strong run today. You two are bonding well, I think.

You're a fine horsewoman, Kathryn. Nathan told me all about your riding prowess, but I thought he was probably exaggerating. I was wrong about that."

Kathryn was pleased to be complimented by Alex, the horse expert; she even blushed slightly all the while realizing she must get his answer about the Saturday gathering.

"Alex, did you know there's going to be an alumni reunion Saturday in the VFW hall? Emmie told me about it yesterday."

After a slight hesitation, he said, "Oh yes, I do think I heard something about it. Are you going?"

"I hope to," she replied "and I would like to have an escort, so I was wondering if I might prevail on you to accompany me...that is, if you aren't doing anything else that evening."

A smile appeared as he answered, "You know, that's the best offer I've had for a long time. I would really like to be your date, and I'm glad you asked me...I probably wouldn't have gone otherwise. I stay here on the farm most of the time and rarely see any of our old classmates. I bet you don't know many of them anymore either." He seemed genuinely pleased. "It'll be good to get reacquainted with them. Thanks again, Kathryn."

She was relieved he had accepted so readily and appeared to like the idea. "Emmie will be with us," she told him. "She's going to see if Dr. Taylor will be able to leave his practice for the evening, so he can be a part of our group. I hear he is a fine doctor, and I'm looking forward to meeting him."

"Sounds good to me. Isn't it strange that I never seemed to be a part of your circle of friends while we were in school? Guess I was always too anxious to get back here to the farm and be with the horses. You'll have to polish up my dancing...I need some lessons, I think."

"No problem," she replied as she thought what a fine man Alexander Adams had turned out to be, handsome, too.

After her invigorating ride, Kathryn went to the house, took her shower, and settled down to do some work for Thayer Enterprises. She couldn't help but think how relaxing it was to work in the home environment; dress was casual, no interruptions, no city noises, and no feeling of urgency. She placed a call to Marcus, who was overjoyed to hear from her. After she had given him a recap of her days at the farm and after he had brought her up to date on his and Emily's activities and after they told each other how much they missed each other, they settled down to company business. High on the company agenda was a promotion to be done for one of their most prestigious accounts, Kingston, a beauty products corporation. They wanted a new line to present for the Christmas season.

"You need to create a name and personality for this new line, Kathryn, and when you have that in place, we can make our presentation, and Kingston will create the products." Marcus went on to say, "I hope, I'm not asking too much of you. I know you want to have plenty of time with Nathan and your friends there in Hawthorne, but you're the only one I will trust with this account."

"Marcus, you could never ask too much of me. I'll just set aside some time each day to work on this. It's a challenge, but I do think I have my 'can do' back...I won't let you down. Tell me, how is Alma doing? Is she handling the day-to-day office work to your satisfaction?"

"Yes," he replied. "She isn't you, but she's doing fine with the office work. We do miss you, though. By the way, Joshua asked about you the other day. Emily told me she had heard he might have a lady friend. Don't know much about that, but when we learn anything, we'll pass it along."

Kathryn spent the rest of the morning working on several accounts that needed promotion updating; she tried to keep all the advertisements new and fresh. Little thought was given to the Kingston promotion, because she knew inspiration would come in its own good time. At noon, when Emmie would be taking time for lunch, she called with her news. "I bet I beat you, Em. My mission is accomplished...Alex said 'yes'!"

"Gosh, Kathryn, you sound like a teenager with a crush. I saw Mark this morning before appointments and he said, 'yes,' too, so I guess we're all set. Can you just imagine the stares and tongue wagging that will happen when we walk into the dance with our handsome dates? You know how this town is...they have to know what's going on with everyone. I really don't mind, because it's not done in a malicious way...It's like we are all just one big family. That's our town...Take it or leave it."

Kathryn settled into a daily routine; an early ride on Rhett followed by breakfast with Poppy, after which she spent time in her makeshift office. She enjoyed her new relaxed approach to work and being able to work at a slower pace with no interruptions. She called Alma each day and received a report on all her accounts and sometimes a little office news. *If the people at Thayer Enterprises could see me working in these quiet beautiful surroundings, they would be so envious. It would surely surprise them to see me working in jeans after all the years I was a real clothes horse each day.* She had placed her work station before a large window where she could enjoy the morning sunrise and the beauty of the land. *Just perfect*, she thought.

One evening, she strolled to the family burial ground. This was the final resting place for generations of Hawthornes, and it encompassed a large area. The area was enclosed with a wrought-iron fence and was shaded on every side by huge oak trees. There was a bench under each tree for the comfort of those wishing to spend some quiet time remembering their loved ones. On this particular evening, Kathryn went inside the iron fence and stood at the graves of her parents, remembering her days with them and the love they had shared. Then she moved to Granna's grave and recalled memories of this beautiful, gentle lady. She needed more time, so she sat on one of the benches to reflect on the stories she had heard through the years about the Hawthornes. *I come from a line of sturdy and fine people. Hopefully, I can live up to their example.* She had never before given much thought to how the responsibility for the farm had passed from generation to generation, but this evening, as she sat pondering, she realized there had always been an eldest son who had inherited the farm; the chain had never been broken until the present. What was to happen now that her father had died so young? There was no one left but her. It was a startling thought. She knew nothing about the farm operation and furthermore, had no interest in the science of farming. This was a troubling revelation. Poppy and she had never discussed the future of the farm, but surely, it had been on his mind. She determined not to approach Poppy on this subject. When the time was right, he would surely discuss it with her.

The night of the alumni dance arrived, and Kathryn had selected her dress for the evening. Kathryn had asked

Emmie's advice on the choice of outfit for the evening and had been told that Hawthorne people didn't dress very formally for these affairs, so Kathryn opted to wear a simple sheath that was the palest of lilac with only pearl earrings and a pearl bracelet as her accessories. She carried a dark lilac Kashmina stole for protection against the spring night air. As she descended the stairs, she heard male voices in Nathan's study. Alex had arrived, and he and Nathan were having one of their conversations regarding the farm. Alex was the one person, other than Kathryn, that Nathan seemed to enjoy the most. They stood as Kathryn entered, and Nathan said, "Isn't she beautiful, Alex? I just wish Anna were here to see her."

Admiration shone in Alex's eyes, too, and he approached her saying, "Is this really the little girl I used to tease when we were kids romping around the farm? I tell you, I'm going to be the envy of all the men at this dance."

Kathryn returned his compliment by telling him how handsome he looked in his dark brown slacks and cream-colored blazer. She had never seen him attired in anything other than the clothes he wore to the stable. As she complimented him, she was thinking how easy he was for her to be with...as though she had known him all her life.

When they arrived at the Hurley's, they were greeted by Emmie, who looked like a beautiful fairy princess dressed in her simple dress of soft yellow lace. Emmie had made an arrangement of daisies to place in her hair which was the perfect accessory for her. She was so small, petite, and feminine that Kathryn caught her breath as she said, "I've always seen you in your nursing outfit...You look just beautiful, Emmie."

Emmie waved off the compliment and ushered them into the living room for introductions all around. Dan and Martha Hurley had played an important part in Kathryn's early life when she lived in Hawthorne, and following the death of her parents, they were her second place of refuge after the farm. Dr. Dan was so much like her father, and Martha had always offered her gentle motherly arms to enfold her. Memories came flooding back as she stood in their presence after so many years. Like the farm, their home had not changed, so she was easily transported back in time. Furnishing and decorating her home had been a labor of love for Martha for years, and the result was a timeless comfort and homeyness. It was comforting to Kathryn to realize, once again, that some things never change.

Alex was introduced all around, and it was easy to see he fit the group perfectly. Then there was Dr. Mark Taylor. Kathryn's thoughts rambled, *Oh my, so tall, dark, and handsome in a quiet, manly way...I must congratulate Emmie on her choice of men...They look so handsome together.*

She hasn't told me much about him...I bet all the girls in Hawthorne are setting their caps for him. Emmie had better keep him hidden.

Dan served wine, and they proceeded to indulge in the usual small talk; how much they had missed being together these past years...how well they all looked...Dan asked about Nathan...They welcomed Dr. Taylor to their town and said they hoped he would continue to make it his home. Speaking of Hawthorne opened the door for Emmie to tell them how distraught Kathryn had been over the decline of the town. They all nodded and agreed that it was very sad. Kathryn reminded them of how vibrant Hawthorne had been when she left. "I just feel something should be done!" she exclaimed.

They told her, as Emmie had, that several ideas had been floated from time to time, but they always hit a brick wall so people felt defeated, and any talk of reclaiming the town had died...along with the town. On that sad note, Emmie said they should be leaving.

As is always the case, the same people do most of the planning for events in small towns; there are the perennial chairpersons and their committees. This night, the VFW hall had been trimmed with everything pertaining to spring; the decorating committee had outdone themselves. The committee chairman for the night's event was an old classmate, Edith Ames, who had married Lloyd Sharr, manager of the bank. Edith and Lloyd had married soon after they graduated, and she had never worked outside the home. Lloyd had worked hard to earn his managerial position, and they were considered leaders in the community. Edith loved her family, garden, crafts, and being chairman of a committee whenever an affair was held in Hawthorne.

Another perennial chairman for all affairs was another classmate, Lucy Smith. She had attended teacher's college for two years, but on one of her visits home, she had met George Smythe, the new lawyer in town. They had fallen in love and married. They, too, were leaders in the community. For this reunion, Lucy was chairman of the refreshments. She and her committee had decided that instead of their usual covered dish buffet, they would splurge and have it all catered. Some people were heard to comment that it probably wouldn't be nearly as good as when the women brought their favorite dishes, but all the women were glad to not have to fuss for once.

A small band had been engaged for the evening by Jack Root, who was in charge of the entertainment. Of course, he would be the emcee...He always was. Jack was married to Lacey Linders and had stepped into his father's shoes as proprietor of the Excel Hardware Store. Everyone said he was an excellent shopkeeper, and his business continued to thrive.

By the time their foursome entered the hall, most of the people had arrived and had been visiting for awhile. All eyes turned in their direction and talk practically ceased, except for whispers. Of course, they all knew Emmie and Mark, and most of them had seen Alex on his infrequent trips to town, but most of them were not sure about Kathryn. When they realized who she was, they all gathered around and welcomed her back to town with promises to stop by their table to speak with her later. Kathryn felt quite overwhelmed and wished she could find a dark corner for awhile in order observe and remember who each of the attendees were. Some had changed a lot since their graduation. She had to admit, though, it was great fun to be back home.

They went to the bar, purchased drinks, and were told which table was theirs. "Emmie, this is such fun! Some have changed a lot, and some are just the same. This brings back so many memories," said Kathryn. "Mark, you must be rather bored with all of this, because it means nothing to you."

"You're wrong there," he replied. "I love everything about a small town. It's one place where most people stay rooted, and friendships continue through their entire lives. I'm getting to know many of these people, and I like them all."

Emmie turned to Alex, "You stay on the farm so much we hardly ever see you in town. In a way, I don't blame you for staying in the most beautiful place around here, but don't you miss some social life?"

"You're right; I don't come to town very much, because I'm usually deep into some project at the farm. Of course, we have a lot of people working and living at the farm, and we get together a lot. Not much need to come to town."

Jack Root was one of the first people to approach their table. "Hi everyone," he said. "It's great to see our two best cheerleaders again and looking so great."

He told everyone he had been Kathryn's date at their senior prom. Kathryn cringed and blushed a little while he was telling about that night, because what she remembered most about the evening were his unwelcome advances and how they had parted. Thankfully, he didn't mention any of that. He wanted her to know he was married to Lacey, and they had three, of course, outstanding children. Everyone was happy for Lacey, because it had been common knowledge that she had pined for Jack all through their school years. He was no longer the handsome football hero but had become rather pudgy, and his hair was thinning. He did, however, retain his bravado and entertaining personality. He seemed contented and happy. This small town was perfect for Jack Root where he could be a big fish in a small pond.

"I hear you're now proprietor of the family business, Jack, and that you are doing very well. I'm happy for you and also for the town, because I don't know what they would do without the Excel. The Excel has been an institution in Hawthorne forever it seems," Kathryn noted.

"Yes, we have our loyal customers. The people in town and the farmers all have stayed with us. I think we carry items the big chain stores don't bother to stock, and we have so many things that are no longer stocked by most hardware departments," he replied proudly.

It was Kathryn's opportunity to mention the sad state of Main Street and to ask him if he had any ideas for revitalizing it. He shook his head no, but he agreed with Kathryn that they were losing the heart of the town.

Many more people came to visit at their table, and finally, between visitors, Alex asked Kathryn to dance, and Mark followed suit with Emmie. They were a handsome foursome as they danced gracefully to the "oldie" music. Kathryn watched Emmie and Mark and thought how perfect they were for each other; they had the same profession, and from what he said, he would be remaining in Hawthorne, and Emmie was not likely to move anywhere else. She was content and happy where she was. *Oh*, Kathryn thought, *I feel so good being back home again...Never realized how rooted I am in this town.*

When they returned to their table, Kathryn remarked, "I never get close to anything having to do with school without feeling my father's presence. He loved the students and school so very much. It was his life."

Emmie explained to Mark that Kathryn's father, Matthew Hawthorne, was a hero to all the residents in Hawthorne. She told him how Matthew had stayed in their little school even though he had been offered more lucrative positions and how he had fostered a love of learning in all of them and how completely devoted he was to all his students. "He was not only our teacher, the best there could ever be, but our mentor, guide, our haven when we had troubles and an example for us to follow in life."

"People like your father don't come along very often, Kathryn," noted Mark. Everyone nodded in agreement.

When the party was over, Kathryn suggested that Emmie and Mark come to the farm the next day, and the four of them would go riding. Mark was unhappy to say he had to decline because he had patients to see, and also, he had to make rounds at the hospital in Wayville. It was then decided that he should join them after rounds, if he was not too tired, and a buffet would be served whenever they were ready, so that Mark would not have to worry about being there at any particular time. After agreeing the reunion had been a big success, they parted in high spirits while looking forward to the next day.

The following morning, Kathryn related, in minute detail, all the happenings of the previous night as she and Poppy lingered over their country breakfast. She could tell how much Poppy enjoyed their time together; he listened intently to everything she had to say. Again, she thought how lonely he must be when he had no family here with him. He loved conversation and sharing stories and ideas, so he was delighted to know that Emmie, Alex, and she were going riding and that they would all be there for dinner. Dr. Hurley had been his doctor for years and he had never met Dr. Taylor, so he was looking forward to meeting him, too.

I was getting to be an old recluse until Katey Sue came. My life is so much better with her here, he thought. He was happy, too, to see Kathryn dragging Alex out of the stables once in awhile…He needed to get out and do some socializing with people his own age.

Emmie arrived in the early afternoon dressed in her jeans and ready for her ride. She remarked that she had not been on a horse since she and Kathryn had spent many hours years ago riding aimlessly around the farm. She gave Alex a shy, tentative smile and said, "You have no idea how much nerve it takes for me to go riding with you two experts. It's probably a good thing Mark will be here later so he can patch me up."

Kathryn smiled saying, "I'm far from an expert; it's Alex who's the perfectionist...and yes, he can be a nag at times. Just don't let him bother you too much, Emmie. We'll just have to remember he means well."

It was a beautiful spring day, the fields were loaded with wildflowers, and when they passed the pond, where Kathryn and Emmie had spent many hours in their youth, Emmie reminded Kathryn of those days and the fun they had shared. Alex started them slowly on their ride, then following his lead, they cantered awhile before returning to a slow walk. Alex made only a few suggestions to Emmie regarding her riding style, and all in all, he told her she was doing very well for someone who hadn't ridden in such a long time. After cooling down the horses and stabling them, they went to Anna's patio and were having cool drinks when Mark appeared and was introduced to Nathan, who told him to shed his jacket and get comfortable.

"Sorry I didn't take the time to go back to my place and change before coming here. I was so anxious to meet Mr. Hawthorne and see the Hawthorne farm. I must say, this is one of the most beautiful places I've ever seen," he said as he stood taking in the view of all the surrounding fields.

It would be hard to ever find any more compatible people anywhere than the five on Anna's patio that evening. They were interested in each other, their professions, their recreational likes and dislikes, and the talk spilled over into many other subjects. Mark was especially interested in the history of the farm, so he was told a shortened version, and Kathryn suggested that after dinner, they take a walk to the cabin. Conversation flowed freely, and ideas were exchanged on many things...They could have gone on and on. When Kathryn went to bed that night, she played back the happenings of the past two days and hoped she could store it in her memory bank forever. It had truly been a special day.

Early Monday morning, after an invigorating ride, Kathryn sat at her desk with the intention of outlining a plan for the Kingston account. However, her mind was filled with the happenings of the previous weekend. It had truly been delightful to spend time with so many of her old friends, and it was surprising to her that so many of them had remained in Hawthorne.

As she sat lost in thought, she received a call from Joshua. Her dear friend was eager to see if life in the country was agreeing with her after her city diet for many years. She leaned back in her chair, looked out the east window, and described to him the beauty and serenity of her surroundings. "Everyone should be able to work in a setting like this. Eat your heart out! Now tell me, what is new with you?"

"I'm so glad you asked," he said. He was bursting to tell her about the wonderful girl he had been seeing. Her name was Madeline Roth, and she was starting her own interior design studio. According to Joshua, she was positively the most beautiful, intelligent, interesting, exciting woman he'd ever met.

Chuckling to herself, Kathryn said, "Well, I guess, this is what happens when I go away...You find a replacement in no time at all."

"Kathryn, you know, you'll never be replaced as my very best friend...not ever."

After much discussion about Madeline, they returned to talk of the farm and Hawthorne. Joshua was told that Poppy and the farm were perfect, but that the town was in a sad state. Kathryn filled him in on all the details of the town's deterioration.

"Joshua, I feel that something has to be done, but most of the local people have given up. I'd like to help, but I wouldn't know where to start. Any ideas, old friend?"

"You sound so distraught, Kathryn. Let me scout around and see if I can come up with any ideas. This is a switch...You were always the idea girl."

"Please, do help me, if you can," she said. "And whatever you do, if Madeline is as perfect as you say, don't let her get away from you. Thank you so much for the call."

It had been good to talk with Joshua, and she was so happy he had found someone to love. Her only hope was that Madeline would be worthy of his special love.

She realized that her life in the city seemed a world away, and she had been only a few days in Hawthorne with old friends and Poppy. "Oh, poor Main Street." She sighed and then said, "I have to stop daydreaming and call Marcus."

As always, Marcus was happy to hear from her. She was told that everything was moving along fine, mostly because she had left a good plan for the day-to-day work with Alma. Also, he said, the workload was always lighter in the summer. However, he was curious about the Kingston account. Kathryn had to tell him that very little was happening with that account so far, but she told him not to worry, it would be taken care of in good time. Marcus knew her word was good, and she would not fail him.

Of course, she wanted to know what he and Emily were doing; to which he answered that they had been doing some redecorating of their home, attending business functions and such, but they did miss her very much and wanted to hear about all her activities at the farm. She promised to call Emily and him on Sunday, so she could talk with both of them.

She placed her daily call to Alma and received the weekly update on all her accounts. After the calls, she continued working in her home office, studying reports and contacting several companies regarding future campaigns.

She was surprised when she spied the clock to see that it was almost noon. Alex had flown Poppy to a meeting at the state capital, and so she would be alone for lunch. *Think I'll just pop into town and snag Emmie for lunch at Walters',* she thought. She knew the doctors did not schedule appointments between noon and one o'clock. She was still wearing her jeans and a white shirt that she had worn for her morning ride, but she wouldn't have time to change if she wanted to be in Hawthorne for lunch. As she hurried out, she called to Gemma, saying she'd be out for lunch. Kathryn arrived at the clinic shortly after noon to find Emmie's office empty and had turned to leave when Mark appeared in the door. "I thought I heard someone come in," he said. "Emmie won't be back until one o'clock. She went to see an elderly lady who couldn't come to the office. Can I help you?"

"No, I guess not. I just thought Emmie might be able to join me for lunch at Walters'."

"Sorry, I can't fill in for her, but I have to cover the office. Do you have time to talk for a few minutes?"

She followed him into his office and sat across his desk from him. The office was neat, like the man, and sparsely but tastefully furnished. She was impressed with all the bookcases and certificates. It all seemed so right for him. "I've been wanting to tell you how much I enjoyed the reunion and especially the day at the farm.

Your grandfather is one of the most fascinating people I've ever met. I couldn't get enough of him and his stories. The history of your family and the town of Hawthorne has stuck with me ever since I heard it."

As she watched his face light up when he spoke of the farm, Kathryn looked into his blue eyes and was drawn to him in a way she couldn't explain. Here was a gentleman filled with quiet strength whose handsomeness almost became secondary. Kathryn agreed with him that the Hawthorne story and Isaac's Dream were special.

"Perhaps, knowing the story of our town will help you understand why I was so adamant about its decline the night we were with Emmie's family. I do feel guilty for my strong feelings and the fact that no one has done anything to preserve what we had. I have no right to point my finger at others, because I haven't been here to help."

Mark had sat back in his chair, scrutinizing her carefully, and after hearing her litany of the decaying town repeated once again, he leaned forward and said, "Since you feel so strongly about it all, why don't you set the wheels in motion for revitalization. I hear you're quite the idea girl, so maybe you're just the one to get the ball rolling."

All Kathryn could do after his suggestion was stare incredulously and say, "Me? This is not what I do....I wouldn't have any idea where to start."

"Well, I know for a fact that most of the townspeople feel like you do. They have always loved this town, and like you, they always say they don't know where they could start. Maybe the first step would be for you to call a meeting or set up time at a council meeting. Get the people talking about the problem again. You might get some constructive suggestions. So far, all the people have done is lament the loss of businesses and the bad economy among themselves, but not in an open forum where there's the possibility of getting something accomplished," Mark suggested. "They need a leader, and since your family gave the land for this town, who better than you to be the one?"

Kathryn was stunned by his challenge. Oh, it had been easy for her to point a finger at the local people and suggest they should do something, but Mark had just put the shoe on the other foot. It was either put up or shut up time. She'd never shied away from a problem before, but this was such a huge problem and way out of her league. Couldn't Mark see this should be in the hands of a professional preservationist? He leaned back in his chair, smiling, confident she could handle it.

"Oh dear, I don't know. Maybe I could at least get something started by calling a gathering of townspeople at the council meeting. I could do that much. Would I have to be put on the agenda? I wonder if Emmie would come with me. This is all so new; I don't know where to start."

"Don't worry, Kathryn, I know you can get something going. You can be sure I'll plan to be at that meeting, and you can count on me to back you up, whatever you say."

It was at that point that Emmie appeared. She was surprised to find Kathryn and Mark leaning across his desk toward each other, and the excitement they generated was palpable; they weren't even aware she was standing in the door.

"Ahem...what am I missing?" Emmie asked with a smile on her face.

"Oh, Emmie, Mark has just convinced me to go to the next town council meeting and try to present a case for revitalizing the town. I can't believe I've even listened to him. What do you think?"

"Sorry, I didn't hear Mark's pitch to you, but it must have been good. I know how much you care about this town, Kathryn, and I think Mark is on to something. I say go for it."

The hour break was over, and patients were filing into the waiting room, so Kathryn had to leave but only after a promise to call Emmie that night. She turned to Mark and said, "Thanks...I think."

As she drove back to the farm, her mind was in a whirl. How had she gotten involved in such a short time with so many people and events. Her work at Thayer Enterprises had its hectic days, but by and large, her days there were scheduled and predictable, while here, every day seemed to present something new and exciting and yes…challenging. Now this latest challenge that had come from Mark might prove to be too much for her. As she drove back to the farm wrapped in thoughts of her short time with Mark, she was not even conscious of driving. Suddenly, it seemed, she reached the lane leading to the house, and her first thought was to turn to Poppy for his opinion. He would know what she should do. Dear Poppy.

She saved her news until after their dinner that evening. However, Nathan was well aware that Kathryn was nearly bursting to tell him something. He knew his Katey Sue well and recognized her every mood. After dinner, they went to Anna's patio to have their coffee and a heart-to-heart talk.

He was well aware of her concern for the town. Now she was telling him of Mark's suggestion that she was the one to try to do something about it. She needed Nathan's blessing and his trust and belief that she could make a difference. After hearing her account of the day, Nathan took both her hands in his, looked her in the eye, and said, "I have to agree with Mark. You, Katey Sue, as a strong Hawthorne, and with all your organizational skills, are probably the only one who might have any chance at all of turning this town around. I give you my blessing as would

Isaac...and your father would be so very proud of you. You can be sure I'll do everything I can to help."

Kathryn got very little sleep that night. She tossed and turned and thought about her meeting with Mark. Her thoughts were all jumbled; what to do first, funding for the project if they decided to follow through...How would the citizens accept the challenge?...Around and around ideas and thoughts raced through her mind, and she couldn't shut them off. Then there was Mark himself. *Why can't I get him out of my mind?* she thought. She still felt his piercing blue eyes that had held her entranced. *He's just perfect for Emmie.*

The days that followed were days of planning. Kathryn was an excellent planner due to her training at Thayer Enterprises. She planned step by step for the actions to be taken. One of the first calls she made was to Joshua, who was delighted to hear from her. The news from Joshua was that he and his love, Madeline, were going to be married after the first of the year. Her decorating business was in full gear, and she would be swamped during the holidays, hence the wait. Kathryn promised to be with them for all the wedding festivities. "I'm so very happy for you, my friend," she said. He questioned her about her love life and received an "Oh no, I haven't found the man for me yet," and she dismissed the subject.

"I can read you like a book, Kathryn. You have another reason for this call besides inquiring about my love life. What do we need to talk about?"

Kathryn proceeded to tell him of her newest venture, and after her detailed outline of a preliminary plan, she asked him if he knew of any grants they might receive for such a project. "At the present time," she explained, "there's no money allotted for such a project, and since the town is very poor, I don't expect we could ever produce the kind of money needed for a revitalization of this magnitude."

Joshua assured her he would try to help her and asked what kind of businesses and industry they had in Hawthorne. She explained the makeup of the town. "It might be well for me to visit with you so that I can get a better feel for the area," he said and added, "I might even be able to bring Madeline with me. We'll see."

Kathryn made an appointment with Jeff Moore Junior, Hawthorne mayor. The Moores were an old Hawthorne family. Jeff Junior's father had been the police chief for years until his retirement. Jeff Junior known as J.J. greeted Kathryn profusely and had set aside as much time for their talk as she needed. They talked long and earnestly about their concerns regarding the deterioration of the businesses and the Main Street. He was more than happy to put Kathryn on the agenda for the next meeting of the council so she could air her concerns, present a skeleton plan, and assess how much interest there was from the council and the townspeople.

"You understand, I don't have a concrete plan in place as yet," said Kathryn, "but we have to first find out if there's enough support here in the town for this kind of endeavor."

"You're perfectly correct in approaching the problem this way," replied J.J. "I'm sorry I can't give you any idea of the support you will receive, but there has been a lot of grumbling all over town for a long time...People just haven't known what they could do to change things. I have a feeling you're just the person they need to help them pull it together, and I can see how persuasive you can be."

She had one week to prepare her presentation. Kathryn felt this was the most important assignment she had ever undertaken, and this time, she didn't have Marcus to guide her. Besides working on her proposal to the council, she went to every business and asked if they would make a special effort to attend the next council meeting. The response she received was very gratifying, if for no other reason than they were curious as to what the young Hawthorne girl was up to. She even got in touch with the Emersons, who had owned and managed the ice cream parlor for so many years. They had retired and closed the door, but all the furnishings were still in place, because they had always been hopeful their nephew would want to operate it. However, with the town in the stages of dying, he, like most of the other young people, was not anxious to take on what he saw as a liability. Maybe this was a boost he needed.

Marcus had heard from Joshua about Kathryn's latest venture, and he called to offer any help he could give her. Once again, he and Emily were there for her, and Kathryn promised he would be first on her "help" list. She also assured him she was still working each morning on Thayer accounts and would soon be coming up with something for the Kingston account.

Every morning, she rose very early and went directly to the stable where Alex would have Rhett saddled and ready for her. Her morning ride was one of the best times of her day, a time to be alone with her thoughts and plans for the day ahead. She loved to be a part of the dawning, which seemed to be a time for cleansing and renewal. After her ride, she joined Poppy for breakfast. It was such a beautiful way to start the day. Most days, she received a call from Emmie with words of encouragement. "Mark and I will be front and center on your big night," Emmie told her. "We might even carry a couple of balloons. Alex told me he'll be there, too."

The attendees usually numbered fifteen or twenty at council meetings, and they met in a small meeting room off the mayor's office. However, word had spread all through the town that Nathan Hawthorne's granddaughter was going to be on the agenda, and the *Hawthorne Weekly News* had published the council agenda, so a large crowd was expected, and the meeting was moved to a large hall. The hall was crowded to overflowing, and a feeling of anticipation and excitement permeated the large room. After the call to order and the reading of the minutes and treasurer's report, Kathryn was first on the agenda.

Her stomach was full of butterflies as she stood and looked at all her old childhood friends, who were now the adults whose shoulders bore the weight of the future of Hawthorne. As she faced them, Kathryn spent some time reminiscing about days past when the town had been vibrant, and the people were full of optimism. There had been pride in and loyalty to their hometown. Heads nodded in remembrance. "It was a wonderful place for children to go to school and to play, to have all the adults as their mentors and examples and to grow into adulthood with others who would be their friends for life. We were living in the mother lode of Utopia. That's the way it was."

From there, she told them how she found it to be now. It was not a pretty picture. The people were the same but Main Street had always been Hawthorne's focal point, and gradually, through the years, all that had changed. It no longer was a place of pride where families congregated to do business with people they had known all their lives.

Why? Was it because they could drive twenty miles to a "discount" for bargains? "Are you really gaining enough to forfeit the integrity of your town and to give up a way of life that most people only dream about? What kind of example are we setting for today's children? What kind of memories will they have of their town?"

She continued to question her old friends and heads started to nod in her favor. Then she asked if they would be willing to form a committee to look into some possibilities of turning the town around. Every hand raised in favor, and the stage was set for the biggest endeavor the town had ever undertaken.

Kathryn was swamped with offers from everyone to help in any way they could. A committee, led by Jack Root, was quickly formed to work with Kathryn, and they vowed not to waste any time putting together a plan. The local newspaper editor, Ed Abbott, knew he had his lead story for weeks to come. Why, the *Hawthorne Weekly News* might even double its circulation, he thought. Everyone was so psyched that they made no move to end the meeting. Kathryn was hoping she could continue to foster this commitment to the restoration. After dispensing with the remaining short agenda, the people finally started to shuffle out, and the meeting was over. It was obvious the people hated to leave, and so they stood in groups outside still discussing the meeting and offering ideas for the newly formed committee.

Emmie invited Nathan, Mark, Alex, and Kathryn to adjourn to her parents' home. Dr. Dan had covered the clinic that evening, and she knew he and Martha were probably waiting to hear all the news of the meeting. All those who had attended the meeting needed time to wind down and to review the events of the evening amongst themselves.

Dr. Dan and Martha were delighted to receive this group of excited people and could hardly wait to hear all the details of the meeting. First, though, Emmie poured wine and led a toast to Kathryn for her wonderful, persuasive presentation.

"I don't know that I deserve all this," said Kathryn. "I think it's the people of this town we should be toasting for their willingness to take on this huge task. I only hope I won't let them down. Really, you know, it's Mark who set it all in motion by pushing me into this. Time will tell if I should thank him."

All eyes turned to Mark who quietly remarked, "I don't think Kathryn needed much of a shove, and there's positively no doubt in my mind that she will succeed with flying colors." As he spoke he looked only at Kathryn...into her eyes and held her there.

The moment left Kathryn flustered as she said, "Mark sounds so convincing; I think perhaps he should have been the one addressing the crowd tonight. Of course, it's easy for him; he just tosses all the workload into my court."

Everyone chuckled and agreed they should toast Mark for being the instigator of this grand plan. Kathryn looked from Emmie to Mark and thought the town would be in good hands with such a couple being a part of it for years to come. They both had said they intended to spend their life in Hawthorne, and in her mind, Kathryn could look down the road and see marriage and children in their future.

It was apparent to everyone the pride that shone in Nathan's eyes when he looked at his wonderful Katey Sue. Deep in his soul, he knew Anna and Matthew were with them this night.

The week following the council meeting was filled with organizational meetings. It seemed everyone wanted to be involved in some way, and no one refused to serve on any committee where they were needed. Jack Root headed up the merchants' group; George Smythe, the lawyer, and Lloyd Sharr, the banker, offered to research the history and present-day status of local industry in Hawthorne, which would be needed if they asked for grants from the government. In his conversations with county and state officials, Nathan made them aware of this new turn of events in Hawthorne and received positive responses.

Ed Abbott had moved to Hawthorne and was owner and editor of the *Hawthorne Weekly News*. Ed liked to think of himself as a big city newspaper editor like he had seen mostly in "B" movies, late breaking news, extras, investigative reporting, scoops, and such. He modeled himself after the early "B" movie editors even in his dress, which usually consisted of bold plaid suits, which made his pudgy figure appear even fatter, and always, always he wore a felt hat set at a jaunty angle with the brim snapped down in the front. He was hardly ever seen without a half-smoked cigar dangling from the corner of his mouth. In truth, for all the self-importance he tried to portray, he had spent the past years writing about the high school sports, social gatherings, births, and deaths. To fill space in the paper, he had added the "Police Blotter," which was read avidly by subscribers in case the grapevine had not already reported one of the items.

Ed had hired MaryLu Ward as his office girl. It was the first and only job MaryLu had ever had. The extent of her training had been a business course in high school which meant, according to Ed, she couldn't demand a high salary. MaryLu was a tiny, wiry, plain, and unassuming girl with her best features being her bright smile and gentle demeanor. Her mother was a seamstress and had always made MaryLu's dresses, which had not changed much in style over the years. She wore flowered cotton dresses with puffy sleeves and sashes in the summer and dark skirts with white blouses in the winter. Her work at the paper meant everything to her, and it would not be an exaggeration to say she lived to go to work each day. The fact that she idolized Ed did not go unnoticed by him, which only fed his ego.

Now Ed had his big story: the rebirth of Hawthorne. He could hardly contain himself and seemed to be everywhere...at every meeting, interviewing people and taking pictures of everything on Main Street, so he would have a complete set of before and after pictures. At some point, he thought, he might even print one of those special supplements, like the big city papers did. He knew all the people in town would buy a copy. MaryLu had never done any reporting or writing for the paper, but now he asked her to pull together some facts about the history of Hawthorne that he might use in a supplement. MaryLu could hardly imagine that Ed would give her such an important job...*I must do a really outstanding job*, she thought, as she poured herself into her project. MaryLu had been an A student in high school, and composition was something she had excelled in. Now was her chance to make use of it. Overnight, the little newspaper office became a beehive of activity with people sending in ideas for future columns regarding the preservation plan and the different town organizations sending in items regarding the part they were going to play in promoting the project. Suddenly, the "Letters to the Editor" more than doubled, because everyone, it seemed, had ideas about what should be done and how to proceed. Overnight, Ed Abbott was in the limelight, and he reveled in it. He started referring to MaryLu as his "girl Friday," which delighted her, and she started blossoming. The change was so gradual that it took people a while to realize MaryLu was not wearing her homemade dresses any longer. They had been replaced by fashionable pants suits and silk blouses. Her long, thick hair was now being styled by Jeanne Rizzo at the Cameo Beauty Shop, and Jean introduced her to a way with makeup that enhanced all her best features. However, the biggest change in MaryLu was in her attitude; she was no longer the shy little wallflower but had assumed the persona of a career woman like those she had idolized on television.

All this change happened without Ed's even noticing because he was so busy with all the happenings in the town, but one day, she asked for some of his time to discuss office matters. As he sat before her and took the time to really see his "girl Friday," it was hard for him to digest the changes...He was speechless for the first time in months as she told him they would need to hire at least two people to take care of phones and mail.

"I will still be responsible for the office procedures," she informed him, "but I'm busy writing some of the Hawthorne history, and I don't have to tell you, we are doing a much larger volume of paperwork now."

Ed was completely shocked in the changes in MaryLu. *When did this all happen?* he thought. *I must have been blind these past weeks.* Of course, he approved her hiring two helpers and even decided she deserved an increase in her wages. After all, she had more responsibility.

Marcus and Emily called to find out about the council meeting. They were delighted to hear the outcome and how all the townspeople were responding. Both he and Emily wanted to be a part of Kathryn's new venture. Marcus told Kathryn he had talked with a highly respected architect named Myles Cooledge. Myles became so interested in this gigantic undertaking by a little proud, but poor town that he offered to advise the town regarding the badly needed face-lift at no cost to the town. Myles was renowned for his designs of modern buildings and huge shopping malls but had never worked in the preservation field before, especially the preservation of so large an area. He was intrigued, and he needed a new challenge. Kathryn welcomed the offer enthusiastically and told Marcus and Emily that when the time was right, they should visit the farm and bring Myles with them. However, she made clear to them that she could not imagine there would ever be enough money in their preservation fund to afford to pay Mr. Cooledge.

"Myles told me, Kathryn, that he would do it without it costing you anything. Myles has made his mark in the architectural world, and he's a wealthy man. At this point in his life, he's looking for new challenges and also for some way to give back. This is something he wants to do. Don't worry about money."

"I really need to see you," she said, "so do plan to stay awhile when you come so we can have plenty of time. I'm sure Mr. Cooledge will be a great help to us; we really need that kind of expertise. Please send me his address so I can thank him…his telephone number, too."

Kathryn was wise enough to know that with all the activity whirling around her, she needed her quiet moments more than ever, and her morning rides had become more important. Alex was always at the stable waiting for her with Rhett saddled. They spoke little when they first met in the morning as Alex sensed her need for quiet and privacy. After her ride, she was ready to talk with him about all the organizational work being done for the town. Many times, he had good suggestions and always asked her to promise to call on him if he would fit into her scheme of things. It was so easy for her to talk with Alex, and with each passing day, she felt closer and closer to him. She was surprised to hear he'd been giving instructions to Emmie in the art of horsemanship. Kathryn and Emmie had very little time of late to talk about what they were doing personally. *We need a good old girly talk*, thought Kathryn.

After her ride and breakfast with Nathan, Kathryn always went to her room to work on her Thayer accounts. She had no intention of slighting her Thayer accounts. One morning after her shower, she sat down at the large dressing table that had been Anna's. While she sat brushing her hair, her eyes were drawn to Anna's picture. She spoke to the picture, saying, "Oh, Granna, you were so beautiful and a real lady. I miss you..oh, how I miss. You're still my ideal...the model of the perfect lady." As she continued to look at the picture, she received her inspiration for the Kingston account. Everything regarding the account fell into place in that moment, and Kathryn knew she had something really special. *I must talk with Poppy about this*, she thought and went immediately to his study.

He listened attentively to her animated presentation, and when she had finished, he looked at her with admiration in his eyes and said, "I'll be so proud to have such a tribute paid to my Anna. You're right, Katey Sue, to me, she was the most beautiful lady there ever was."

After gaining his approval, Kathryn went back to her room and proceeded to outline her plan. Ideas seemed to flow without any effort, and she knew it was perfect. It had to be right...the inspiration had come from her heart.

Before the morning was over, she called Marcus and told him she was all set on the Kingston account, and she proceeded to lay out her preliminary plan. With the right inspiration, it had all been so easy for her.

Women had, for a long time, accepted the bold, bright coloring which was a badge of their liberation. Now that they were more and more secure in their new place, and knowing that women liked change, Kathryn felt intuitively the time was right for this new line. Kathryn could see this change affecting clothing styles, too, and she would have to promote this new theme in her other accounts.

If the new Kingston line was to be ready for Christmas, it was important for them to move fast. Kathryn put a priority on the account and spent hours preparing charts and layouts for the presentation. E-mails and faxes flowed between the farm and Kathryn's staff at Thayer regularly and often. It was a full-court press. All of Kathryn's dealings with Mr. Kingston in the past had been more than successful and had resulted in her being the only person he allowed to handle his account. She was looking forward to making this presentation.

With her plans pretty much in place, Kathryn was ready to move to the next step. After discussing her idea with Nathan, she called Marcus and Emily and suggested they plan to visit the farm the following week. She also wanted Peter Kingston to join them, because she was ready to discuss his new line. Kathryn apologized for the short notice, but she explained if she made the presentation at the farm, they would be away from the pressure of the city and could discuss business without interruption, plus they could enjoy the farm and the little town. She wanted to show them the "before" town so they would be able to compare it, someday, to the "after" town she hoped to produce. Once again, she had to tell them how proud she was of all the Hawthorne citizens, who were working so hard to make the "after" town a reality. Marcus and Emily were positively delighted at the prospect of a visit.

"I'll call Peter tomorrow—maybe even tonight," said Marcus. "I'm sure he would like a working vacation in the country. This is a fine idea, Kathryn."

The Thayer jet landed at the Wayville Airport the following week. Kathryn, Nathan, and Alex were on hand to welcome Emily, Marcus, and Peter Kingston. Tears spilled from her eyes when Emily saw Kathryn...her dear girl...and their long embrace was evidence of their joy at being together again. Peter was introduced to Nathan and Alex before proceeding to their cars. Alex was driving the men, and Kathryn and Emily would return to the farm in Kathryn's car. Peter Kingston, who had spent most of his life in the city, took in all the sights around him and inhaled deeply of the clear, clean air of the country.

Emily was happy to have Kathryn all to herself during the ride back to the farm. "My, you looked so good to me, Kathryn...all flushed and spirited. I can see you really did the right thing in coming back here to the farm. I've been worried that you have taken on too much in accepting so much of the responsibility for your town's preservation planning, but I must say, I think it's really agreeing with you. Just promise me you'll slow down if it starts to overwhelm you."

Gemma and her household staff had worked hard all week preparing the guest rooms, cooking, and baking for the meals ahead. Cut flowers were in every room, the silver was polished, and the crystal sparkled. The grounds of the farm were in pristine condition; flowers were blooming in profusion, and the tree-lined lane leading to the house was at its most beautiful. As they approached, Peter said, "Can this be for real?"

Kathryn had outlined a rather loose itinerary. The morning after their arrival, she would present her Kingston proposal, and they could take as much time as needed to go over every aspect of the plan. She apologized to Peter for taking so long in deciding the direction they should take, but she was hopeful he would agree it had been worth all the delay. It only meant they would have to work diligently to have everything in place in time for the holidays.

"You've never let me down," replied Peter, "and I'm sure this will be no exception."

Kathryn had Peter, Marcus, and Emily gathered in Anna's room for the presentation. It took over an hour for Kathryn to introduce the new product and her planned promotion. During her presentation, she received rapt attention, not a word, not a query, not a smile or frown. As sure as she had been about ANNA, Kathryn began to feel skeptical about her faith in her new idea. When she had finished, there was a moment of silence before Peter said quietly, "I've never before been so impressed by any idea for a new product or as sure it was completely right for its time. Kathryn, you're a dreamer and a genius. This cannot fail."

Marcus was nodding and smiling broadly, so proud of "his" girl. Emily showed her pride through her bright, glistening eyes. It was at this point Kathryn called their attention to the painting of beautiful Anna that hung over the hearth. After all, she was the inspiration for all of this: THE LADY LINE BY KINGSTON. The first LADY LINE product would be "ANNA" and introduced soon.

When Nathan returned from his daily farm inspection, the door to Anna's room had been opened, and he heard all the kudos being given to his wonderful granddaughter. He joined them saying, "I'm so happy you are all here so I can share in the celebration. Kathryn has been gone for a long time, and I've missed many of her triumphs," and he continued, as he looked around the room, "It reassures me to know she's been with such fine people."

Peter was so full of enthusiasm he could hardly wait to get started. He called his staff, his perfumers and cosmetic gurus for a high-level planning meeting as soon as he returned to the city. His head was full of ideas. Kathryn assured him she could make some trips to the city if and when she was needed by him. *Now*, she thought, *is the time for me to claim those plane rides Alex promised me.*

They adjourned to the terrace for an extremely tasty buffet of summertime country fare. The talk remained on the subject of the new account...everyone was keyed up. Finally, when that subject seemed to be exhausted, Marcus said, "I'm looking forward to a tour of Hawthorne. Peter, this is another important project Kathryn is tackling at the present time and one that's very close to her heart. Let's see if we can help her in any way."

"Tell us some of the history of the town, Kathryn," said Emily. "After all, this is all new to Peter, and it will help him understand why this is important to you."

Kathryn proceeded to tell them about the founding of the town, about the wonderful people who lived there, and about her happy childhood in those surroundings. Peter had been born in a small town in the west, but his family had moved to an eastern city when he was still a baby so he had never experienced the small-town life Kathryn described.

"The town you are going to see will not look as it did when I was a child...oh, the same houses are still there and the people keep them trim and maintained, but our wonderful Main Street looks tired and worn. However, the heart of any town is the people who live there, and the people in Hawthorne are among the best; loving, compassionate, loyal, hard working, and, oh, I can't find enough adjectives to describe them. They're the backbone of the revitalization project, and they have so much hope for the future of their town. We just can't fail," she told them with a touch of uncertainty in her voice.

Emily spoke immediately. "Don't you ever doubt that you can make this happen, Kathryn. You'll make it happen just as you have always been able to work your magic. Like it or not, you have become the leader in this undertaking, and you must leave no doubt in anyone's mind that this town will turn around." She went on, "And now, I think, its time to go see just what Kathryn has been talking about."

Nathan had work to do in his study, but he told Kathryn to drive his SUV so they would have plenty of room. It was a beautiful summer day, not too hot and with a light breeze to keep them comfortable. This was a world new to Kathryn's passengers, and the more she showed them, the more intrigued they became. The Excel Hardware was a highlight...like something out of a novel about the past. The store was a large wooden structure, three stories high, and painted barn red, which had been built circa 1900. The stock was unbelievable, a mixture of new and very, very old items. No one was sure they ever had a complete inventory even though Jack Root had been trying to get it all on computer. Most of the salespersons had worked there for years and were familiar with all the stock and always seemed to be able to find anything a person needed. All the Amish communities shopped at Excel, because it was the only hardware that stocked old tools and hardware...items the new stores did not stock. Jack was pleased the city visitors stopped in his store, and he launched into the plans for putting their town "back on the map." Peter and Marcus had their cameras and the flashbulbs were going off continually while they took pictures of the Excel, inside and out, some with Jack proudly displaying some of his old wares.

From there, they went by the other establishments: Knowles Dry Goods, Murphy's Shoes, Krogers, Harris Drugstore, Rialto Theater, the old Emerson Ice Cream Parlor, and on and on. Kathryn had a story to tell about each place and about the proprietors. "I know in this day and age, most people would call these stores old and drab, but when we have finished with our preservation, they're going to call them charming," she said. She had her friends agreeing with her as they nodded in the affirmative.

"I really enjoyed meeting the two Knowles sisters in their dry goods store. Oh yes, their names were Lottie and Harriet Knowles. I loved seeing the stacks of materials and oh, the little drawers full of spools of thread. You just don't see stores like that anymore. People in your town must do a lot of sewing to keep them in business," noted Emily. "Of course, people do a lot of crafts, and quilting has made a big comeback."

"Aren't they wonderful....like characters out of a 1900's novel. Neither of them ever married, and their lives have been spent, for the most part, in their little dry goods establishment. The Knowles family goes back to the early pioneers in this area, and the building in which they are located was built by their ancestors many years ago. What makes it so valuable is that they have maintained it beautifully, and they haven't changed anything about it. Thankfully, they didn't even erect a modern facade for the front as so many of the other stores have done. That building and the sisters, too, are a treasure." Kathryn loved to praise the people in her town.

She drove them up and down tree-lined streets and by neat frame homes...all with porches...typical of the Midwestern architecture. She took them by the school complex and told them about her father and his commitment to the young people of the town. The school was now named Matthew Hawthorne High School. They passed two of the small factories on their way to see the park and the beautiful river that flowed by the town and where, she told them, she had spent many youthful hours swimming. Their last stop was Walters' Restaurant.

"I think it's time for a break and some refreshment," Kathryn told them, "and you cannot leave here without tasting the pies they have at Walters' Restaurant. Like most of the places you've seen, this is a landmark and has belonged to the same family forever. Except for this awful facade, the decor of the restaurant and its furnishings have changed little, and we wouldn't have it any other way."

During their whirlwind visit, Marcus, Emily, and Peter had soaked up the sights and sounds of Hawthorne and all the areas of the farm. They would never forget riding the grand horses across the fields, by the ponds and rivers, and sometimes into the forests on this historic farm. Nor would they forget the stories about the many generations who had lived there. However, it was the people that would leave the most indelible impression; from Nathan, who personified all the Hawthornes, to the families, who worked the farm and took great pride in their work. Then there were the people in Hawthorne, spirited people determined to save their little town. This was a week none of them would ever forget. They were all sad to be saying goodbye, but they were already gearing up for their next projects, renewed and inspired.

After their leave-taking, Kathryn started preparing for the next set of guests, who would be Joshua, his Madeline, and the architect, Myles Cooledge. Kathryn had already extended the invitation, and they were to arrive in two weeks. Joshua, with his national legal knowledge and Madeline, interior decorator, along with Myles, renowned architect, should all compliment each other. Nathan was enjoying all the visitors. It reminded him of his days with Anna, when they had entertained often. Both of them had enjoyed meeting new people and being with old friends. All these visitors did keep Gemma and her household staff extra busy, so Nathan told her to hire extra help any time it became too much for them to handle. After all, up until Kathryn came to stay, they only had him to tend to except when he had some state or federal officials to the farm.

"I can always call on some of the women on the farm to help out when we need extra hands," Gemma told him. "They're always happy to lend a hand. Don't you worry about us, Mr. Hawthorne."

The Hawthorne project had been named by the various committees, HAWTHORNE—OUR TOWN. Of course, the name was shortened to HOT. The week before the arrival of the new advisors, Kathryn called a meeting of all the HOT committees, so they could bring all their ideas to the table and interact. It was now time to state their visions and goals for the project. Kathryn was gratified to see the enthusiasm demonstrated by all the committees, and she was more confident than ever they would not fail. "HAWTHORNE—OUR TOWN" banners were posted at the entrances to the town and on Main Street. They sold HAWTHORNE—OUR TOWN bumper stickers to everyone for a nominal fee. Everyone caught the fever, and excitement ran rampant.

Kathryn was waiting for Joshua, Madeline, and Myles when they arrived at the Wayville Airport. When he spied her, Joshua found himself almost running toward her, his dear beautiful friend, and they embraced enthusiastically while Madeline and Myles stood patiently waiting as the two friends told each other how much they had been missed. Finally, Kathryn met Madeline, and it didn't take her long to realize that Joshua had found his true love. Madeline was a petite, pixie-like lady, who wore her love for Joshua on her sleeve. Joshua kept his arm around her as though she might disappear.

They all turned toward Myles as Joshua made the introduction. Myles was an imposing figure; tall, over six feet, lean, muscled, blue-eyed with a face lined in a good way, and a head of long, shaggy grey hair. Who would not be impressed? was Kathryn's first reaction.

Kathryn said, "The people in this little town owe you all so very much, and I'm afraid we can never repay you. All we can do is thank you from the bottom of our hearts for the time you're donating to our project. We welcome any and all the advice you can give. Today, we'll go to the farm first so you can get settled, and maybe later, we'll take a drive around the area. That will give you a feel for this part of the country. All the committees are anxiously waiting to meet you, so I've set up meetings for tomorrow."

As she drove them toward the farm, her guests drank in the beauty and serenity of the Midwestern countryside, a real contrast to the city. The neat homes and waves from the people they passed along the way, plus the obviously unhurried pace of life did not go unnoticed by Kathryn's three passengers. As they drove the lane leading to the farm, it was hard for their eyes to take in the beauty before them, and as most first-time visitors, they sat quietly, not wanting to miss anything or break the spell. The trees and flowers Anna had started so many years ago had flourished and now greeted everyone proudly.

Myles turned to Kathryn and stated, "This place is magic."

Kathryn took them on a tour of the house and introduced them to the household staff before showing them to their rooms. After a short respite, they were to meet on the terrace for a late lunch. Nathan would join them when he returned from his daily farm inspection.

Kathryn was always proud to introduce Poppy to all her friends. People always felt instinctively the strength as well as the soft, compassionate side of this imposing man. He had an impact on everyone who met him. As for Nathan, he was delighted to have a house full of knowledgeable and interesting people.

Toward evening, Kathryn took her guests on a little hike to the cabin, so she could tell them the story of the Hawthorne family and the story of the town of Hawthorne. She had been telling that story often lately, but it seemed necessary for these city folk to know the local history. As they sat on the porch of the cabin in the twilight, she told these first-time visitors about Isaac's dream and the dedication of the succeeding generations in order to fulfill that dream. Not only were they entranced by the history lesson, but it grounded them in the present endeavor. They wanted to be a part of keeping this history alive.

The week following their arrival was spent getting to know the townspeople and meeting various committees. Each HOT committee had done its work thoroughly and was anxious to present its findings and proposals. Joshua met with the town attorneys, while Madeline and Myles surveyed the town and familiarized themselves with the buildings and culture of the area.

Ed Abbott was everywhere. He reported on every meeting so thoroughly that all the surrounding county waited anxiously each week to read about the planned rebirth of Hawthorne. After a short time, the story was picked up by the Associated Press as one of their human interest articles. All eyes were on Hawthorne, which didn't go unnoticed by politicians and investors.

Peter Kingston was in daily contact with Kathryn regarding the LADY LINE. He had been so smitten with Hawthorne and its people that after much consultation with his management team, he made the decision to build a facility in Hawthorne for the new line. He explained to Kathryn that his other facilities would be too overloaded if they took on the new product, and as he said, "What better place for the new LADY LINE product to have as its home?" They would start building as soon as land could be procured, and they could have an architect submit plans.

"Oh, Peter, thank you, thank you," Kathryn replied breathlessly. "You're an angel. We just happen to have a wonderful architect here right now...Myles Cooledge. He's studying the town and has offered his services to us. Perhaps, if he has the time, he would be just the right person to work with you. Oh, I'm so excited. It's hard for me to believe all this is happening."

Peter asked Kathryn to speak to Myles and get back to him. He trusted her judgment. He went on to say that there would be jobs for some people in Hawthorne, and he would provide a training team for them. Of course, the new building wouldn't be in place for the presentation of ANNA, but he would give it priority and have the first ANNA products produced at an existing location so that they could have it ready for the holiday season.

The week was filled with intense meetings, but there was time left for Kathryn and Madeline to spend time getting to know each other, and since they both loved Joshua, they had an immediate common bond. Small-town culture, which manifested itself in loyalty, caring for each other, revering the past they had all shared...all of this fascinated the city dwellers, the continuity of the small town.

After Kathryn bid her friends goodbye, she went back to the farm and took stock of all that had been accomplished. After laying it all out, she knew they were on their way. All the committees were organized and had their goals in place. The most important element was the enthusiasm and belief the citizens had in the project. It was difficult for her to accept how easily the project was falling into place.

I must get away from all this for awhile, she thought. It was time for a ride on Rhett to clear the cobwebs. She called Alex and asked him to saddle Rhett while she donned her riding clothes. Poppy met her as she was leaving, and he told her that as much as he enjoyed having her friends spend time with them, he thought she needed some downtime and encouraged her to return to her daily rides. "You need time for yourself," he advised her. After an embrace, she was off to the stable.

"Well, Kathryn, it's about time you got back to your daily rides. You've been keeping up too fast a pace," was Alex's greeting. "I think, Emmie, Mark, you, and I should get together again soon. I really have enjoyed our times together. Being with you all has made me realize just how much I've been missing by holing up here on the farm all the time. If you're in favor of another night out, I'll get in touch with Mark and Emmie, and we'll set a date."

"I would like for us to get together again. I really haven't seen Emmie, one on one, for too long, and I, too, have enjoyed our little foursome. Just let me know when there's a good date for our medical friends." Jokingly, she poked a little fun at him, "By the way, I'm glad you've discovered the horses will be just fine if you leave them once in awhile."

By the time Kathryn returned from her invigorating ride, Alex had arranged for the foursome to go to the Wayville Inn on Saturday for dinner and dancing. For a man who seldom dated, Alex seemed happy about his planned get-together. Kathryn observed that Mark and Alex were becoming very good friends; they reminded her of Dr. Hurley and her father. *I'm lucky to have these good friends in my old home place. They're dear, interesting people and so comfortable to be with. Friends like these had been lacking in the city,* thought Kathryn.

It would have been hard to find a more handsome group on that Saturday night at the inn than their foursome, with the men in light sport jackets, Emmie in a lovely, summery flowered dress, and Kathryn in a chic sleeveless bold-printed linen sheath. They were in a merry mood, and after congratulating Kathryn on all the fine work she had been doing in the town, Alex said, "Let's not talk about any of that for the rest of the evening. Kathryn needs a break." It was agreed.

The Wayville Inn was a historic landmark and a favorite place for special celebrations...reunions, weddings, engagement parties, and such. Dinner was always a gourmet delight and served in the grand style. After dining, they adjourned to the dance area where a small band played for their enjoyment. Alex had chosen the perfect venue for their night out, and he seemed to be improving in his dancing, which made Kathryn wonder if he had been taking some lessons. Mark was a fine dancer. Kathryn felt so comfortable in his arms, and their steps were in complete harmony. When asked where he had learned to dance so well, Mark replied that he had to credit his young sister. "She is almost a professional ballroom dancer now, but when she was first starting, she needed someone to practice on...It turned out to be me until I was replaced by a really good dancer," Mark informed her. "I didn't have time for dancing when I went to med school, and now I'm too busy."

As they drove home through the warm night, it was agreed that these outings should continue. Mark said he would like to make a reservation at the Hawthorne Country Club for their next outing, and they set a date for two weeks later. In the meantime, Kathryn suggested they all meet again at the farm the following Sunday for a ride, swim, and buffet. Fortunately, Mark was not on duty that day, and it was agreed.

Kathryn couldn't remember a time when she had been so busy. She kept the Thayer accounts uppermost on her schedule; she worked on them each morning and talked with Marcus and Alma. Now that the Kingston account was on track, the New York operation seemed to be flowing along fine. After tending to the Thayer accounts, the rest of her days were taken up with meetings. All the planning and organization was now paying off. Joshua, along with the local lawyer, George Smythe, and the banker, Lloyd Sharr, had received approval for sizeable government grants. Of course, the respect state and federal officials had for Nathan had a lot to do with the speed with which these grants were approved. Now that funds were assured, Myles and Madeline went to work with the local merchants. This trio from New York had blocked out time from their busy schedules to spend time in Hawthorne at the local inn. They wanted to stay in the town where they would be close to the work they would be doing. At this point, changes started coming fast. The committees had done their jobs so thoroughly, goals were clear to everyone, and now it was time to implement them. The cheap, fake facades came down, revealing the true character of the old brick two-story buildings. Merchants ordered new stock; grocery stores started purchasing once again from the local farmers and dairymen, which meant that all their merchandise was fresh daily. Melvin refurbished the movie theater and had a contract to receive all the latest movie releases. The Emersons' nephew decided to reopen the old confectionary and serve the same scrumptious treats that everyone remembered from days gone by. New streetlights in the style of the gaslight era were ordered along with huge planters for flowers at each store, and benches were placed strategically. Due to all the publicity about Main Street, inquiries from proprietors of unique specialty stores requesting information regarding locating in Hawthorne were received daily. Most importantly, the local citizens were deciding that it would be much better to shop in Hawthorne than to drive to Wayville, even though prices there might be a little cheaper. After all, there was the gas used to get there and back and then all the time spent. Besides, they remembered how pleasant it had been to deal with their local merchants, and in the process, to meet their friends on Main Street. It had really been very nice.

Regardless of how busy Kathryn was with all her responsibilities, she always set aside time to spend with Nathan. After all, he had been the main reason she'd wanted to be at the farm again. Both of them were realizing the summer would be coming to an end all too soon, and she would have to return to Thayer Enterprises in the city, but neither spoke of it; as if by not acknowledging the end of summer, it would never come. It had been a precious time for both of them.

Nathan was summoned to the state capital for some high-level meetings and would be gone for two days. Alex had flown him there and activity at the farm was nil. It was a respite for Kathryn, which she needed badly. She felt as though she'd been on a merry-go-round for too long. In the evening, after a light dinner, she took a twilight walk to the family burial plot. Somehow, she felt the need to be as close to her father and Granna as she could get. It was a beautiful, balmy evening with the stars faintly appearing in the darkening sky. As she approached the site, she was astonished to see a woman kneeling and softly sobbing at her father's grave. Intuitively, she stood back so as not to intrude on this moment. The woman had brought flowers and placed them on his grave. *Who can this be?...And why?* she wondered. Finally, the woman stood, still weeping, and turned toward Kathryn. It was Marcy Adams, Alex's mother.

The two women faced each other in silence for minutes before Kathryn spoke. "Please, tell me why this visit to my father's grave and why you're so upset. Come, let's sit here on this bench...Maybe I can help."

Slowly, they walked to the bench under the huge oak tree where they sat for minutes before Kathryn once again said, "Marcy, I really do need an explanation. I never knew you and my father were such good friends. Please don't leave me to wonder."

With bowed head, Marcy replied, "I've never told this story to anyone, because it belonged only to your father and me. Maybe it's time for it to be told."

MARCY'S STORY

"AS CHILDREN, MATTHEW and I played together on the farm with all the children who lived here. After I graduated from high school, I went to a state university where I majored in education. It had been my dream for years to teach literature. After I received my degree, I applied to Hawthorne High School for a position and was accepted. I, like Matthew, was a dedicated teacher with high ideals and hopes for my students. I was living my dream, and I spent long hours at the school, as did Matthew. Naturally, we exchanged ideas about how best to serve the students. Matthew was my inspiration and mentor.

"I attended the wedding reception, along with all the other teachers when Matthew and Ivy were married. We all loved Matthew and respected him so much that our fondest hope was for his happiness.

"A couple of years into the marriage, I sensed a subtle change in Matthew. He seemed a little withdrawn, and there were fewer smiles. We continued to be friends and met often regarding various students and their problems. Matthew started spending longer hours at the school, and he never seemed in a hurry to leave a discussion we were having. On the contrary, he would prolong our time together as though he had nowhere else to go. In fact, Matthew started to seek me out and would suggest we have a cup of coffee and talk.

"It was inevitable that we could not remain just friends. We would look into each other's eyes, and we knew, without a word being spoken, we could not stay apart." Marcy hesitated and looked nervously at Kathryn before proceeding. "One day, Matthew asked me to meet him at the old cabin on the farm. That evening, he told me of his unhappiness with Ivy. He was so sad. He said their marriage had been broken for a long time, and he confessed his love for me. I'm sorry to be telling you this,

Kathryn, but I want you to know that Matthew is the only man I've ever loved."

Kathryn was stunned by what she was hearing. It was too much for her to process quickly. However, she had to ask, "If my dad was the only man you have ever or could ever love, how do you explain Alex?"

Marcy hung her head and looked away as she replied, "This is the hardest part of the story to tell you. You see, Matthew and I continued meeting at the cabin, and we knew we wanted more than these secret meetings. We wanted to have a life together. Matthew never wanted to hurt anyone, but he felt that Ivy had pretty much made a life of her own without him, and after the initial rage, hurt, and tears, she would be perfectly happy without him, so the decision was made to ask Ivy for a divorce. It was just at that time Ivy announced to Matthew that she was pregnant, and your father, being the dear man he was, didn't feel he could leave Ivy and the baby she was having."

Marcy took some deep breaths and continued, "I hadn't confided to Matthew that I, too, was expecting our child. I just could not do that to him...I loved him too much to see him torn between two babies. So I told him I understood why he had to stay with Ivy. Shortly after that, I left my teaching job at Hawthorne High School, took my savings, and moved away. Our baby was born in a city far enough away that I would not see any of the local people. When Alex was a few months old, I got another job teaching. It was so hard being alone...not having Matthew. I loved and needed him so much, and I kept thinking how proud he would be of his beautiful son."

After Marcy's announcement that Alex's father was really Matthew, both women sat in silence still holding hands...both speechless at this point. Marcy was emotionally drained and not sure she should have told Kathryn. Kathryn was completely stunned and trying to deal with all she had just heard. The two women were sitting quietly in this serene place as birds flew to their nests, and the stars grew brighter in the darkening sky. Marcy closed her eyes and prayed that she had done the right thing. Kathryn was processing what she had just heard...a life-changing revelation. Now she knew, Alex and she were surely bonded for life.

After a few more minutes, Kathryn put her arm around Marcy, who was crying softly, and said, "You did the right thing in telling me. It will take me some time to get used to the idea that my dad experienced the deep love he had for you. I'm sure there is more to the story, and I would really like to hear it if you think you can go on tonight."

"Oh yes," replied Mary. "Now that I've gone this far, I really want you to know the whole story." And she went on, "I told you I had moved to a city, and after Alex was born, I got a job teaching. I was fortunate enough to find a nice elderly woman to leave Alex with each day. I knew I had to have a story to tell my family. I had never lied to my family before, but times were different then, and I wanted to protect my son and them from any scandal. I was thinking about Matthew, too, and his family. The story I told my family was that I had met and married a Navy man after a whirlwind courtship. Shortly after our marriage, he went to sea and was killed in a skirmish. They had always trusted me and had no reason to question this. About six months after Alex was born, my mother had a heart attack and died suddenly…My father was crushed and lost without her. He needed me, so I returned to the farm. By this time, everyone had heard the story of my marriage to Richard Adams which had ended so sadly, and there were no questions. Having Alex at the farm perked Dad up, and he had a reason, once again, to face each day. Of course, Matthew heard by way of the grapevine about my marriage. We tried to never see each other; it would have been too hurtful. We both turned our attention to our babies. The real tragedy is that Matthew never knew he had a wonderful son, and Alex never knew his real father. I explained to Alex that we did not have a picture of his dad, because he and I had such a short time together. I'm sure he's missed having a father to guide him, but my father, Abel, took him under his wing. That is where Alex learned so much about horses; he was always tagging behind his grandfather." After a long pause, she sighed, "I told so many lies, but I didn't know what else to do."

They continued to sit in silence, each with her own thoughts and emotions. Marcy was consumed with her love for Matthew; he would always be a part of her, and she knew he never stopped loving her.

Kathryn's thoughts took her back to her life with her parents. She remembered what life had been like with Ivy and Matthew when she was a child. Now, on reflection, she realized there had never been any demonstration of closeness or love between them. She remembered Ivy as a spark that flittered here and there, never really warm or loving, never grounded. On the other hand, Matthew was always Kathryn's safe haven, always tender and loving and admiring of all she did. As a child, she had paid little attention to the detachment between her parents. Now, she was seeing their lives clearly. Ivy had been happy in her social life, and Matthew had immersed himself in the love and care of his daughter and his work at the school. *Oh*, she thought, *I'm so glad he experienced a true love even if he and Marcy were fated to have only a short time together.*

Finally, Kathryn turned to Marcy, took her hand, and said, "Marcy, you're surely a very strong person to have carried this load all these years in order to protect others. Your reward is the fine son you have raised. I only wish his Dad could have known him; he would be so proud. Thank you for trusting me enough to let me know I have a half brother." Then in typical Kathryn fashion, "Now we must think carefully about how we're going to proceed. Why don't we meet at the cabin two days from now in the evening after we've had time to think more about it? This is life changing for all of us."

They embraced and parted. Life would never be the same.

The old cabin had always played an important part in most events in the lives of the Hawthornes, so it seemed to be the perfect venue for this momentous meeting. Kathryn greeted Marcy by placing her arm around her shoulder and leading her to one of the rocking chairs.

Marcy spoke first. "I'm still not sure I should have told you about Matthew and me. I would never want to do anything to upset Mr. Hawthorne or you. And then, most important to me, there is Alex. If he's told, will he ever forgive me for my lies all these years, and what will it do to the identity he has thought was his all his life? These last two days, I've been thinking that maybe we should just keep everything as it has always been.

Kathryn leaned forward, looked Marcy in the eyes, and replied, "You positively did the right thing in telling me... please don't have any second thoughts...I would have it no other way. Just think what I have gained...a brother and new member of the Hawthorne family! I love you, Marcy, for all the years you gave to your son; he's such a wonderful human being. I love you, too, because, I know my father loved you, and you were an important part of his life. You gave him happiness." After a brief pause, she went on, "My only regrets are that we didn't know sooner and, of course, that my father didn't ever know about Alex."

They spent the next few minutes quietly, each with her own thoughts, as they stared at the glorious sunset. Finally, Kathryn turned once again to Marcy and said, "We both know the next step is to decide where we go from here. I really don't think, Marcy, that we can keep this a secret any longer. Nathan needs to know that the young man he so admires and cares for is really his grandson. He just has to know! It then follows that if Nathan is told, Alex must be told also. I strongly feel he is entitled to know his true identity. However, this is your life we are dealing with, and I'll follow your lead. Whatever you decide, I'll respect. You've listened thoughtfully to how I feel; now it's your turn."

Again, there were moments of silence, while Marcy thought about what would be ahead for all of them if Alex's true identity became known. However, she realized that having told her story to Kathryn, Alex and Nathan were entitled to know, too. It must be done. She turned to

Kathryn, nodded, and replied, "You're right. We will do it your way."

"You're doing the right thing, Marcy. I know it won't be easy. I'm sure you would prefer to be alone with Alex in order to tell him in your own way. Poppy will be in for quite a shock, so I think perhaps I should tell him privately, too." Marcy nodded in agreement. "We'll have to be patient, I'm sure, and give them time to come to terms with all they learn. Then, at some point, we must all get together and go from there. I can't say where we're headed, but we must tell them."

When Nathan and Alex returned from the capital, they were in high spirits. High spirits because the meeting had gone well and also because they truly did enjoy being together. Alex had been accompanying Nathan to his meetings for quite a long time and was becoming known and respected among Nathan's peers, very influential men. It was not unusual for Nathan to ask Alex for his opinion during many of the meetings, and his ideas were usually well received by the other attendees. Alex had gained a position of respect and was recognized as Nathan's protégé.

The day they returned, Kathryn was busy with all her Thayer accounts, so there was little time to speak with Nathan. Therefore, they were both eager for the evening when they could catch up on each other's news. After dinner, Kathryn suggested they adjourn to Nathan's study for their "latest news" talk, because it would be private with no distractions and because it was a place most special to Nathan.

After they were settled comfortably in his study, he turned questioning eyes toward Kathryn, and she said, "I have learned something of the utmost importance to you and me. I think it is wonderful news so don't be worried, please. I'll try to relate the story to you just as I heard it three days ago, and I would appreciate it if you would not interrupt me during the telling."

He was filled with apprehension as he settled back in his large lounge chair while she sat on the ottoman, and as she began to tell the story, she took his hand. Kathryn told the tale slowly and carefully so as not to omit anything. After the telling was over, they sat quietly in the dimly lit room while Nathan processed all he had heard, and Kathryn waited nervously to learn his reaction. After many minutes had passed he smiled and said, "Damn! This is the best news I've had since Matthew and you were born. Just think, Katey Sue, we have another member in the Hawthorne family and...what a guy! Marcy surely did do a fine job of raising and guiding him. I can understand why Matthew loved her so much. Matthew and Alex were cheated out of knowing each other, but, Darlin', it's time for us to give thanks for the time we have now to love each other as a family."

"Marcy is telling Alex tonight. I wonder what his reaction will be. Not knowing Alex's identity has robbed all of us of the joy we might have had for many years, but Marcy did what she thought was right for everyone at the time. I know you'll want to acknowledge Alex as your grandson, but I promised Marcy we would let her make the decision as to how to handle this situation."

"Yes, I definitely want everyone to know he's a Hawthorne, but I guess you are right, Marcy may not want it known that she had a baby out of wedlock. It may have to be enough that only we know the truth."

Kathryn answered, "My opinion is that Alex should claim his birthright, and we should announce he is Matthew's son. After all, Poppy, we're living in the twentieth century, and people are not so quick to judge this sort of thing. Alex is loved and respected by all the people in this area, and I think they will accept all this without a ripple. Of course, our local grapevine will be hard at work for some time. We can count on that. We'll just have to wait now to hear from Marcy and Alex."

Alex was happy to be home. He enjoyed nothing more than spending time with Nathan, and their meetings had been successful. However, he always felt the pull of the farm; it was the center of the world to him. He called to his mother as he entered their home, and she hurried toward him with open arms. They had been everything to each other ever since his birth, and their deep love and devotion was evident to everyone. Marcy was feeling riddled with guilt and worry now that she knew her secret must be told. How would he react? How was Mr. Hawthorne taking the news? *Oh, Matthew, I wish you were here. Please help me tell our son*, she thought.

During dinner, he related all the details of the flight, the meetings, and the names of all those in attendance at the capital. The list of people was impressive. He was happy and relaxed which made Marcy dread all the more having to burst his bubble. Finally, Marcy steeled herself and asked if they could sit for awhile in the living room, because she had something important to tell him.

"Is there a problem?" Alex asked when he saw the worry lines on his mother's face. It was then he realized she had barely touched her food.

Marcy turned on the lights but kept them dim so their emotions would not be too evident, and they took chairs on opposite sides of the fireplace. "God, help me," she prayed. Then she told her story in just the same way she had told it to Kathryn. Alex sat tensely in his chair, looking into his mother's eyes, not saying a word until she announced that Matthew had been his father, and then he uttered a loud questioning, "What?" Marcy paused for several minutes to allow Alex time to digest what he had just heard before repeating again that Matthew Hawthorne was his father and Nathan Hawthorne was his grandfather.

"Please try to understand how much Matthew and I loved each other and the circumstances surrounding that love. Our love is forever, Alex, and you were conceived in that love...that will never change. I never told Matthew, but I know he would have loved you with all his heart. At the time, I did what I thought was the only right thing to do for everyone concerned. I lied to you about your father, and you missed all those years when perhaps you should have known the truth." Alex continued to stare with blank eyes as though she were talking about someone else. He had lived a lie all his life. Marcy finally said through tears, "Please forgive me."

With that, his eyes came to life, "I love you, Mom; nothing could ever change that. I just need some time to get used to what you have told me. Would it be all right with you if I went to the stables and spent some time alone? I need to be alone. Oh, and I want you to know there is nothing to forgive. You have always done the best you could."

Marcy nodded, and they stood. Alex embraced her, turned, and started the solitary walk to his haven in the stable. Marcy's announcement had shaken him to his core. His old identity had been stripped from him and a complete new one put in its place in the matter of one hour.

All the participants in this new turn of events had a sleepless night. Nathan couldn't stop talking with Kathryn; he needed to keep sharing with her this wonderful revelation. To think, the young man he cared so much about and admired was his grandson. Matthew had left a part of himself in a son. If only Anna could be by his side to share in his joy.

Kathryn was still getting used to the idea that she had a brother and such a fine one. No wonder she had always thought he reminded her of someone. Now that she knew he was Matthew's son, the picture came into focus. He reminded her of her father in many ways, but it was Poppy that he most resembled. Now that she knew, she realized that Poppy and Alex were like two peas in a pod. It was all so wonderful, another fine, strong Hawthorne man.

Early the following morning, Kathryn phoned Marcy. She could wait no longer to hear an account of the meeting between Alex and his mother. In a weary, tremulous voice Marcy recalled for Kathryn every detail of the previous evening. Poor Marcy, she was such a tender soul, and all the events of the past few days were taking a toll on her. "Alex received my confession in his usual quiet way, but I could tell he was completely stunned. He wanted to be alone and spent the night in his little room in the stable.

I know we had planned for the four of us to sit down together and talk this out after I told Alex. Now, I think we have to wait till we know how Alex is going to react. I don't want to do anything more to hurt him."

After the call to Marcy, Kathryn went to Nathan's study to tell him what Marcy had to say, to which he simply nodded and patted her hand. From the study, Kathryn left for her morning ride. On arriving at the stable, she found Rhett saddled and a hollow-eyed Alex standing in the door. She walked over to him and said, "I know you have a lot to deal with right now and probably don't want to discuss it yet, but I want you to know, I think your mother, you, Poppy, and I should sit down at some point and talk it out. Let's not wait too long." He simply nodded. Kathryn turned, mounted Rhett, and rode slowly away. It was not a morning she wanted a swift ride, but a morning to simply keep the horse to a walk while her mind, which was filled with so many thoughts, did the racing.

A few evenings hence, they all gathered in Anna's room. Gemma had provided tea, tiny sandwiches, and fancy cookies before pulling closed the pocket doors so that they would have no interruptions. Each person came to the gathering having played different roles in this drama; each having lived a different history in the story. Marcy and Alex sat in matching wing chairs, while Nathan selected a comfortable lounge chair, and Kathryn sat on the ottoman at his feet. After each person had been served tea, Kathryn started the dialogue. "Since Poppy is the elder of this group, I think he should let us know how he is feeling."

Nathan looked tenderly at Marcy and spoke. "I want you to know, Marcy, that my heart is full of love and admiration for you. I can understand why you made the decision you did regarding the identity of your baby. It was an unselfish act. We can all sit here now and say we should have known sooner that Alex is truly a member of the Hawthorne family, but at the time, years ago, you wanted to spare Matthew, and you courageously made the decision to go it alone. You are a strong woman, and you have reared a fine son." Nathan then turned to Alex. "Now let me say, Alex, that there is no one...no one I admire more than you, and to think you are a member of our family just compounds my feelings...I'm overjoyed. I'm praying you will take Hawthorne as your name and assume your rightful place in this family. I truly do love you, my boy. I only wish Anna could be here to know you as her grandson."

If a stranger had entered Anna's room that evening and surveyed the participants, he would never have guessed that Alex was the subject of the meeting or that his future might be defined by the actions decided on that night. He sat through Nathan's remarks, seemingly relaxed and with a stoical expression which made it impossible for anyone to know what he was thinking. Kathryn could not help comparing him to Nathan when he was delivered important news…always strong and unreadable, *two peas in a pod.*

All eyes turned to Alex at this point, and without preamble, he spoke. "First of all, let me say I agree wholeheartedly with Nathan regarding my wonderful, strong, and loving mother. She is all that and more, and I'm only sorry things could not have been different for her through the years. Needless to say, when she told me about my father, I felt as though we must be talking about someone else, not me. When I acknowledged it really was about me, at first, I didn't want to deal with it. I wanted life to go on as it always had. I needed time. For several days, I've stayed at the stable except when I went in the evenings to the cemetery and tried to get in touch with the father I have never known, really, except for having him as a teacher when I was in high school. I willed my mind back to those days and the many times he spoke with me and advised me. I always looked up to him, and he was the man I turned to when I had questions…questions about anything…and he was always there for me. To think, he was really my father, and we never knew. Then I went through a phase of anger at the hand I had been dealt…I was really angry!" Alex was now sitting upright and a little forward in his chair, using his arms and hands to put emphasis on his remarks. Passion was flowing from him. Everyone else in the room listened raptly.

When he had finished venting his anger, he sat back and seemed to look into space. There was complete silence, and everyone sat as though in a trance waiting for Alex to go on. Minutes seemed to pass before he spoke again, this time calmly. He turned to his mother and said, "Mother, I love you and thank you for being everything to me all these years. I'm only sorry the love you and Matthew had for each other could not be openly acknowledged."

After Alex spoke, the entire group sat quietly, each lost in his or her own thoughts. Kathryn looked at Nathan, Marcy, and Alex and realized they were her family. In her heart, she thanked God for making it so. *Are the others feeling it, too?* she wondered.

Nathan turned to Alex. "There's nothing I want more in this world than to acknowledge you as my grandson, but the decision has to be yours. You know, Alex, I've always felt this affinity we have for each other, and now, I know it's because we're both Hawthornes. You have also inherited fine traits from your grandfather Ellis, which only add to your character. You have become a fine young man, and a lot of that we owe to your mother, Marcy, and her guidance all these years."

As Nathan spoke, the men looked at each other with a steady gaze. Alex squirmed in his chair, ran his fingers through his mop of disheveled blond hair, and looked down at his feet because it was hard for this humble man to accept so much praise from Nathan. How had all this happened to him? Finally, "Thank you, Nathan, for all you've said just now and for all the times you've been here for me. You have always inspired me to do things that at first, I thought were beyond me. My grandfather Ellis really had to take the place of my father when I was a little boy and in my youth, but through it all and beyond those years, you have always been here doing what grandfathers do...We just didn't know you really were my grandfather. Thank you. I've wrestled with this news ever since I was told, and it all boils down to this...I really am a Hawthorne and proud of it. I'm still getting used to it and suppose I'll be working on that for quite some time."

Everyone had been listening to Alex and practically holding their breath until they finally heard his decision. As he declared his decision, Alex turned to his mother first and observed the glistening in her eyes and her proud and happy smile. Then Alex went to Nathan, and they embraced. Nathan was so overwhelmed that words would not come, but none were needed between these two. Lastly, Alex pulled Kathryn to him; they both smiled tentatively, acknowledging they were brother and sister. Emotion ruled the night.

Kathryn thought Marcy's feelings had been overlooked in all the soul searching. "I think we should hear from Marcy. After all, she is the prime character in this drama and could be affected in ways we cannot know. Please, Marcy, let us know what you're feeling."

Marcy took some moments to gather her thoughts before she replied. "As I have always done, I think of Matthew and what he would want for his son. This I know, he would have loved Alex more than I can ever tell you. Alex is Matthew's son and a Hawthorne. I've felt guilty ever since Alex was born because of the lie I have lived. Now we have a chance to make it all right, and I know Matthew is smiling down on us." Her voice was strong as she spoke, but tears were spilling over. "I'm so happy to finally be able to speak of Matthew with you and to acknowledge our love for each other."

All the players in this scene were too overwhelmed with feelings to let go, and Kathryn realized this when she said, "We can't leave each other without a toast to our future. Why don't we adjourn to Poppy's den where, I'm sure, we'll find the ingredients for a toast to the decision made this night." Nathan and Marcy led the way to the room where Alex and Nathan had spent many hours. Alex took the orders for the drinks, while Kathryn and Nathan told Marcy about the history of the room and the daily journals that were the pride of the Hawthornes and their true treasure. Marcy's heart was at peace at last, for in truth, her son was finally home.

They raised their glasses as Nathan said, "Here's to the next chapter in the Hawthorne saga."

As this new family circle finished their drinks and the evening came to a close, Nathan told them, "I will enter the events of this evening in the present day's journal, and I'll say how blessed we are to know Alexander is one of us."

Kathryn, as always the planner, told them, "We all know there is still much to be done. We must plan for the name change for Alex and how we're going to announce all this to the public. Tonight is not the time for all that, but I suggest we all get together in a day or two and set the wheels in motion." It was agreed.

A week after the family's momentous meeting, Nathan invited George Smythe, the local attorney, to join Alex and him at the farm. They sat in Nathan's den, and the situation was explained to their lawyer. He was entrusted to handle all the legalities of the name change and any other legal items that needed to be done. Nathan explained that while they wouldn't be shouting the news to the winds, they had no intention of being secretive in any way.

The next order of business was to relate all of this to Dr. Dan and his family. They had been Matthew's best friends, and Emmie was Kathryn's dearest friend. Kathryn called Emmie and between them, they set a date for the Hurleys to have dinner at the farm. "Come early," Kathryn said, "so we have time for cocktails and talk before sitting down to dinner."

When the Hurleys arrived, they were greeted by Nathan, Kathryn, and Alex. Marcy had declined to join them; it had always been her nature to stand in the background. Drinks were served in the beautiful living room, and Dan, Martha, and Emmie settled back for what they thought would be some light chatter. However, Nathan took the floor and explained that they had been invited to share some good news with the Hawthornes. Then he went on to tell them of the love Marcy Ellis and Matthew had shared and a result of that love being their son, Alex. He continued to explain to them that Matthew had never known about Alex because of circumstances at the time of his birth. It was only recently they had all learned they had another family member...and a fine one... in the Hawthorne family. Alex would now be known as Alexander Hawthorne.

It was Kathryn's turn to add to the story. "As Dad's best friend, Dr. Dan, you needed to hear about this from us. Of course, before long, all the town will know...by word of mouth...; the good old grapevine is very efficient. You're probably wondering about Marcy. She has been carrying this load for years while she raised a fine son alone, but she is happy, and I might add, brave to have it all out in the open at last so that Alex can take the place his father would have wanted for him. She was invited here tonight, but Marcy doesn't like the limelight and prefers staying in the background. We respect her wish."

Dan spoke, "You all know, Matthew and I spent many hours together, and there were no secrets between us. Everyone should have a good friend to whom you can tell anything and everything; it's the best therapy in the world. Oh, how I've missed those times we had. Every time we got together, he talked about nothing but his love for Marcy... His heart was full of her. I know for a fact that he was all set to ask for a divorce from Ivy until he learned she was pregnant. My good friend was probably the most ethical person I have ever known, and his love for children knew no bounds, so he felt compelled to stay with Ivy. If he had known Marcy was pregnant, he would have told me... He just did not know. I know one thing for sure...You're positively doing what Matt would have wanted...making his son a part of the family." Turning to Alex, "You do your father proud, Alex. I'm just sorry you never got to know him."

"Let's drink a toast to my grandson," Nathan said. They all rose and raised their glasses.

"I don't think I have to tell you, I'm completely overwhelmed." All eyes were on Alex as he spoke, "My mentor and inspiration is my grandfather, and I have a sister, too. Just haven't gotten used to all this yet. It will take time."

Kathryn had always been sensitive and intuitive when it came to the feelings and actions of people around her. She had been watching all the characters in this little scene, and it became apparent to her that there were two people in the room who had eyes only for each other...Alex and Emmie. *When did this happen?* she thought. *I should have seen signs of this before. It's as if there's no one else here.*

It was not necessary to make a public announcement regarding the new member of the Hawthorne family. In small towns, where the same families have shared all their ups and downs with each other for generations, there are no secrets. It's the nature of small-town life. The "town" family loves each other, chastises and forgives, encourages, and above all, tries to understand each other. The news of Alex's relationship to the Hawthornes was discussed for days. The school staff, who had served when Matthew and Marcy were teachers at the local school, agreed they had observed them together often. Others said they always felt there was more than friendship between them, but Matthew and Marcy were so admired by everyone that nothing was said at the time. "Besides," many of them said, "Matthew did not have much of a home life with Ivy... Who could blame him for turning to Marcy Ellis? They were perfectly suited for each other, and it was just a shame it all turned out as it did." Not a person could be found who didn't admire Marcy. She was beautiful, unassuming, gentle, and kind; what was there not to like? Now that her story was public knowledge, Marcy was admired even more for her courage as a single mother, who had raised a wonderful son. The fact that she had been the chosen one of Matthew Hawthorne only added to her stature. Marcy had never sought the spotlight, and at this point in her life, she, more than ever, wished to remain in the background.

Nathan invited Alex and Marcy to live with him in his home, but she declined saying, "Alex may do as he pleases, but I'm happy in the little home I've always known. Since my parents' deaths, it has been my home where I do as I please, and I am very happy here. I do thank you, Mr. Hawthorne. You're so kind, but I think you understand. Alex will have to speak for himself, and I'll be happy with any decision he makes."

"I don't want you calling me Mr. Hawthorne anymore, Marcy...Call me Nathan."

Even though he knew he would still be close to his mother if he moved in with Nathan, Alex decided to stay in the little home with her. Nathan made it clear to him that someday, he would be in charge of the farm, and it would be up to him to carry on the Hawthorne legacy, at which point, he definitely should live in the big house. Alex had a lot to learn about managing the farm, but Nathan was anxious to teach him. "I'll be here to show you the ropes," Nathan told him. "I can't tell you how happy all this makes me. I feel that only God could have arranged our destiny so beautifully."

HAWTHORNE—OUR TOWN

SINCE THE EVENING Kathryn had sat with Marcy by the Hawthorne burial ground, family matters had taken precedence over everything else she was working on. However, the Thayer accounts had been in good order and moving ahead before that life-changing meeting, and the town restoration plan was being handled by the capable committees formed by Kathryn. This had given her some breathing room. In the meantime, Peter Kingston had found the property he wanted for his new Hawthorne facility, which would house all the operations pertaining to the new LADY LINE.

Myles Cooledge had given top priority to the designing of the building, which would be built by the beautiful river in Hawthorne, and Peter was so pleased with Myles that he asked Kathryn to recommend an interior decorator for the offices when the building was complete. In Kathryn's mind, no one but Madeline Roth would do. She had spent a lot of time in Hawthorne working on the Main Street restoration and becoming familiar with the character of the town as had Myles. What a team they made! When Madeline was approached, she was more than happy to accept the assignment, which meant she and Joshua would be spending more time in Hawthorne, much to Kathryn's delight.

Kathryn had kept in close touch with the offices at Thayer Enterprises through her daily phone calls to Marcus and Alma. However, she had not told him about Alex, because she wanted to be able to sit down with both Emily and him when they would have no interruptions and plenty of time. The opportunity presented itself when Marcus called asking if she could meet with Peter Kingston and him to make some decisions on the presentation of the new LADY LINE. He invited her to please stay with Emily and him.

"Oh, you dear, dear people. I've missed you, and I have so very much to tell you...a big surprise!"

Alex drove her to the Wayville Airport. She had decided to take a commercial flight rather than have Alex away from the farm at this busy time. As he drove to Wayville, they remarked about the strangeness of the change in their relationship, but both agreed, it was great they were Hawthornes...brother and sister.

Kathryn turned to Alex and said, "Now, I think, as your nosey sister, there is something else I should know about you. Lately, when we've been together with the Hurleys, I felt a new dynamic in the air between you and Emmie. Am I wrong?"

Alex smiled, in fact you might say he beamed, as he turned to her. "No, you surely are not wrong, my nosey sister."

"How long has this been going on?"

"Well, it all started after that first day we all went riding at the farm. Emmie told me how much she had enjoyed the ride and would like to do more of it, but she was sure she needed to take lessons. You were busy with all your work and projects, so you weren't aware that Emmie was coming to the farm for lessons regularly after that. I felt drawn to her from the first, and the feeling grew and grew. You know, I've always been pretty much a loner, but suddenly, the days when I didn't see her were empty for me. Finally, one day, when we stopped by the pond to take a break, we just looked each other in the eye and fell into each other's arms. Both of us just knew...There could never be anyone else for either of us. Loving each other as we do, it's a puzzle to both of us that we could have grown up and gone to school together all those years without ever really seeing each other. If it hadn't been for your coming back here, we might have gone on without ever getting together. Thank you...sister."

"If you weren't driving, Alex, I'd give you a great big hug, but I'm sorta' miffed with both of you for not telling me sooner. All this time since being here, I've thought Emmie and Mark were a pair, but now that I've heard from you, I realize that the two of you are positively right for each other. My brother and my best friend! How much better could it be!"

Marcus was at the airport to meet her with a huge hug and fond greetings. They were saving all the personal news for when they were with Emily, so they turned to discussing the Kingston account without wasting any time. A meeting had been set up with Peter Kingston at which time Kathryn would lay out her promotional ideas. It was going to be a massive campaign and must be done just right and soon. The first order of business would be to select a model to represent ANNA. Kathryn was looking for a fresh face...someone not familiar to the public, someone new to the business, a model who could be presented as a woman when she is young, middle-aged, and older...

always a lady. It would entail perfect coiffures and classic clothing. It was a lot to get done in a short time. However, Kathryn felt reinvigorated and ready for the challenge. Marcus could see that her time spent in Hawthorne had been good for her.

Kathryn's first stop upon arriving at the offices of Thayer Enterprises was to meet with Alma. The Kingston account had been Kathryn's main focus during the summer because of the urgency to get the new line into production, but she could not ignore her other accounts. She was glad to have time to spend with dear, efficient Alma, who had all the information on all her accounts organized perfectly. Alma had been Kathryn's right hand for so long that she could anticipate the information Kathryn would require which always saved a lot of discussion and direction on Kathryn's part. *How did I get so lucky as to find this perfect jewel to work with me?* thought Kathryn. *We must give her a new title and a raise.* Alma, a subdued person, who dressed in dark suits with her hair pulled back severely, always seemed to be a part of the background. However, she did everything to perfection, neatly with all the t's crossed and i's dotted. She never talked about her private life and never was seen socializing with anyone in the office, but all her coworkers liked and respected her. She was totally dedicated to her job and never missed a day's work. Dependable but a real loner—that was Alma.

Kathryn was quick to compliment Alma on her work and dedication. "I would never have been able to spend this summer with my grandfather if it had not been for you, Alma. I just hope it was not too heavy a load for you."

"Oh no," was the reply. "I'm glad you felt you could rely on me. I really enjoyed working with the different accounts, and even though you were not in your office here, you kept in close touch with me, and I knew I could reach you at any time. I'm just glad I was able to handle everything to your satisfaction."

After two hours with Alma, Kathryn joined Peter Kingston and Marcus for lunch. Peter was literally beaming. He spent the entire lunch time paying tribute to Kathryn for her inspiration of the new LADY LINE. He showed Marcus pictures of the site and beginnings of his new Kingston facility in Hawthorne. Located by the beautiful river and standing in a grove of Maple trees, it was like nothing else in the Kingston family of buildings. Marcus had never seen his friend, Peter, so enthusiastic and full of new life.

"Marcus, this girl not only proposed a wonderful new product for my company, but she found the most remarkable architect, Myles Cooledge, and the best decorator, Madeline Roth, for my new building. I'm sure I wouldn't have been able to put this all together without her. Young lady, you can expect a nice bonus for all the extra time you've given me. Another benefit we've discovered by our locating this department in Hawthorne is the people in that town we have hired to work for us. They're innovative and industrious, and they are, I am happy to say, lacking in the 'world owes me a living' attitude we see so much of in the city. We're just delighted to have them as members of our group. Yes, Kathryn, I owe you a lot."

Marcus glowed and Kathryn, rather embarrassed by all the praise, blushed a bit, smiled, and replied, "Please, Mr. Kingston, this is what I do. My reward is in knowing you are happy with my work. We still have a lot to do in order to get LADY LINE'S—ANNA—launched before the holidays. I have a lot of ideas, and so I suggest we get back to my office and brainstorm."

The days in the city flew by, and her visit with Emily and Marcus was not nearly long enough for any of them. There was so much Kathryn had to tell them, mainly, the turn of events with Alex. They were astounded when they heard this news but delighted in the knowledge that Kathryn had gained a brother and Nathan, a grandson. In the short time they had spent in his company, they had recognized all Alex's fine attributes. Emily wanted to hear also about how the preservation of Hawthorne was progressing. The Thayers could not help but see the light in Kathryn's eyes as she described all the work being done in her little hometown by the people there that she loved and admired. Marcus thought, *How are we ever going to get her back to the city?*

"I know he's a very strong man, but how is Nathan handling all this excitement? Just the work in the town would have been a lot for him to be involved in...however much he is delighted in all that is being done. But this business with Alex would have been too much for many people to handle. He seems to have taken it all in his stride. What a man!" said Marcus.

"Yes, isn't he. He's happier and more vigorous than I have seen him in years, and none of this has fazed him one bit. He seems younger every day. I love him so much, and it makes my heart sing just to be with him these days," replied Kathryn.

On her return, Kathryn was met by Emmie. Alex had flown Nathan to the state capital for another conference. They were happy to see each other and to have some time alone. Kathryn was anxious to know more about Alex and Emmie's plans which launched Emmie into her favorite topic...Alex. The glow she exuded shouted love, love, love. The exquisite, old-fashioned engagement ring was small but beautifully detailed to suit the petite Emmie. The main diamond was surrounded with many small ones, and all the exquisite stones sparkled in the afternoon sunlight. Emmie told Kathryn they were not rushing to the wedding day, because they wanted to savor every moment of this time...not hurry through it.

Finally, the farm came into view, and Kathryn asked Emmie to stop the car. She felt the need, once again, to sit at the bottom of the hill and take in the sight. *This is home to me*, she realized. *How can I ever be satisfied to spend my life anywhere else?* After a few minutes spent in silence, Kathryn motioned that they should proceed. These two friends were so in tune that Emmie felt the depth of Kathryn's emotions on returning to the farm. They drove up the tree-lined approach to the house and parked by the terrace. "Let's rest here on the terrace, and see if Gemma has some of her wonderful iced tea or maybe lemonade for us," Kathryn suggested. They still needed more time together...It had been weeks since they'd been able to hear the news from each other. Rocking chairs welcomed them, and with a sigh, they sat back to experience the beauty of the day while reflecting on the many joys that had been a part of their history.

"We're at the most special time in our lives," Emmie said. "It seems to be the culmination of all our experiences. Just couldn't be any better...except that I wish you had a person to love as I have. Oh, Kathryn, there aren't words to describe how it feels to be totally in love with a wonderful person like my Alex...It's beyond description. There are no words...You just have to feel it."

Kathryn thought about the people she knew who had experienced total love for each other; Poppy and Granna, Marcus and Emily, Alex and Emmie, and now she could add Matthew and Marcy to that list. For the first time, she felt the loss of a person who could be her "world," a world full of love, devotion, and, yes, passion. What was wrong with her? Was she doomed to always present a persona of warmth toward men but remain icy inside? This was her mother's legacy. It was clear to her that Ivy had never known real love. *I realize now my mother was a very tragic figure.*

Talk was never necessary between these two friends, and this day, they rocked gently, each lost in her own thoughts. Their reverie was broken when Nathan and Alex returned and joined them. Kathryn thought Nathan looked very tired and suggested he have a refreshing drink of lemonade and then take time out for a rest. He readily agreed that she had a good idea.

After Nathan departed for his nap, Emmie, Alex, and Kathryn refilled their glasses and sat back, reluctant to part. Kathryn had been busy with all her responsibilities, and Alex had taken on more at the farm, so there had not been time for lazy gatherings. Alex reported that Mark had called him to say he still wanted to make reservations for the four of them at the Wayville Country Club whenever they were free.

"What do you say?" asked Alex. "We haven't all been together for a long time. Let's give Mark a date."

Mark called Kathryn the following day to say there was going to be a dinner-dance at the country club the following Saturday and asked if she would be free to go. He had already spoken with Emmie and Alex, and they were in favor of that night.

"Sounds perfect to me," she replied. "I'm looking forward to all of us being together again." To herself, she was thinking this outing might seem a little strange, because they would be changing partners.

Kathryn continued to handle all her duties for Thayer Enterprises during the morning hours. Alma now called her each morning with reports on all the accounts and to receive direction from Kathryn. After digesting all the details, Kathryn called Marcus with her reports and updates. The Kingston LADY LINE was proceeding swiftly, and the advertising campaign was in full gear. The model had been chosen while Kathryn was in the city, a beautiful young girl with long chestnut hair, soft brown eyes, and a beautiful smile. A good choice, Kathryn was sure. The Kingston facility in Hawthorne was moving along swiftly at the prodding of Myles, and Madeline was ready to do the interior decorating at a moment's notice.

Peter Kingston was delighted. He bragged to Marcus that it was one of the best moves he had ever made. "In fact," he said, "I might even move to Hawthorne myself one of these days, enlarge that building, and make it my headquarters. I've fallen in love with that little town."

The next order of business for Kathryn was another meeting with all the HOT committees for a progress report. They came together in the school auditorium full of excitement and enthusiasm. More had been accomplished in the past few months than anyone would have ever felt was possible. Now, they all knew the sky was the limit; they were ready to spread their wings and keep soaring. Main Street was regaining the charm it had displayed in the early days. All the shopkeepers were working hard to have the best merchandise and to display it attractively. New specialty shops had moved into vacant buildings and were offering a variety of goods. Most gratifying to Kathryn was that the majority of the original shopkeepers were staying in business and for some, returning after thinking there was no future for them in Hawthorne. The Emersons fell into the latter category, because they had convinced their nephew, Harry, to take over the business. Now there would once again be Emerson's. Walters' Restaurant continued in the same fashion except the cheap facade had been removed, revealing all the old brick. The wooden floor had been stripped and oiled, the chairs and tables were refinished, not replaced; no one wanted to lose the decor they had always known. The Excel Hardware had never changed much in all the years of its existence. Now Jack Root was promoting its historical significance and displaying historical hardware items.

After hearing all the reports, it was agreed they were ready for the next step of beautification. Areas behind the stores had been set aside for parking, which meant they could now have a park in the center of the square... no cars allowed. The plan called for the planting of trees, benches to be placed strategically, and a gazebo to grace the center of the park. The committees envisioned summer band concerts where everyone could gather for summertime entertainment and singing. In front of the stores, huge planters of flowers were planned with flowers being donated by the local nursery, and the Hawthorne Garden Club offered to do the planting and maintaining of these planters. All the clubs wanted to be involved; the Rotary was donating the gazebo; the American Legion, the benches; the Elks and Eagles, the trees. The Women's Club announced they would purchase a drinking fountain for the little park. People had all come together for one cause: the rebirth of their town. Pride showed on every face. Kathryn, remembering her father's love of children, thought he would be saying, "This is a wonderful example for the young people of what can be accomplished when everyone works together for a good cause."

Ed Abbott had the story of his lifetime and found it impossible to sit still for more than five or ten minutes; he bustled about continually cornering committee members for quotes on their progress, always looking for a tidbit that had not been reported as yet. People chuckled and asked each other when they thought Ed found time to sleep. Ed had gained a sense of importance that had always been lacking in his life. Since he was devoting more and more of his time to the HOT news, he was glad to have MaryLu do the reporting of the social life in Hawthorne along with the birth announcements and obituary columns. The city newspapers had used the Hawthorne experiment as a human interest story, never expecting the response they had from their readers. People in the cities were intrigued by the little town and the ingenuity and spirit of the Hawthorne citizens; it called for future columns. Also, the fact that Kingston had built a facility in Hawthorne was big news for the papers' business sections. Reporters came to town to interview Kathryn, but she kept the spotlight on the townspeople, who had worked so very hard. The city reporters soon found the place to go in order to learn about HAWTHORNE—OUR TOWN was to the office of the Hawthorne newspaper.

The committees decided at the meeting to give themselves three weeks to get as much in place as possible, and at the end of that time, they would have the grand celebration. Ed Abbott was chairman of the publicity committee, and he reported his committee was ready to proceed with news coverage, flyers, and banners. Everything was in order, and Kathryn could see that her work with HOT was coming to an end. It was good, she thought, because her stay with Poppy was nearly over, and she would need to return to the city. Marcus had been understanding during the past months, but it would not be fair for her to prolong her time away. This was a bittersweet time for her; she was extremely happy about all the town accomplishments but sad to be leaving it all.

Before the meeting adjourned, Kathryn spoke. "You know now that there is nothing you can't accomplish if you all continue to work together. You should be very proud of yourselves. I've been honored to have been a part of your endeavor, and I will never forget you or these days."

The applause was thundering, and as the noise continued, Jack Root took a place beside Kathryn, held up his hands for quiet, and said, "Without you, Kathryn Hawthorne, we would not be celebrating this night. You have been the heart and soul of a dream that has come true. I only wish you could stay here with us forever, but since that is not in the cards, we hope you will return often, and may I ask if we can call you from time to time...whenever we run into a problem?"

A few tears trickled down her cheek as she replied, "Oh yes, please do...anytime."

Saturday, Mark arrived at the farm earlier than necessary so he would have time to visit with Nathan before collecting Alex, Kathryn, and Emmie for the drive to the dance. Mark had not seen Nathan for a long time, and he missed their conversations. Nathan was dressed in his well-worn jeans and an old, faded plaid shirt when he greeted Mark, explaining that he was going to take his favorite stallion out for a ride later.

"The sun will be going down soon; you won't have much daylight time," said Mark.

Nathan shook his head, "Don't have to worry about my riding in the dark, because this horse and I know every trail on this farm intimately. It's good to see you again... Let's go into the den and visit until Kathryn is ready to leave."

While the men were in the den, Kathryn was getting ready for the evening. She had chosen one of her favorite dresses to wear, a flowered chiffon. The background of the dress was white and the print was of flowers in various shades of peach with accents of green. The dress was loosely fitted, with a flare at the bottom, ankle length, and had spaghetti straps and a small cape of the same material, to be worn or not. Her sandals consisted mostly of rhinestone straps. *I really need a change*, she thought as she pulled her hair up loosely at the neckline and affixed two tiny peach roses at that point; just the right touch. It was good to be going out for an evening of fun with her good friends. *I must have been psychic when I packed these clothes for a stay in the country.*

When she finally appeared in the den, she found Mark, Nathan, and Alex deep into a discussion of the farm and all the people who lived there. They looked at Kathryn with approving eyes, and Nathan said, "I say this all the time, but I have to say it again. I hope Anna is looking down on us this night so she can see our lovely granddaughter. Katey Sue, you look beautiful." Alex and Mark nodded in agreement.

The trio proceeded to the Hurley home where Emmie was waiting. Emmie was her usual petite, dainty self, wearing a soft green pique dress that totally suited her. The foursome was complete. It seemed strange to Kathryn to be sitting with Mark. There had been many changes during her short stay at the farm, and this was one of them.

As they entered the club, Kathryn was impressed by all the attention paid to Mark. It was apparent that he was highly respected in Wayville due to his work at the hospital. She observed his special way of making each person feel special, and of many of them, he inquired how a member of their family was doing since an illness in which he had been involved. One could not help but admire such a man.

As they made their way to the table Mark had reserved, all eyes were focused on the striking foursome, but they were wrapped up in each other and unaware of the stir they were causing. Alex and Emmie had eyes only for each other and wanted to be touching or in each other's arms all the time so they danced nearly every dance together. Kathryn and Mark, therefore, were partners most of the evening. Kathryn was like no other girl Mark had ever known; she had it all. She was intelligent, a leader, an accomplisher, a lot of fun to be with, and to top it all off, she was the most beautiful girl he had ever seen. However, he wanted to protect himself against caring for her except as a friend for several reasons. She would be leaving Hawthorne soon to return to the city, where she belonged. Her lifestyle was completely different from his; he wanted a family and to remain a small-town doctor. Besides, Kathryn gave him no encouragement…She actually appeared a little cool toward him, which made him believe she was already committed to someone else…probably someone high on the corporate ladder in the city.

An evening like this was just what Kathryn needed, and she enjoyed it completely. She had to admit she really was glad Mark and she danced most of the time together; he was such a good dancer and so easy for her to follow. He treated her gently and made no moves to take them beyond friendship; it was just the way she wanted it to be. For the first time in months, she felt relaxed with no pressures... totally carefree.

Well into the evening, Alex was paged...He had a phone call. A call at this time of the night alarmed them all so they accompanied him to the phone. The call was from his mother, Marcy, telling him that Nathan had been thrown from his horse and had been taken to the Wayville Hospital. The medical team told her he was not awake or responding. Nathan, Matthew's dear father, had become a very important part of Marcy's life. She begged Alex to call her as soon as he saw Nathan and talked with the doctors. He could tell she was weeping softly as she spoke.

The usually strong, competent Kathryn actually fell apart and was glad for Mark's strong, steadying arms around her. "We really don't know anything yet," said Mark. "Don't think the worst. Let's just get moving." And with his arm around her to steady her, he led her to the car with Alex and Emmie trailing after them. It was obvious that Mark had taken charge.

On their arrival at the hospital, Kathryn and Mark ran inside while Alex and Emmie parked the car before joining them. Mark found a place for Kathryn in the lounge and told her to stay there, while he located Nathan and talked with the resident doctor. "I'll take care of this and get back to you. We'll know soon. Tell Alex and Emmie to stay with you after they park the car."

Kathryn was grateful for Mark's strength and thankful, too, to have her brother there with her. *I know he's just as worried and distraught as I am*, she thought.

Mark returned after having seen Nathan and been informed as to the tests that had been taken. "You have a lot to be thankful for," he said, "because it appears to be nothing more than a concussion. He is a bit disoriented, nervous, and weak, but we'll keep him here for a couple of days if he responds as I think he will, and then he can go home. Nathan is a strong man who's in good physical shape. He'll be alright."

Kathryn had been sitting stiffly, holding her emotions in check. Upon learning of Nathan's condition, she succumbed to her emotions; tears streamed down her cheeks. She went limp into Mark's strong arms without thinking. She had found a safe haven, and she remained there for several minutes while Alex and Mark discussed Nathan's prognosis. Finally, Kathryn's mind took over, and many scrambled emotions surfaced. She thought, *I'm so glad I have a brother to share this with...Why did I move into Mark's arms?...It feels good having someone to lean on... Oh no, this is foolish because I don't need anyone to take care of me; I can do it.* Self-consciously, she backed away from Mark and asked, "Can we see Poppy? Just a minute? We know he needs to rest so we'll make it brief. We just need to see for ourselves that he's alright."

When they entered his room, Nathan's eyes lit up, and he said, "Sorry to cause all this fuss. Damn fool horse was spooked by something, but it was partly my fault, too. I know better than to relax completely while riding."

"Poppy, now you will have a few days' forced rest, and that won't hurt you a bit. We are just happy you're okay," was Kathryn's response as she took his hand.

Alex informed Nathan that he would take care of everything at the farm, and he didn't want Nathan to fret about anything. "Just lay back and get a good rest; you have it coming."

Mark took Kathryn home last and walked her to the door where she turned to him. "I'm so thankful you were with us this night; don't know where I would have turned. I really needed a friend to lean on and someone to get me through the rough spots. I hope you'll monitor Poppy during his recovery. Will you please call me often? I think I need a lot of reassurance right now."

Mark so wanted her to come into his arms again but intuitively knew it was not the time, so he promised to call and to keep a close watch on Nathan. He turned and walked away.

Nathan recovered quickly and was anxious to return to the farm, but he bowed to Dr. Hurley's order that he remain in the hospital for four days. After all, this was the doctor's territory, and he set the rules. Everyone fell into an adjusted daily routine. Alex went to be with Nathan every day at eleven o'clock and stayed through the lunch hour until two o'clock at which time, Nathan took a nap. Kathryn joined Nathan for the dinner hour until eight o'clock. Mark always looked in on them during his evening visiting hours, making Nathan's room his last stop for the night so that he could stay as long as possible. Dr. Hurley was Nathan's doctor, but Mark asked Kathryn if he might visit with Nathan after he left the hospital; they had gotten to be good friends.

"Of course, anytime," was her reply, and she realized she would enjoy seeing Mark more often. She had seen him every day during Nathan's hospital stay.

During Nathan's hiatus, Alex assumed leadership at the farm. It became apparent he had learned more than he had realized from tagging around with Nathan, and while the stables were still his passion, he was enjoying working with every aspect of the farm. Truly blessed is the person who finds his Eden early in life doing work that fulfills him every day. God had smiled on Alex.

At the end of four days in the hospital, Dr. Dan gave permission for Nathan to return home with the proviso that he not go riding for two weeks and that he conduct all his business from his den and take naps often. "You're very lucky to have such good health; don't take it for granted. We want you around here for a long time."

Nathan was happy to return to his beloved farm, and he settled into his new routine without too much grumbling on his part. Gemma and her helpers shed a few tears of thankfulness to have him home again, and every meal consisted of his very favorites. Gemma had given orders to everyone to work quietly so as not to disturb him...They were on tiptoe most of the time. Alex made the daily visits to the various sites on the farm and reported to Nathan every evening.

At a meeting to finalize the unveiling of the Hawthorne project, it was decided the celebration would be held on Labor Day. No one wanted to be overlooked as part of the gala. From Washington D.C., the Republican Party would be represented, and not to be outdone, the Democratic Party was also sending representatives. This was too good a story for them to miss. Of course, many state government officers had written and asked to be part of the program. Interest in the Hawthorne project was sweeping the country. The Associated Press had been reporting on the HAWTHORNE—OUR TOWN project, and now reporters from all the city newspapers were making plans to cover the celebration. Their readers had been following the progress in the little town as it had been unfolding. Now many of them were eager to see the results and were planning to attend the celebration. Motels and inns in Wayville and Hawthorne were completely booked for the holiday weekend.

"This is all well and good," was Kathryn's reaction, "and it will give us publicity which will benefit us in the long run. However, I would like us to recognize all the contributions of the townspeople before any others. After all, it is because of them that all of this has been possible. We will build a large platform, which will accommodate everyone on the program, but we'll ask the outside dignitaries to limit their remarks to one paragraph (she smiled)...They'll just have to be creative. All the committee chairmen for the preservation project will be on the platform and will be introduced by Mayor J.J. Moore, and he will acknowledge all the citizens of Hawthorne for their contributions. It took everyone to breathe new life into our wonderful little town. Since we don't want our program to be so long that people get edgy, Ed Abbott will be in charge of issuing a commemorative booklet about the town's history, so we won't have to go into that in a succession of speeches. In this booklet, we will list all members of the HOT committees. I'm sure Ed will have more ideas for this little tribute, which everyone can have as a keepsake." Ed was smiling and nodding importantly. "Oh yes, another thing we must add are names of all the clubs and organizations listing their contributions. I'm sorry to be so longwinded, but we must not forget to acknowledge our friends from the city, too, whose advice and help have been invaluable, so they will be introduced and their names listed in the booklet." Ideas kept popping into her head as she continued, "I have heard that we should expect hordes of people to join with us and the motels and inns in the area are booked to capacity, so I have thought some of the townspeople who have an extra room might like to have a boarder for a night or two. Do you agree we should organize to do just that?" She received applause and nods of yes from everyone. "I can think of two women that we can always count on, and they are Edith Sharr and Lucy Smythe. Why don't we ask them to take on this job? I know they'll do it well." Heads nodded in agreement. "It will be a rather big job, because they'll first have to get a list of people who have extra rooms. Ed, you're in touch with the large newspapers, so you could ask them to run the phone numbers for Lucy and Edith. Also, let's give those numbers to the motels and inns for referral." No one seemed to have any doubt that Lucy and Edith would accept the challenge. After all, they had all those years as chairladies...They could handle anything.

The final items to be discussed at the meeting were extra parking areas and the directing of traffic, which the Moose Lodge had offered to oversee. It would be a big job, and the lodge received a round of applause. Several of the clubs were planning to be vendors of food and some arts and crafts; at the Legion they would sell barbequed chicken, the Elks planned to sell hamburgers and hot dogs and cold drinks, and the Girl Scouts had made plans to sell cookies and lemonade.

After the meeting, Kathryn returned to the farm feeling gratified that it was really going to happen. *What great people we have here*, she thought. Now she was reaching the time when she would have to bid them goodbye. Marcus had been making plans for her return to the city, and she knew her wonderful summer was coming to an end. It was hard to envision her days without Nathan and Alex. Thoughts of leaving were uppermost in her mind as she told herself, *It eases my mind knowing Poppy has Alex. And then there is Emmie. After being together this time, I'm going to miss her more than ever. There's no one I can share my joys, sorrows, doubts, and fears with like I can with Emmie. No one else can take her place.* Now she had to add Mark to the list of people she would most hate to leave; they were just getting to know each other, and she had such respect for him. *I must stop thinking this way,* her optimistic side said. *After all, I can come back often. Alex can fly to the city from time to time and bring me back for a visit. It won't be too bad...After all, I will have Emily and Marcus and my other friends in the city. I love the work I do for Thayer Enterprises, and I have the new Kingston line to promote, and that is going to be really exciting. I know we have a wonderful product.* Kathryn's innate optimism was in full bloom. She had always been able to count on it.

Celebration Day arrived to the hum of voices as busy citizens put the finishing touches on their projects while happy laughter sailed through the balmy air. Nature was rewarding them for all their efforts by providing a perfect day of sunshine and soft breezes. Main Street had taken on the appearance of a Grandma Moses painting. The proud merchants displayed their wares under new bright awnings; windows were sparkling and streets swept. The new park in the town square was alive with activity. A large platform had been erected and was festooned in red, white, and blue bunting. The band members were arranging their chairs and instruments; the food vendors were starting to cook their barbeques, hot dogs, and hamburgers; the Girl Scouts were busily making lemonade and arranging their cookies...It was a sight to behold. The Celebration Committee had decided to add another feature to the festivities. A dance band had been hired for the evening hours and a platform for dancing had been built.

By eleven o'clock, throngs of people had descended on the little square for the dedication. All the dignitaries were in their places on the festive platform and had been instructed to keep their remarks short. Mayor J.J. Moore was the master of ceremonies. Nathan sat in a place of honor flanked on each side by Kathryn and Alex, the three Hawthornes. To open the ceremonies, everyone proudly faced the giant flag that Nathan had donated for the park and sang "The Star Spangled Banner." From there, the program proceeded as planned. The mayor introduced the Hawthornes, followed by the dignitaries, after which each made just a few remarks. Then Jack Root stood at the microphone to name all the local committees, who had worked so diligently. This announcement was followed by minutes of loud applause. Finally, Mayor Moore stepped to the microphone and said, "There is one person here, who was the dreamer, the planner, the prodder, and the organizer, without whom we would not be having this celebration: our own wonderful Kathryn Hawthorne."

Everyone jumped to their feet once again and applauded, whooped, and whistled while Kathryn was pulled to her feet by Jack Moore. Kathryn had no clue this was going to happen and to say she felt numb would be an understatement. As she stood there before this noisy crowd, she thought, *These are my people...wonderful people*, and tears streamed down her cheeks.

The mayor managed to call for quiet, so he could continue with his remarks. "We'll never be able to repay Kathryn for her foresight and belief in us, but there is something we all wanted to do. From this night on, this park will be called the Kathryn S. Hawthorne Park. We'll never forget what she has done for our hometown."

The applause and whistles started again until Kathryn was led to the microphone.

"This is all a surprise to me, and I'm overcome by it all, because I don't feel that I had a lot to do with the result that has been achieved...It is the people of this town who deserve the accolades. I do want to say, we must not forget the help we received from our city friends and all the people who worked on our behalf so that we could get the necessary funding. Thank you all for the honor you have bestowed on me by naming the park after me. Just one thing I ask...please, always keep our small-town values alive and please keep working together in harmony as you have these past months. This is a beautiful little town, so don't let your guard down and always protect it by never allowing the standards we have set here today to ever be lowered. You are all wonderful...I love you all."

To end the program, everyone stood and sang "God Bless America."

The commemorative booklets chronicling the history of Hawthorne along with a map of all the venues and times for different events had been handed out by the Boy Scouts. There was something for everyone. The food vendors were doing a big business, but the local stores were not overlooked in any way, and from the size of the crowd, they were assured of making a good profit. It didn't take long for first-time visitors to the town to hear about the world-class pies at Walters' Restaurant or the old-fashioned Emerson Ice Cream Parlor, and lines formed at both of those establishments.

After a rather long break, the school band congregated in the gazebo and started playing many favorite tunes, which brought most people back to their chairs, and it was not long before they raised their voices to sing along.

Emily and Marcus, Madeline and Joshua, Peter Kingston and Myles Cooledge were all in attendance. They had flown from the city together in the Thayer jet. The Thayers were staying at the farm while the others had booked reservations at the Wayville Inn. All the city contingent met Nathan, Kathryn, Alex, and Emmie for lunch at the barbeque chicken stand. It was a new experience for the city dwellers, and they were enthralled by it all.

"I wouldn't have missed any of this for the world," commented Emily.

"This is truly a Kathryn production," said Marcus as he turned to Nathan. "You have one hell of a granddaughter!"

Nathan nodded, smiling in agreement, while Kathryn shook her head saying, "I keep saying, the credit for all of this is not mine. Mark Taylor nudged me to start this, but it was really and truly the people of Hawthorne who made it happen."

"It's all well and good for you to give credit to the fine people in Hawthorne...They deserve it. But, Kathryn, I think all of us know you and the kind of work you do, especially when you believe strongly in something. Don't try to tell us you weren't the spark that kept the fire going here these past months...We know better," Emily said firmly as everyone nodded in agreement.

"Come on, Kathryn, let us brag on you, and just accept our love and congratulations on another job well done," Joshua offered as he gave his good friend a bow. "I'm just glad we could all have a hand in this great achievement."

Kathryn held out her arms as though she were hugging all of them. "I feel like the richest and most blessed person in the world at this moment. What did I ever do to be a part of this family?" She turned to Nathan and Alex and then faced the others. "I can't tell you how much I love you all, my dear friends. Don't know what I would do without you. And then to have my roots in this little town and the farm." Everyone held their arms out toward her in return make-believe hugs.

"Let's buy some cookies and lemonade from the darling Girl Scouts," suggested Madeline. "They are the cutest little girls and so enthusiastic. I wish little girls everywhere could be part of such a group. Do they have

Girls Scouts and Boy Scouts for young people in the city? I've never heard anything about such clubs...Have I missed something?"

After the cookies and lemonade, Kathryn stretched and yawned, saying, "It's time for Poppy's nap, and I'm feeling the need for some downtime. Maybe it's the letdown after so much activity. How would you all feel about taking time out for a siesta so we can be ready for the dance tonight? Let's meet back here about nine o'clock."

"Kathryn, I think Mark would like to be included in your plan for the evening. After all, if it hadn't been for his famous nudge, we probably wouldn't be celebrating," came from Alex. "I'll call him; he's on duty today, and Dr. Dan is going to cover tonight."

"By all means...call him."

That evening, when they all came together again in the park, it had taken on the look and feel of a fairyland. Paper lanterns had been strung over the area, tiny white lights in all the trees were glistening, and the band was playing a love song. Most of the people were dancing, and their group joined them. Mark asked Kathryn for the first dance. "May I have a dance with the princess of the day?"

She went into his arms, and he held her close...closer than ever before. As they danced, Kathryn let her head rest on his wide shoulder, and they danced in perfect harmony. She was so lost in her thoughts that she stayed in his arms after the music stopped, but Mark, feeling her mood, kept moving and holding her until the music struck up again. Mark was happy to keep her in his arms as long as he could.

Marcus and Emily had remained at the farm with Nathan. It had been a full day for them, as it had for Nathan. That left only the young contingent to attend the dance. The band set the romantic mood of the evening by playing mostly love songs, and these couples, now the best of friends, seemed to draw closer in their embraces, realizing that this night signaled the end of one chapter and the beginning of another in their lives. Madeline and Joshua would be returning to the city the next day to make plans for their wedding in the New Year, while reestablishing themselves in their professions, so much of their time had been spent in Hawthorne of late. Alex and Emmie would start planning for their wedding and their future. Kathryn realized she needed to do some serious scheduling for her move back to the city. Until this night, she had not given it much serious thought. The move away from the farm was made easier, however, knowing that Alex would be with Poppy, but oh, she was going to miss them terribly. Mark's thoughts were on Kathryn's disappearing from his life soon, leaving him to wonder how he was going to manage when every time he walked down Main Street or looked at the park, it would be a reminder of his time with her. This night, his head was full of memories; the first time he met her, the day he had prodded her into taking the lead in the restoration of Hawthorne, the visits to the farm, the time Nathan was in the hospital, and she needed him, and most of all, the times he had held her in his arms when they were dancing. "Get real," he told himself. "She has never given any sign that she could be interested in me except as a friend...In fact, she's kept herself a safe distance from me...I'm sure she has many men in the business world, her world, who are more suitable for her than a small-town doctor."

All too soon, it seemed, the band was playing the traditional final number, "Goodnight Sweetheart," and the festivities had come to an end.

"We will all be parting soon, and I think we should all go back to my home and drink a toast to our wonderful friendship," suggested Emmie. Everyone was delighted to prolong the evening, especially since Joshua and Madeline would be leaving the following day.

When they arrived at the Hurley home, they were disappointed to find that Dan and Martha had retired after the long day. However, they had a lot to talk about. Everyone seemed to be in a mood to relive the past weeks and the accomplishments of everyone. It had really been a momentous time.

"I know I probably bore you with this, but once again, I just have to say how impressed I am with all the people in Hawthorne. They just pitched in and got the job done beyond all expectations," Kathryn said. "They were clever too with so many good ideas...Now, if they will just keep working together..."

With a chuckle, Alex poked a little fun. "What is Ed Abbott going to write about in the *Hawthorne Weekly News* now? He's been flying high and feeling very important... This is going to be a really big letdown."

"You don't have to feel sorry for Ed," said Mark. "I heard the other day that a city newspaper has asked him to write a weekly column entitled simply, 'HAWTHORNE.' It seems their readers have enjoyed the news from Hawthorne, even to the point where some of the local people, who were mentioned often, like Jack Root and J.J. Moore and Ed, himself, have become celebrities. So we don't have to worry about Ed's balloon being deflated anytime soon. He's strutting around like he rules the world, and I say good for him."

"Have you taken notice of MaryLu lately? She's really blossomed, and I think she will figure a lot in Ed's future. You know, she turned out to be a really good reporter and writer when Ed gave her the chance," was Emmie's observation. "She used to be such a wallflower, and Ed was hardly aware of her, but since her transformation, he can hardly keep his eyes off her. And have you noticed, she's really the one in charge in the office now?"

The week following the celebration saw the influx of people continue...Hawthorne had become the place to experience. Its uniqueness and charm were enjoyed by all, and many people started thinking about the joys of small-town living. There were so many visitors to the town that many of the homes had been turned into bed-and-breakfast establishments. Edith Sharr and Lucy Smythe, the perennial committee women, had been so successful handling reservations during the celebration that they decided to start a little business. They had a sign painted that read "Bed and Breakfast Reservations by Sharr-Smythe." They found a small room on Main Street for an office and started advertising. It was the first time they had ever been paid for their efforts. All the committees that had worked on the preservation project were reluctant to disband, and so they decided to stay in place as watch dogs in order to insure nothing would derail their good works.

It was time to set the wheels in motion for Kathryn's return to her city life. Marcus was so anxious for her return that he was sending the jet for her. If she needed a car in the city, the company would lease one for her. Emily was planning a dinner party to celebrate Kathryn's return, and of course, they wanted her to spend the first weekend of her return with them. Emily had missed her girl.

Kathryn said her goodbye to Nathan at the farm. "Remember, I'm only a jet ride away from you. That works both ways, too. You can have Alex fly you to see me sometimes. Oh, I know, my apartment is too confining for you, but you can handle it once in awhile." Her heart was sad at this leave-taking, so she tried to keep the conversation as light as possible.

Nathan enfolded her in his arms. "This has been a special summer for me. So much has happened and all of it good. I love you, Katey Sue."

He is still a strong man; reminds me of a strong oak tree, she thought. "Poppy, it has been just as special for me. Just one more thing, please see as much of Marcy as you can. She tends to stand quietly in the shadows, but she's part of our family now, and my dad would want us to take care of her."

As Alex drove her down the lane, Kathryn turned for a final glimpse of Nathan as he stood on the porch waving to her.

When they arrived at the airport, Emmie and Mark were waiting for them. It was at this point Kathryn could hold back the tears no longer. Emmie gave her a hug as the tears spilled from their eyes. "I don't know why we're crying like this...We'll be seeing each other often, I hope. And besides, you'll be sure to be here for our wedding."

Then it was Mark's turn, and he took advantage of it by putting his strong arms around her and holding her tightly, but gently, for as long as he could without feeling foolish. Kathryn made no move to pull away; this seemed natural to her. They all agreed it had been a time they would never forget. "We could fill a journal with everything that has transpired in these past few months. Let's just store it away and bring it out again when we may be feeling a little 'down.'"

Alex moved to her for a hug, saying, "If there's anything you might need or if you want me to fly Nathan's jet to bring you back for a little visit, just call me. You know I'll keep a close watch on Nathan, so don't worry about anything here. Just know we're all going to miss you."

With that, Kathryn hurried to the jet because she couldn't trust herself to say any more without getting maudlin. She waved and disappeared inside the plane.

Weeks passed, and Kathryn resumed her busy schedule. She found that Alma, her girl Friday, had left no stone unturned to make sure everything was perfect for Kathryn's return. All the staff welcomed her with open arms and smiles, everyone telling her how much she'd been missed. Kathryn rather doubted she had been missed that much since Alma had done such a magnificent job. She was once again ensconced in her beautiful suite of offices, high atop the Thayer Building. She had forgotten how large a staff she seemed to need in order to accomplish her objectives. Kathryn found herself comparing her routine in the city with the simplicity of the operation she had established at the farm while the city contingent worked miles away from her. At the farm, her head had seemed clearer, and she could totally focus on each project. She remembered the clear early mornings when she would greet the sunrise as she rode Rhett through the dewy countryside. It had been her nourishment for the coming day. As much as she tried not to, she found herself making comparisons all the time. For instance, her apartment with its sleek modern furnishings, which had appealed to her several years ago, now seemed cold and discomforting in comparison to the warmness of the farm.

Kathryn poured over her work with new dedication, all the time presenting a happy smile to everyone. She was among the first to arrive at the office in the morning and the last to leave; she had put herself back on the treadmill in order to crowd out as much as possible any thoughts of Poppy and Alex. She missed having Emmie to talk with about important ideas and the insignificant, silly things as well. And then there was Mark. She found him creeping into her thoughts more than she would have thought possible. Really, why should that be? In her few quiet moments, she remembered their dancing together, and she could feel his arms around her at which point, deep down inside, she felt a tingling, her face would become flushed, and her knees might have buckled if she'd been standing. *What is this feeling?...It's like nothing I've ever felt before, a little scary but delicious.*

Peter Kingston called to see if Kathryn could spare some time for him in her busy day. She was delighted to sit down with him and hear about the LADY LINE from his point of view. He was fairly bursting with enthusiasm. "I've not felt this high about any product we have ever introduced before. Everything about it is falling into place, and I'm positively mad about your presentations of this new line. I know its going to be our biggest seller ever."

"You make me very happy, Peter. I, too, feel confident about the future of the LADY LINE. The best part is that we'll present ANNA this year, and next year, we'll introduce a new product in the LADY LINE that we might name, for instance, BARBARA, whatever strikes us at the time. We can go on and on with this, giving each a name and new personality. I think women are going to find it exciting."

"You are so right, Kathryn. I feel it, too. I have to tell you once again how happy I am to be building the headquarters for the LADY LINE in Hawthorne. I fell in love with that little town and the people in it. I love it so much, I've decided to buy or build a home there. It will probably take me some time before I settle there, but we should be able to start operations there soon after the first of the year. I'm so proud of the facility that I'm going to have guided tours so people can see how cosmetics are fastidiously prepared. This will be a first for any cosmetic firm. I just have to show it off...I am that proud of it."

"Peter, building your plant in Hawthorne has given the town a real lift, and I'm sure the people there will stand behind you in anything you want to do. The Kingston plant is a big asset for the area."

"I'm proud to be a part of remarkable Hawthorne. Now, why don't we call Marcus and have him join us for lunch? I haven't seen him for quite some time."

During lunch, Peter repeated for Marcus all he had told Kathryn about his feelings and plans for the division he was starting in Hawthorne. As Peter spoke, Marcus watched Kathryn and was struck by the sad, faraway look in her eyes. *Where is she? Can she be missing Hawthorne and the farm this much?*

The weeks marched on. The city was festooned in Christmas lights and finery, and Santas greeted the shoppers on every corner. Salvation Army bells could be heard at the entrance to most stores, and carolers were out in full force to add to the holiday spirit. Little wide-eyed tots, accompanied by parents, visited Santa Claus in order to tell him what they wished and hoped would be under their Christmas tree...promising solemnly to be really good boys and girls. Cameras flashed so their parents could document this momentous occasion. In the midst of all the lights, music, bells, and laughter, Mother Nature wanted to get into the act, and so she sent soft fluffy snowflakes to brighten the city.

Christmas had always been Kathryn's favorite holiday. She had wonderful memories of the times, when, as a little girl, she had walked through the wonderland of lights with her dad in Hawthorne and the excitement of climbing up on Santa's lap. She always wondered where the reindeer were hitched, and Matthew told her Santa had a secret place for them to rest away from the prying eyes of people. All of that seemed like a dream to her now, but she loved to stroll along with the crowds as she shopped for just the right gifts for friends. In past years, she had not gone to the farm for the holidays but had remained in the city to participate in the fancy galas and parties. In years past, the city had spelled more excitement, and to be truthful, she had enjoyed hobnobbing with leading society figures. She had soothed her conscience by telling herself that Poppy was having a joyous time with all the people on the farm, and she would not be missed at their little homey affairs.

This year was going to be different. She had spoken with Marcus and told him she felt compelled to spend the holidays at the farm and in Hawthorne. After all, Poppy was getting older and the times she spent with him had become more and more precious to her. She explained further that she needed to have this time with her Hawthorne friends and her newfound brother... It would be their first Christmas as brother and sister. Marcus nodded his head in understanding even though he knew how disappointed Emily was going to be. Kathryn had always spent Christmas with them in past years. He thought, *We'll just have to adjust to missing her.*

Kathryn had told Nathan to include Marcy in more of the activities at the farm, because she was so very unassuming and shy and could easily be overlooked in the pattern of life at the farm. Kathryn had not been aware that Nathan was already determined Marcy would be a part of their lives. Every day, during his ride, it had become a habit for him to stop mid-morning to visit with her. He always wanted to know if she needed anything or if there was anything he could do for her. Marcy looked forward to his daily visits, and she always had fresh-brewed coffee and a plate of cookies or muffins waiting for him. Their favorite topic was Matthew. Nathan would tell Marcy about Matthew's childhood and youth, and she, in turn, would talk about the years they spent teaching. Both of them looked forward to their morning visits; gradually, Marcy came out of her shell and smiles took the place of a somber countenance.

Kathryn called to tell Nathan of her plans for spending the holidays at the farm. Immediately, his mind started spinning with plans. He could hardly wait to tell Marcy and to invite her to be with them. "We are once again going to have a family Christmas. Just to think, we'll have more members in our family this year. You and Alex and I know Anna and Matthew will be smiling on us. I want us to decorate the house with greens, bows, bells, and whatever else we can fit in, just as Anna would have done. We'll wait until Katey Sue is here before we decorate, because I'm sure she'll not want to miss being any part of the planning or festivities. We all know what a planner she is."

Marcy stood by his side laughing and replied, "Slow down, Nathan. You're going off in all directions. Don't worry, we'll get it all done, and it will be a glorious holiday for all of us."

Alex flew to the city for Kathryn the week before Christmas, and she planned to stay until the New Year. Kathryn had outdone herself shopping, and when Alex saw all the packages to be loaded on the plane, he laughingly said, "Did you leave anything for Santa to bring?"

During their flight back to Wayville, Alex filled her in on all the plans he and Emmie had been making. They were planning to be married in April, and Nathan was giving them a trip to France for their honeymoon. He wanted them to visit some of the places he and Anna had seen. After the honeymoon, they were going to move into the big house with Nathan. Alex had thought Emmie might want a new home, but she was in favor of making the farmhouse their home. After all, she said, Alex was next in line to carry on the farm tradition, and they should make it their home from the beginning.

"In fact, she's very excited about it all," said Alex. "Nathan and I have both told her she should feel free to make any changes she wants in order to make it truly her home. So far, she has made no suggestions. Emmie wants to continue working with her dad and Mark, and as she says, she won't have to worry about the house, because Gemma and her staff will continue as they always have. I think it will all work out fine. The person who seems most happy about it is Nathan. I'm sure he's been lonely."

"Your plans sound wonderful," Kathryn told him. "Everything is falling into place just as it should. Alex, I have to tell you once again how blessed I feel that you are my brother. You and Emmie will be great caretakers of the farm. You two had better produce a son to carry on for you."

"We'll try," he replied smiling.

Nathan greeted them saying, "I have received the best Christmas presents I could ever have hoped for...having my two grandchildren here with me. Guess you can tell how proud I am of both of you. You represent the best of the Hawthornes."

Gemma had prepared a fine lunch for them, and while they enjoyed the small sandwiches, fruit, cookies, and coffee, Nathan suggested they round up some of their friends to scout the woods and fields for greenery, and afterward, they could decorate the house...tree and all... for the holidays. He told them Anna had always used greenery from the farm, and he would like to see the tradition continue. He had already taken the ornaments out of storage. "Katey Sue, you'll remember most of the old things we had when you were a little girl. Your eyes were always filled with wonder when you looked at the tree, and it never failed to delight Anna to see how awestruck you were."

"Oh, Poppy, I love the idea of gathering greenery... Don't you, Alex?! I think we certainly want to include Emmie and Mark, and we mustn't forget Marcy. Alex, why don't you see if Dr. Dan and Martha could arrange to join us, too. Maybe they could have Mary Jo, their medical secretary, cover the office and get in touch with them or Mark if there is an emergency. I so want them to be with us."

Jokingly, Alex said as he poked at Kathryn, "I really have a sister who takes charge, don't I?...Always organizing us all. That's okay, Katey (the first time he had used that name), I guess we need someone to keep us in line. To answer your question, I'll be glad to see what I can do about getting the Hurleys here."

"I guess I needed that," as she nudged him back. The warmth and love between these Hawthornes was felt by each of them. It was a real bonding.

Everything worked out as they planned. Marcy was feeling more comfortable with the Hawthornes' friends so she seemed very much at ease. A lot of that had to do with all the time she and Nathan had spent together. Mark arrived later than the others, because he had early rounds at the hospital, and by the time he got there, Alex, Emmie, and Kathryn were all ready to go to the woods and fields to gather greens. The older contingent decided to stay at the house and put up the tree so it would be ready for decorating. It was a chance for the Hurleys to spend some time with Nathan and Marcy. Marcy and Martha were very much alike, and they took to each other quickly.

While Gemma and her staff were busily preparing a late lunch, Nathan prepared his special eggnog; he had a special recipe, and he made a ritual of the preparation. The eggnog was one of his specialties. The other was mint juleps that he made with great care and ceremony, down to making sure the glasses were well frosted. The juleps were always served in the spring. Now it was eggnog time.

The scavengers, equipped with cutters, heavy gloves, and huge and medium-sized baskets, trooped off into the woods. "Oh, what fun!" shouted Kathryn. She felt carefree, secure, and happy as she turned to the others and asked, "Don't you agree?"

Alex and Emmie nodded, and Mark smiled and replied, "Totally."

After two hours, these eager beavers had gathered almost more than they could carry and headed back to the house with their pine branches, holly, and various other greens. They unloaded all their loot on the terrace and sorted it. However, before the decorating started, everyone gathered at the long table in the kitchen to enjoy Gemma's bounty.

Each person had a hand in the decorating as CDs played carols, and they hummed and sang along. Alex and Mark decorated the porch with swags that Marcy and Martha had put together, and they tied them with huge red bows. Kathryn did remember many of the tree ornaments from her childhood, and she thought of all the times she had stood before previous trees with her dad. This day, in this place, he seemed very close to her and her eyes filled. She had become that little girl again, looking at the tree in wide-eyed wonder.

Greenery was placed in all the right places, the tree glowed with tiny lights, candles were lit, and the hearth emitted a warm glow. Everyone agreed the house looked almost unreal...like something out of an old novel.

"One more thing we need to do," was Kathryn's observation, "but we can't do it today. We need wreaths to hang outside on each window."

"Might know, Katey would not be through with this project," Alex added as he shook his head. "Hate to admit all the time that she's right, but I concede...she's right once again! It's tough having such a perfectionist sister."

Everyone chuckled...Kathryn blushed.

"I agree with Kathryn. The wreaths will put the finishing touch to the holiday decorating," agreed Emmie.

"Guess it's settled then. Alex and I will get together and put up the wreaths," offered Mark.

They toasted the holidays with Nathan's eggnog.

The following day, Alex and Nathan went to a seminar at the state capital. The seminar had been called to discuss and make decisions pertaining to usage of farmland and possible aid to small farmers. Nathan was a champion of the small farmer, who, in his mind, was the backbone of the country and according to him, always had been from our earliest days. Now, they were having financial problems trying to compete with agribusiness. If our food supply should be taken over by big business and ultimately, end up in the hands of a few, Nathan felt, the quality of food would suffer tremendously, and prices for food would surely soar. Word had gotten out that Alex was Nathan's grandson and heir, and his opinions were starting to be considered seriously by all. He was recognized as a new bright star in the state.

While the men were gone, Kathryn took a ride on Rhett...It was so good! During her ride, she paid a visit to Marcy, whose friendship she had come to treasure. Marcy was happy to welcome Kathryn to her cozy, sunny home which was decorated tastefully for Christmas. They enjoyed each other's company...these two women Matthew had loved above all else.

When Kathryn returned home, she surveyed the decorations and decided she needed to go to Betty's Nursery and buy scads of poinsettias. She wanted them everywhere. However, before leaving on her Poinsettia errand, she went to the kitchen for a late lunch. She wanted to ask Gemma if it would be too much trouble for her staff to prepare for a small open house two nights before Christmas.

"Not a lot of food, just Eggnog, which Poppy will prepare, of course, hot mulled cider, and perhaps some wine. For snacks, we could have finger foods, cheese platter, finger sandwiches, fruit, and such. Just want to keep it simple. Maybe you have some better ideas; you've been doing this for a long time."

Gemma beamed. "Miss Kathryn, getting ready for a party will be no trouble at all. It's always a happy time when you're here. I can almost feel this old home smiling."

"I'll have to talk with Poppy first, but I think he will be in favor of it. I'll get back to you. Thanks so much, Gemma. By the way, I'm going into town this afternoon, and I don't know when I'll get back, so don't prepare any dinner for me. I'm sure Alex and Poppy will be eating out, too."

It was late in the afternoon when Kathryn finally got to Betty's Nursery. She bought so many plants that Betty's would have to deliver them the next day. Kathryn wanted every stair step, nook, and cranny to sport these bright red flowers.

All the stores were staying open evenings for the holidays, and Kathryn had a yen to savor the Main Street sight. *I hope Emmie is free to meander with me*, she thought, as she headed to the medical office. By the time she got there, it was five o'clock, and there were no people waiting. Emmie and Mark were standing by the office desk discussing some of the patients they had tended that day.

"Hi, you two. Enough work for one day, Emmie. Come and join me as I walk the square. I want to soak up the sight. It can be a memory walk for us."

"Darn, Kathryn, I wish I could go with you, but Mrs. Hayes is just home after an operation, and I promised to change her bandages every day. That was the only way the doctor would release her, and oh, she so wanted to get back to her home."

"Please don't look so disappointed, Kathryn. I'd really like to take your memory walk with you, if you'll have me," offered Mark hopefully. "And if you've not had your dinner, I would like you to join me at Walters'. We might even have our dessert at Emerson's and see if their goodies are as good as you remember."

Kathryn thought, *What is it about this man?* Whenever she was near him, she felt warm and fluttery, feelings she had never experienced before. She was definitely drawn to him as she replied, "I accept it all; the walk, dinner, and even Emerson's. Mark, I fear you've found all my weak spots."

"Hope so."

Emmie watched her two friends, who seemed to have already forgotten she was there with them. *When are they finally going to break down and admit how they feel about each other?*

Kathryn and Mark went to Walters' first and were greeted by all the customers with smiles and handshakes. Mark ate a hearty dinner, but Kathryn opted for a salad so she could have a treat later at Emersons'. Kathryn was gratified to see that the restaurant had not been changed during the work on Main Street. There were café-type curtains for the window, walls were repainted, and the floor and furniture refinished. The tin ceiling was intact, and the ceiling fans were the same as was the counter section. It was just brighter looking. After dinner, they strolled the street taking in all the quiet decorations and listening to the carolers. During the holidays, carolers were singing on Main Street every night, which really helped set the stage for this special season. Once again, people were shopping on Main Street and visiting with friends along the way. Walters' Restaurant had been filled to capacity with mostly local citizens having dinner before setting out on their shopping. All the stores were staying open evenings during the holidays. Kathryn and Mark talked little as they strolled. Words didn't seem necessary and would only have intruded on the sensations they were feeling. Mark was so conscious of Kathryn's mood of remembrance and wonder that at the end of the walk around the square, he took her hand and led her to the gazebo, so they could sit and experience everything a little longer. Finally, he took her hand once again and led her to Emersons' just as her father had done years ago. It was a beautiful night.

"I'm joining Alex tomorrow so we can get the wreaths for the windows, and we'll put them in place for you," Mark told her as he walked her to her car. "Drive carefully."

The days slipped by fast, and it was the night of the open house. Gemma and her staff had outdone themselves in the food presentation. Nathan prepared, very carefully, his famous eggnog, and Kathryn fixed the mulled cider. It was a cold night, but they were all warmed by a well-laid fire in the huge fireplace. The pocket doors between living room and dining room were open, making a large expanse for easy maneuvering, and it was made more magical by glowing candlelight.

Nathan, Alex, and Kathryn stood by the door to greet their guests, while Mark and Emmie mingled. Emmie paid particular attention to Bertha and introduced her to everyone as a person who was important in Kathryn's life. Old age was taking its toll on Bertha, so when the introductions were over, Marcy invited her to a chair next to her. Marcy recognized Bertha as a lonely person who needed a friend, so she stayed by her side most of the evening. Even though Bertha, like everyone else, knew the story of Matthew and Marcy's love for each other, and she might have resented it because of her love for Ivy, Marcy, in her gentle, sweet way, won her over completely. She would always love Ivy, but that was in the past now.

◇◇◇

Mark had brought a video camera in order to document the evening for Kathryn. She was such a sentimentalist. That was just one of the things he loved about her. Emmie had been observing Mark and Kathryn for days. *Someone ought to knock their heads together. Don't they realize how much they care for each other?* She turned to Alex and said, "Can't we do something to wake them up?"

"Don't worry, honey; they'll find their way to each other. We did." His arm tightened around her.

During the party, Kathryn was summoned to the phone. Joshua and Madeline were announcing the date for their wedding...Valentine's Day...and they wanted Nathan, Alex, Emmie, Mark, and Kathryn to share their day with them. Of course, they said, invitations would be in the mail, but they were calling to give them plenty of time to clear their calendars for that time.

"How sappy can we get, Kathryn, getting married on Valentine's Day? But then we're giddy with love. You know that, my friend."

Everyone agreed this Christmas gathering would be remembered for years. Nathan glowed as he surveyed all his friends and particularly his family. He felt confident now that the future of the Hawthorne family was in good hands. Yes, the Hawthorne legacy would be lovingly tended, and Isaac's dream would be preserved by future generations of Hawthornes, who would add exciting new chapters to the family's journals.

The holidays proceeded in the traditional ways of the season. There was the Christmas Eve church service. The Hurleys and Hawthornes sat together in order for Alex and Emmie to be together. Alex, Marcy, Nathan, and Kathryn spent Christmas Day together. Gifts that had been selected with care were exchanged with a great deal of exuberance and a lot of oohs and aahs. Every minute was savored, because in the back of each person's mind, was the knowledge that there would likely be a lot of changes in the coming year. By evening, Nathan showed signs of fatigue and announced he was going to his den to write in the journal. Alex had promised Emmie he would join her, and Marcy, like Nathan, was tired after all the activities of the day, and she excused herself. Kathryn had assured them she needed some quiet time, too, and not to worry about her being alone for a time. After everyone had gone, she had a compelling urge to visit the family cemetery and the old cabin.

When Kathryn told Nathan of her yen to visit the cemetery and cabin, he said, "I understand perfectly; I've felt that need many times. I always think the past is speaking to me when I'm there, and it gives me a feeling of serenity and rightness...Somehow, it takes away any loneliness I might be feeling."

There had been a light snow, and it was cold, but Kathryn found it invigorating. She dressed warmly and wore lined gloves and boots. In her hand was a lantern provided by Gemma's husband. Except for her daily rides, Kathryn had been indoors most of the time, and it was good to be out in the fresh, cold air in the quiet of the night with the stars shining brightly overhead. They always seemed to shine brighter on cold winter nights. There was a light snow falling, and she welcomed it as the perfect touch. First, she went to the graveyard and stood by Ivy's grave. "I'm sorry, Mother, that your life appears to have had so little meaning. I can only hope you found happiness in your own way. I'll always remember you as a bright little sprite, flitting from place to place and never landing anywhere. I hope you're resting in peace at long last." Then she moved to Matthew's grave. "Dear Dad, we've all gotten to know you better this past year. It's tragic that you and Marcy could not have had a life together, but you did share a wonderful love that is still alive in Marcy. Many people never know such a love. Then, there's Alex, your fine son. Alex is a wonderful gift to all of us, and we love him very much. Thank you, Dad, for all the wonderful memories you left in my keeping of our times together. I keep missing you." Her voice broke, and she couldn't go on, while her heart was brimming over with love for this man, who had been her world.

She moved on to the cabin. It was cold, but the old rocking chairs were on the porch, and she wanted to sit there for a spell. She put the lantern down, brushed off a chair, and sat down, leaned back, and rocked slowly. She was caught up in the romance of the night, and this special place. A large evergreen wreath had been placed on the door, and with the lantern for soft light, it was almost magical. As she rocked, she closed her eyes and let herself be transported back in time when the cabin was home to earlier Hawthornes. She could almost hear voices and laughter from the past. *If we all would only take time from our busy lives to reflect, we would realize that all our generations are connected,* she thought. We're all a part of the past, as the past is a part of the present. She sat there long enough that the snow was deepening and the cold wind was making it crusty. Her reverie was interrupted by footsteps noisily crunching the snow. She opened her eyes to see Mark approaching.

He stopped at the foot of the steps. "Nathan told me I'd probably find you here, and I felt the need to see you. I wish I had words to describe the picture you make sitting there in the soft light. I wish your grandmother Anna could be here to paint you." He stepped back. "I'm sorry to be interfering with your private moments. I can see how important this time is to you."

Kathryn left her chair and stood at the edge of the porch. For some reason, she felt the importance of Mark's being there, and she motioned him to join her. He went up the steps until they were eye to eye, and he could go no farther. "I can't let you leave again without telling you how deeply in love with you I am, Kathryn. I think I fell in love with you the first time we met, and it has grown to the point where I can think of nothing else...You have become my world."

Kathryn stood speechless, looking into his eyes.

"Every time we were together, it was all I could do to keep my hands off you, but you seemed to hold yourself distant from me. I know I'm asking a lot to think you could care for me. If you have someone else you care about, please tell me...I need to know if my case is hopeless. I can't go on not knowing."

Kathryn was thinking, *This beautiful, wonderful man loves me!* It was like an epiphany. Ivy's legacy suddenly lost its power. *Why has it taken me so long to realize I love this gentle man? I trust him with my life. Yes, I want to turn myself over to him forever. God has smiled on me once again.*

Mark saw her eyes light up and her expression soften as he opened his arms, and she went into them without hesitation. They had been transported to a world of their own, lit by the winter moon and stars. At last, they stood together, not wanting to part.

"It took a long time, Kathryn, but when you finally came into my arms, it truly felt like it was always meant to be. It's so right. All I want to do is love and treasure you for the rest of our lives."

Finally, Kathryn said, "This is the final piece for my crazy quilt. Someday, Mark, I'll tell you the story of my dream. Not tonight...just hold me."

After a time, they returned to the house exuding a happiness that only love can cause. As they approached Nathan, he smiled and said, "I think I know from your expressions what you're going to tell me."

"You are right, sir; we love each other."

"Poppy, I'm finally experiencing what you and Anna had for so many years. I have never been so happy!"

"Mark, let's invite Alex and Emmie to go to dinner with us tomorrow night, so we can surprise them with our news. I want everyone to know. Poppy, why don't you plan to join us?"

Nathan declined, because it would be more of a surprise if he weren't there, and besides, he said, it should be a young people's evening.

The next evening, the foursome assembled at the Wayville Inn. Mark ordered a fine wine. Before the toast, he said he hadn't given Kathryn her Christmas present, and he produced a small ring box and handed it to her. By that time, Alex and Emmie realized the significance of the evening's celebration. Kathryn was awed by the large pear-shaped diamond Mark slid on her finger. Their eyes locked, and Mark pulled her to him for a kiss full of desire.

"Well, you two, it took you long enough," was Emmie's first comment. "Alex knows I've been wanting to knock your heads together for a long time."

"I told her you would wake up sooner or later...We hoped it would be sooner," added Alex.

Questions filled the air. Had they thought about a wedding date? What was Kathryn going to do about her work? Where were they going to live?

These were all things they would have to deal with, but it was too soon. Mark and Kathryn wanted to relish their newfound love before diving into practicality. "We'll get to those things, but please, don't topple us from our special cloud nine yet," said Kathryn as she smiled at Mark and received a nod in agreement.

"Well, I must say, Katey must be love struck, if she hasn't dived into her organizational mode. Will wonders never cease?" Alex couldn't help but poke a little brotherly fun.

"You know, Alex, you're right. Love, love, love is my only agenda right now. I don't want the world intruding into these private, precious moments." Mark drew her close and kissed her lightly.

When Mark took her home that evening, Kathryn told him, "I really don't know how I'm going to leave you in two days. You know, for years, I was in a box, wrapped tightly and never expecting the box to be opened. Now that it has been opened, I never want to go back inside. Mark, I do love you so much, and I never want us to be separated. You realize, though, I can't just walk away from my work at Thayer. I love my work there, and I owe Marcus so much, but I can never be away from you for long; and furthermore, I've come to the realization since being here this past summer that Hawthorne will always be home to me, and it's where I want to live for the rest of my life. My roots go too deep here. I'll talk with Marcus as soon as possible."

It was her first day back to work in the city, and she had arrived at Thayer Enterprises early in order to read Alma's report of account activity during her absence. It was going to be an eventful day for Kathryn, because she planned to announce her engagement to Marcus, and her plan to move back to Hawthorne. No sooner had she started to read Alma's report than Marcus appeared, all smiles and with arms outstretched for an embrace.

"It looks good to see you back behind that desk. We've all missed you more than I can say."

Kathryn walked into his arms and held him in a firm hug as she said, "I always miss Emily and you when I'm away. I'm glad you're here because we have to talk. I have a lot of news."

Immediately, Marcus sensed this news was not going to be to his liking. His smile faded, and his stomach started to churn. For quite some time, he and Emily had watched the signs of Kathryn's growing involvement with the farm and Hawthorne.

They sat in the two large wing chairs facing each other as Kathryn told him first of her engagement to Mark. Marcus looked into her bright shining eyes and felt the happiness pouring from her. He had never, as long as he had known her, seen her this aglow. This was what he wanted for Kathryn, the beautiful young woman he thought of as a daughter. Everything else was secondary to her happiness. Emily would feel the same way, he knew.

Kathryn had told her secretary there were to be no interruptions, and she and Marcus talked for most of the morning. After her engagement announcement and shared joyousness, they finally turned to talk of her work and how to best continue. Of course, she informed him, she would like to continue, but she just could not be in the city with Mark in Hawthorne. They had proven that Alma could continue to carry on the daily routine at the city office, but Marcus knew Kathryn was really the creative genius.

"I don't want to lose you, Kathryn. Tell you what... I'll give all this a lot of thought. You plan to spend the weekend with Emily and me, and we will try to work this out by then. I know you are anxious to get back to that handsome young man of yours." Kathryn beamed. "Emily is going to be so very happy for you even if we are going to lose you to Hawthorne."

They embraced once again, Marcus departed, and Kathryn sat down to review her accounts. All seemed to be doing well, but the Kingston LADY LINE had outdistanced them all. It had really caught on. Women liked the big change in make-up it offered, and the LADY LINE clothes styles had set the designers scrambling to make changes in their designs. It was the year of the lady look. Kathryn's agenda for the day was crammed, but Mark kept creeping into her thoughts, and a tender smile would flit across her face. She could hardly wait to talk with him that evening, as they had planned. Oh, how she missed him.

The weekend arrived, and once again, Otto was driving Kathryn and Marcus to the Thayer estate. During the drive, they kept their conversation light with little snippets of events during the past months. Emily met them at the door with a smile and tears in her eyes. "Some of these tears are sad ones, because I hear we'll be losing you, and the others are happy tears because of the beautiful future you have ahead of you."

After their greetings, Kathryn proudly displayed her sparkling ring and her tender "I'm in love" smile before drinking a toast to her upcoming wedding. They took time to freshen up before meeting in the sitting room for a discussion of their future plans. The subject of Kathryn's leaving was uppermost in all their minds. They needed to deal with it.

Marcus started the discussion by saying he had spent a lot of time with his advisors and had given all their suggestions a lot of thought...Now he believed he had a solution. He hoped Kathryn would like it. He went on to say he had met with his board and advisers with an idea that had been with him for quite some time. It had been evident to him for several months that Kathryn was sinking deeper and deeper into her life in Hawthorne. He couldn't blame her; it was a life and a place many people dream of experiencing. Add that to the success of their operation during the past months, and he felt the solution had been staring them in the face.

"But, Marcus, I don't see how I could continue there and be of worth to the company without more staff close at hand. What we did this past summer worked for a short time, but I don't know how it would work on a steady basis," was Kathryn's observation.

"We can take care of all that, my dear girl, by building offices in Hawthorne, like Peter Kingston has done. It will be the Hawthorne Division of Thayer Enterprises, and I want you to be in charge of that division."

Kathryn was stunned at this proposal, and she had her doubts. "There are many aspects of the business that should be located in the city, aren't there? The representatives of many large accounts feel comfortable in being able to visit the Thayer city offices often. How many of them would travel to Hawthorne?"

"Don't let that worry you, Kathryn. You'll have just a few of our elite accounts to oversee in Hawthorne, and when any of their people want a meeting, we'll simply fly them there in the company jet. We should move Alma up the ladder and give her a title, which should please her. Must say, she has earned it. However, I'll want her to report to you just as she did during the past months. Really, I don't know why this shouldn't work in this age of computers and jets. Of course, we have a lot of organizing to do, but you're the queen of organization, Kathryn. If you agree to all this, I'll call Myles Cooledge and ask him to plan the building with our engineers. I think I'll ask him to go to Hawthorne and look for the perfect site for the building, too. Peter seems to be more than happy with the location of his building. Do you think there is property near his that would be available and appropriate? Of course, Kathryn, I want you to have the last say in just where we build, the type of building, choosing your staff, and everything else to do with this division. It's yours."

Emily sat by quietly; she had known what Marcus was going to propose. It was going to be a huge wrench for her to have Kathryn making her home far away, but she wanted Kathryn to be happy and fulfilled in every way just as she would have wanted for her own child. Furthermore, she had liked and admired Mark when she had met him, and she was sure he would be good to and for Kathryn. It wasn't hard to see how head over heels in love Kathryn was with her handsome man. Emily believed there was nothing more important in this life than to be fortunate enough to meet and to love your soul mate. She knew firsthand, she thought, as she smiled tenderly while she watched her Marcus help make Kathryn's dreams come true. She felt sorry for all the people who never found their true love and ended up settling for less.

"Marcus, I'm overwhelmed! So much to think about. I can see you have given this much thought, and you seem convinced it will work well. I do want to continue being a part of your organization, but I'm sure you and Emily can appreciate that I can't be away from Mark any longer than necessary. I'm finally experiencing a love like you have known for a long time, and I don't want to miss a moment of it. Mark will always come first in my life." Her eyes sparkled as she sighed, "Oh, how I do love that man!"

"I think, we had better move quickly on our plan." Marcus smiled, followed by soft chuckles from Emily and Kathryn as they nodded their heads in agreement. "We can work out any kinks."

Kathryn could hardly wait to phone Mark later that evening, when he would be home from the hospital. Most of all, she just wanted to hear his voice while at the same time imagining his arms around her. Oh yes, that was the most important reason for the call, but then, she did have a lot to report about the new plan Marcus had offered.

Mark listened without interrupting while Kathryn described her meeting with Emily and Marcus and the plan for the future division in Hawthorne. He listened patiently as she told him about all the reservations she had felt when she first heard about this proposed arrangement, but, she continued, Marcus was so sure it would all work that he had convinced her it was doable.

"I don't know how long it will take to build the facility and get everything in place but we'll have it on a fast track. I can't stand to be away from you any longer than absolutely necessary. I'll fly back to Hawthorne every weekend. If you have any doubts about my working, Mark, let me know. I don't want to do anything if we're not in complete agreement."

"Kathryn, darling, I want you to do what makes you happy. If you're happy, I'll be happy, too. You have to remember, you'll be married to a doctor who has crazy hours, and it will probably be good for you to have your own work. I just don't want us to ever drift apart by letting our work become more important than our love. Let's keep our priorities in the right order."

"I totally agree; our love for each other will always be number one. Poppy and Anna are the example we can emulate. Their love is still felt by everyone who ever saw them together. My poor dad was unfortunate in his marriage; instead of love for my mother, I'm afraid, it started as a strong infatuation, and that all faded after a few years. When he did find his true love, they didn't have a chance. Thankfully, Dad and Marcy did have some time together. My mother just didn't have a clue about love; she was really a pathetic figure. Oh, Mark, we must never take our love for granted."

Madeline and Joshua were married in the early evening on Valentine's Day. Both of them, coming from the ranks of high society, insured that many financial and professional leaders from the city were in attendance. The Hawthorne contingent was flown to the city in Nathan's jet by Alex. Kathryn, having been Joshua's most special friend for years, was a bridesmaid. Madeline had planned everything down to the smallest detail, and everyone agreed it was one of the most glamorous weddings they had ever attended. Madeline, in her stunning white satin gown and long veil, carried red roses. The bridesmaids' dresses were pink velvet except for Madeline's sister, maid of honor, who wore a red velvet gown. Roses were the flower of the day and were everywhere in colors of red, pink, and white. It was breathtaking.

Madeline's parents had reserved the Four Seasons for the reception. This truly was a memorable experience for everyone. At the reception, Nathan had time to meet again and talk with Marcus and Emily and to be introduced to many of their friends. Kathryn proudly introduced her Mark to all her city friends as she clung to his arm and leaned against him. Everyone Alex and Emmie met were told that they were the next couple to be married in the spring. This wedding was rather overwhelming to them, and as beautiful as it was, they agreed their wedding would be simpler and more intimate.

It took Nathan longer to make his entries in the daily journals these days. He continued reporting the daily workings of the farm, as he had always done, but now he had all the family happenings to record as well. He wanted future generations to have all the details. The events of the past year might have overwhelmed a weaker man, but Nathan knew it had been his happiest year since his years with Anna. He still had trouble realizing that Alex, this fine young man, was his grandson, the Hawthorne who would carry on Isaac's dream. With beautiful little Emmie at his side, the Hawthorne bloodline would continue.

Then there was his wonderful Katey Sue, the light of his life. She had it all: beauty, brains, and compassion for others. She, and her chosen Mark, would be leaders in Hawthorne. With them at the helm, the town was in loving, capable hands and, he was sure, would always be an example of good small-town living.

God had been good to him. He had lost his son at an early age, but Matthew had left two strong Hawthornes to carry on.

The holidays were over, and everyone fell back into their routines with new vigor. Marcus set the wheels in motion to get the division in Hawthorne established. Myles Cooledge cleared time in order to make a trip to Hawthorne for selection of property for the new building. Fortunately, he found the perfect place not far from the Kingston property. It sat by a bend in the river on a lot surrounded by huge trees. The land had been farmed by Jake Lyons who was wanting to retire and had no children interested in agriculture. The deal was made between Jake and Thayer Enterprises, and immediately, Myles started making drawings for the building. It had been made clear to him by Marcus that this was Kathryn's division, and she would give final approval for everything pertaining to it. Myles had spoken with Kathryn before setting out for Hawthorne, and he had an idea of the sort of layout she wanted. It was to be a one-story building, built of red brick, and would have white trim. She wanted a wide veranda across the entire front of the building on which would be placed country rocking chairs, flanked by low tables with ceiling fans overhead to stir the air on hot summer days. She envisioned the building to be in the shape of a wagon wheel, with long corridors, which would house the different departments. Kathryn's suite of offices was to be placed at the back of the building with a view of the lazy river. Floor-to-ceiling windows would constitute the outside walls in order to satisfy Kathryn's love of space and light. Once again, they asked Madeline to do the interior decorating. She had done such a magnificent job for Kingston.

Kathryn and Mark managed to be together every weekend. If Mark couldn't get away, Kathryn went back to the farm. It was difficult for them. After all, just as they had acknowledged their love, they had so little time together to nourish it. When they weren't together, each of them felt incomplete. After a lifetime of shunning romantic love, Kathryn could not believe the feelings she was experiencing. It was the first time she was able to remember all the sordid details her mother had told her regarding romance and making love, and she could say, "You had it all wrong, Mother. I'm sorry you missed it all. I believed you for a long time, but now I know different... I'm free!"

Nathan offered them any plot of land at the farm on which to build their future home and was delighted when they accepted his offer. Kathryn and Mark spent many hours riding the many acres, and they finally found the perfect spot for their dream home. It was west of the farmhouse on a high knoll which would afford them a view of a large pond, a playground for ducks and other wildlife. Here they would find the serenity they both were bound to welcome after their busy days. This setting was perfect for the home they were planning with a local architect. They spent hours pouring over drawings. It was to be a low, rambling western-style ranch house with a porch extending across the entire front of the house. They wanted double doors leading into the house and floor-to-ceiling windows. Kathryn never got far from her preference for porches and big windows.

Kathryn said, "It will be necessary for us to have some staff here to handle the cleaning and cooking. That means we should build some servants' quarters." She copied the layout for those quarters from the farmhouse plan. Gemma's daughter, Jade, was a natural to be in charge of their household. She had learned well from her mother and grandmother. Jade's daughter, Ruby, was old enough and experienced enough to work with her grandmother or mother as needed. They had all learned their trade well from the first housekeeper, dear Jewel. Once again, life on the farm was passing gently from one generation to another...the unbroken chain.

Many days, Kathryn felt it must all be a dream. *How is it possible*, she thought, *that on this huge planet, two people so perfect for each other managed to meet and recognize that this is the one person for me.* There must be some heavenly plan. "Mark and I will always treasure our love and treat it tenderly," she told herself.

On a rare day, when they could make the time, Emmie and Kathryn met at Walters' for lunch. They met early in order to get a table in the corner, where they would not be disturbed. When Susie, their waitress, brought their first cup of coffee, they told her they would probably be there for quite some time unless the table was needed. Sue smiled at two of her favorite people and said, "No problem. Stay as long as you want."

"How do you do it?" asked Kathryn. "You're the next in line to be married, and you seem so calm and organized. I feel overwhelmed most of the time."

At the mention of her wedding, Emmie's eyes lit up, and she smiled, "Well, I don't have nearly as much to plan for as you do. After all, Alex and I will just be moving into the farmhouse, and I'm continuing to work in the same place. There are no huge moves. Besides, I have always known I wanted a small but beautiful wedding. Oh, Kathryn, isn't it wonderful to be so in love and be loved the same way in return? How did we get so lucky?"

"Are you planning to make many changes to the farmhouse? Any redecorating or additions to the house? After all, this will be your home."

"Alex has taken me there often, and we have walked through the house, sat in every room, imagined Nathan and Anna's bedroom as being ours, looked at the views from every window, and, you know, I can't find a thing I want to change except one. I really, really want you to have Anna's piano. Please don't say 'no' because I've already spoken with Nathan, and he agrees the piano belongs with you. All the ladies who lived there before me have made it the perfect home, and I don't want to change a thing except to move the piano to your house."

The gift of the piano was a complete surprise to Kathryn, and no gift could have meant more to her. She suddenly remembered all the hours she had spent with Granna learning to play. She would cherish this gift forever.

"You will want to replace the huge piano with something. What will it be?" asked Kathryn.

"I don't think I ever told you that for years, I've been keeping journals about the people and events in Hawthorne, and I think I would like to write a history of our town. I have thought so often about the times your father had his students spend time digging into the history of the founders of Hawthorne, not just the Hawthornes, but many of the families who lived here. I'm sure he must have kept many of those reports. Do you know if that's possible?"

"Gee, what a wonderful idea, Emmie. We all talk about our history, but no one has taken the time to compile a book. Why didn't someone think of this before? Let's get busy and try to find out if any of my dad's papers are still around. Maybe the school has some of them, or maybe Poppy. Of course, Poppy has been keeping the Hawthorne daily journals safe and guarded. We'll talk with him."

"I don't know if I am capable of writing something that will do it all justice, but I want to try. I plan to replace Anna's piano with a comfy chair and ottoman, where I can sit, look out that marvelous west window, and dream about all the people who have been a part of this small community." Emmie paused for a short time before going on. "I believe all small towns are pretty much the same, and their main denominator is the people. Of course, I've always lived in Hawthorne and probably should not make generalizations, but I think small-town folks are all grounded in the same values...They, for the most part, are patriotic, hard working, have deep faith, and are devoted to their families. They love their town and like living there, even though they grumble from time to time. Your father made us all aware of our heritage."

There was silence for a few minutes before Emmie chuckled and said, "Gee, I didn't intend to get on my soap box. Sometimes, I think your dad's classes left me with this need to write about Hawthorne and the people here. He was a great influence in the lives of most of his students, and if you haven't guessed by now, I sorta' love this town."

"Emmie, you have just paid the highest tribute to my dad; wish he could have been here to know his teaching meant so much to you. Thank you for sharing with me. Just want to say, you have a wonderful dream, and I'll help you with the research, but you're the writer. I really had forgotten how you were always writing stories and essays when we were in school, and to think, you never stopped. I think it's wonderful! You're going to find that you will want a computer installed in order to make your writing easier. I think you will have space in your special room for it. If I can be of any help in setting it up, let me know. I had some good help when I had my computer system here."

The restaurant was very busy, but no one bothered Emmie and Kathryn. The regular clientele was all there for their favorite repast, and since it was a Saturday, there were a lot of strangers. Hawthorne had become a bustling place most days with visitors from everywhere, but on weekends, the crowds almost doubled. All the news coverage during the renovation followed by the weekly columns written by Ed Abbott had beckoned people from many urban places to come and enjoy the small-town pleasures. They were never disappointed.

After their long lunch, they went to the medical office. Mark was covering for the weekend. Kathryn didn't want to miss a chance to spend some time with him, and they were fortunate he was alone. "Am I dreaming?" he said. "I was just sitting here thinking about you." Kathryn went into his arms, while Emmie smiled and thought what a beautiful couple they were; Mark, tall, dark-haired, broad-shouldered, and Kathryn, tall and lithe with her beautiful auburn hair and dark brown eyes. One could not be in their presence without feeling the love. While still holding Kathryn close to him, Mark made a suggestion. "Emmie, if you and Alex are free tonight, why don't we four go to dinner at the old Amish restaurant in Hopperville? I can take you out to the farm when I go for Kathryn, and we'll pick up Alex. How does that sound to you?"

"Wonderful," was her reply.

◇◇◇

In April, they all gathered at the small Methodist Church in Hawthorne for the marriage of Alex and Emmie. It was a simple ceremony and so very perfect for this couple. Alex was tall and strong with his brown eyes eagerly waiting to see his bride, as he stood by the altar in a handsome navy blue suit. Mark, his best man, stood by him.

Finally, the strains of the "Wedding March" filled the church, and Emmie appeared on the arm of her father, Dr. Dan, little Emmie in the perfect dress for her; a long, white voile with sweetheart neckline, fitted bodice with buttons down the front to the waist. The skirt was just the right fullness for her petite figure. Her veil, which spilled around her, was held in place by a tiara of spring flowers. The bride's bouquet consisted of daisies, crocus, daffodils, and Queen Anne's lace. Kathryn, maid of honor, wore a lovely yellow voile dress. She had sprigs of Queen Anne's lace in her hair and carried a miniature bouquet of Queen Anne's lace with daisies.

Surrounded by family and all their friends in the little church, it was the ideal setting for the uniting of these two. People were heard to say, "That was the dearest wedding ceremony I have ever witnessed." After the reception, the happy couple set off for their honeymoon to a destination unknown except by family members.

After the excitement of the wedding, everyone settled back once again into their routines. Kathryn was still spending much of her time in the city while the facility was being built in Hawthorne, except for the long weekends she managed to spend at the farm. Mark spent as much time as he could working with the builder, who was in charge of erecting their new home. Every night, he called to report on the progress that had been made that day at the work site. At least that was his excuse for the calls, but the real reason was his need to hear her voice. Both of them were finding it very difficult to be separated.

The date for their wedding was set for early October, the time of the annual fall celebration at the farm. Kathryn wanted to be married at the farm, and she planned to have all the farm people invited to the wedding. Of course, all her friends from the city would be there, too, along with the Hawthorne contingent. She mustn't forget to include Miss Bertha, poor, lonely Miss Bertha, who had been almost like an aunt to her when she was a child and who had loved her mother, Ivy, so very much. Bertha was very frail, and it was necessary for her to have live-in help. Mrs. Couts, a widow, lived with her and tended to her needs. Kathryn would send one of the men from the farm to drive both of them to the wedding.

Alex and Emmie returned from their honeymoon and settled into their new home. Life at the farm continued with little or no interruptions in the daily routine. Nathan was the patriarch of the clan and was loved and revered by everyone more each day. He continued to visit all the farm operations every day, and more and more, he looked forward to his daily visits with Marcy. Each morning, she baked some goody for them to share. They still spent many happy hours sharing remembrances of Matthew, sometimes shedding a few tears and other times, sharing laughter. She had become like a daughter to him.

Emmie moved into the farmhouse and settled in as though she had always lived there. She was able to continue with her nursing due to the capable Gemma, who continued to manage the household operation. Gemma and her staff had turned the house inside out before Alex and Emmie's wedding so that there was not a speck of dust to be found, and everything was sparkling and neat. Life moved along without a hitch.

Shortly after their return from their honeymoon, Emmie started collecting all the historical facts about the Hawthorne family and the town of Hawthorne. Of course, Nathan was delighted to help her in any way and offered the journals for resource material. Emmie went to the school to inquire of the high school principal if some of the materials Matthew had used in his teaching about Hawthorne families might still be available. She also asked Ed Abbott, editor of the *Hawthorne Weekly News*, if he would research old news items. It took very little time for the entire town to know about the project, and, true to form, everyone wanted to help. After all, this was their town, and they wanted their family histories included; no family should be overlooked. Men and women, who had been students of Matthew's and had spent many enjoyable hours researching their own families, offered materials they had saved from that time. Emmie was inundated with mounds and mounds of material. All this information needed to be sorted and organized. Edith Sharr, the banker's wife, was president of the Women's Club. She made the suggestion to the members that it would be a worthy project for the club to undertake. The motion was made by Lucy Smythe, seconded, and passed. The Women's Club offered the facilities of their clubhouse for collecting and storing the materials and promised hours of help in the sorting process. Emmie was on her way. Once again, the townspeople had come together to work on a worthy project. Emmie announced that if she were lucky enough to get the history published, all the profits would go to the HOT committees that were still functioning.

By August, Kathryn had finished with her operation in the city and had moved back to the farm where she took charge of the Hawthorne Division of Marcus Enterprises. Madeline was finished with her decorating; the window treatments were completed, and all the furniture had been selected, large and small living plants and other decorative items were all in place. Business machines were waiting for installation. Kathryn had chosen Beryl King to be her executive assistant in Hawthorne, and while Alma had taken on more duties in the city office, she would still be answering to Kathryn.

A NEW DAY

IT WAS THE end of an era for Marcus. It would be strange having Kathryn so far away...She would always be like a daughter to him...However, he and Emily had to realize daughters do leave the nest.

On September first, many state, city, and business dignitaries descended on Hawthorne once again; this time for the dedication of the Hawthorne Division of Thayer Enterprises. The city contingent of attendees included Marcus and Emily, Joshua and Madeline, Peter Kingston, and Myles Cooledge. Of course, most of the town of Hawthorne attended, and the music for the day was provided by the Hawthorne High School Band; they had been practicing most of the summer. Ed Abbott continued to bask in the limelight as he met with all the visiting news media. However, he was no longer a solo act; he kept MaryLu by his side all the time. She had become so attractive and essential to him that he was taking no chances that she might meet someone else more to her liking.

Promptly at ten a.m., Kathryn walked to the microphone. As always, she made a striking figure dressed in a beautiful soft black suit enhanced by a crisp white blouse, and a huge red rose on the lapel of her jacket, the perfect understated costume for this important day. As this young hometown girl with the beautiful shining auburn hair and bright eyes approached the edge of the stage, she was greeted with a roar of applause, whistles, and calls of "Kathryn…Kathryn…Kathryn!" The media people would have a lot of material for days to come, and cameras kept clicking because they didn't want to miss a minute of this accolade. When they finally quieted, Kathryn made a few remarks and then introduced Marcus, who made a short speech, because, as he said, he wanted to leave plenty of time for everyone to enjoy the open house. He introduced several more dignitaries, who, following the lead of Marcus, kept their remarks brief.

Edith Sharr and Lucy Smythe were in charge of the long buffet tables laden with delicious Midwestern home cooking. Edith and Lucy had enlisted every able-bodied woman in Hawthorne to contribute a delicacy, and they were not disappointed. Fried chicken, beef barbeque, potato salad, baked beans, corn on the cob, green beans, slaw, and homemade breads, cakes, and pies of every description. One of the newsmen was heard to say, "I've always heard a lot about Southern hospitality...Well, this Midwestern hospitality wins my vote."

Two days after the dedication, the doors to the new facility were open for business. In true Kathryn form, all details had been so well planned, personnel trained, and work stations in place that everyone fell into their jobs as though they had been doing this work for a long time. Kathryn's long hours of preparation previous to the opening had paid off. Now she could turn her efforts toward the planning of her most important day...her wedding.

By noon on October first, all the family and friends of Kathryn and Mark were seated in front of the old Hawthorne cabin. Mark with Alex at his side stood at the foot of the steps awaiting his bride. Emmie emerged from the cabin first, and after a very short interval, Kathryn appeared. Complete adoration shone in Mark's eyes as he stood breathless at the sight of his love. However, no one attending this ceremony could have feelings to compare with those experienced by Nathan. There stood Katey Sue wearing the same dress his Anna had worn on her wedding day, and the only jewelry was the huge diamond pendant Nathan had given Anna their first Christmas together. As she approached the edge of the porch, Kathryn looked at Nathan and smiled. That she had chosen to wear Anna's wedding dress and veil was her surprise to him. Nathan's eyes clouded over as Marcy sent a tender look and smile steeped in her love for him.

The string quartet played their music softly, and nature heralded the event with a profusion of color. Fall colors were everywhere, in the variety of trees surrounding them and the banks of fall flowers.

Before their friends and family, Kathryn and Mark spoke their vows, and the glow of their love touched everyone.

HAWTHORNE EPILOGUE

THEY HAD LONG since finished the first pot of tea. From the dining room, they had moved to large country-type rocking chairs on the veranda. Sarah was so enthralled with the Hawthorne story, she almost missed inviting her friend to lunch. Goldie Bassett, being the nurturing motherly type, wouldn't let that happen. She interrupted to ask if maybe they would like for her to serve them a salad or sandwich and something cool to drink. They gave their order and moved back to the dining room after thanking her for her thoughtfulness.

Goldie had lived in the large Victorian house all her married life and raised five children there. After her husband died and the children left the nest, she decided to stay on in her home but to share it with others...hence the bed and breakfast. Goldie was used to mothering, and she took good care of all her lodgers.

After lunch, the two women strolled down Main Street while they continued to talk about the history of this town and small-town life in general. They spent some time at the quaint ice cream parlor feasting on huge chocolate sundaes...The best, Sarah said, she had ever eaten. Finally, they sat on a bench in the little park and watched the sun bid the day goodbye. The story, past to present, had been told.

"This has been one of the best days I have had for a long time. I will be forever indebted to you for taking the time to spend it with me," said Sarah. "As promised, I will submit my article to you for approval before I let it go to print. It is such a beautiful and inspiring story that should be enjoyed by people in all walks of life, a true story of the indomitable human spirit. I think I might print it as a series...one chapter at a time. Once again...thank you so very much."

"It has been a good day for me, too. I always enjoy reliving those times," replied Emmie.

About The Author

Molly Sheppard's roots are planted deep in her Midwestern hometown where she spent her early years. In 1985 after retirement, she and her husband moved to Florida where she has been active in her local historical society and historical museum.

It was after her move to Florida that her love of writing became evident. HAWTHORNE is her first novel.

Printed in the United States
53973LVS00001B/10-12